Amanda ran towar
"Are you okay?" sh

"Fine," he said, but she did... ...p ...r. ...e wrapped her arms around him in a fierce hug. Laughing, he held the pot away. "Careful, you're going to make me spill the blueberries we worked so hard for." But his other hand ran up and down her back, soothing her.

"You were so brave," she whispered. "I thought that bear was going to attack you."

"He was more interested in the salmon, fortunately," Nathan told her. "Are the girls all right?"

"We're okay," Paisley said, as she and Lyla came running up.

"Do you still have the blueberries?" Lyla asked.

"I do." Nathan showed her the almost-full pot. "So let's head down the hill before that bear changes his mind."

Amanda squeezed his arm. "I'm impressed. You managed to dissuade the bear without anyone getting hurt. You should be a professional diplomat."

He smiled. "I can just see the business card. Bear-negotiation specialist."

Dear Reader,

How do you feel about birds? I love them. As I'm writing this, I can hear magpies bickering in the trees outside. In the summer, waterbirds populate the lakes and ponds here in Anchorage. Robins sing, swallows dart over the lakes like acrobats, and seagulls and eagles soar overhead. In the winter, most of those birds fly south, but the ravens return from the mountains, and the chickadees, nuthatches and stellar jays are always around.

I'm excited to bring you a new series, set in the tiny fictional town of Swan Falls, Alaska. Named after a nearby waterfall, the town has a number of landmarks, but its main draws are Swan Lodge, a rustic inn built by Harry and Eleanor Swan, and Swan's Marsh, a bird sanctuary adjacent to the lodge. Nathan Swan, Harry's great-nephew, has returned for Eleanor's memorial service. So has Amanda Flores, Eleanor's great-niece, and her daughter, Paisley. Little do they know what adventures the charming spot has in store for them.

I hope you enjoy your visit to Swan Falls. I'd love to hear what you think. You can find all my contact info at bethcarpenterbooks.blogspot.com.

Happy reading, and may your spirits soar.

Beth Carpenter

HER ALASKAN SUMMER

BETH CARPENTER

H Harlequin

HEARTWARMING

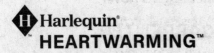

Harlequin®
HEARTWARMING™

ISBN-13: 978-1-335-05150-9

Her Alaskan Summer

Copyright © 2025 by Lisa Deckert

Harlequin Enterprises ULC
22 Adelaide St. West, 41st Floor
Toronto, Ontario M5H 4E3, Canada
www.Harlequin.com

Printed in Lithuania

MIX
Paper | Supporting responsible forestry
FSC® C021394

Beth Carpenter is thankful for good books, a good dog, a good man and a dream job creating happily-ever-afters. She and her husband now split their time between Alaska and Arizona, where she occasionally encounters a moose in the yard or a scorpion in the basement. She prefers the moose.

Books by Beth Carpenter

Harlequin Heartwarming

A Northern Lights Novel

The Alaskan Catch
A Gift for Santa
Alaskan Hideaway
An Alaskan Proposal
Sweet Home Alaska
Alaskan Dreams
An Alaskan Family Christmas
An Alaskan Homecoming
An Alaskan Family Found
An Alaskan Family Thanksgiving

Love Inspired Suspense

Alaskan Wilderness Peril

Visit the Author Profile page at Harlequin.com.

I'd like to dedicate this first book in my new series to my wonderful husband. If not for him, I'd never have moved to Alaska and discovered all the wonders of this special place. Thank you for all those years of support and encouragement. Love you.

Thanks and appreciation to my agent, Barbara Rosenberg; my editor, Kathryn Lye; and all the people at Harlequin and HarperCollins who work behind the scenes to get my stories out to readers. And thanks to the Alaska Department of Fish and Game for the excellent resources about the birds of Potter Marsh.

CHAPTER ONE

THE AIRLINER BUMPED once and then slowed to a crawl along the runway at the Anchorage airport. Nine-year-old Paisley Flores pressed her nose against the airplane window. "Look, Mom! Is that a moose?"

Amanda leaned forward to peer around her daughter's dark curls toward the fence running parallel to the runway. She could just make out a brown dot weaving through the woods outside the fence. "I don't think so, honey. It looks like a big dog to me. But I'll bet we'll see a moose sometime this week."

The plane turned toward the main terminal. A friendly voice came over the speaker, "Welcome to Anchorage. Local time is approximately three fifty-seven."

Amanda laced her fingers together and stretched her arms while her daughter tucked a bookmark inside the last pages of her book. As soon as the plane pulled to a stop at the gate, Paisley unbuckled her seat belt, pulled her backpack from under the seat, and zipped the book inside. Their flight from Albuquerque early this morning had been Paisley's first time on an airplane, at least the first she was old enough to remember, and she'd been wide-eyed, watching and listening. Almost ten hours and two connections later, Paisley could probably have filled in for one of the flight attendants if the need arose. Amanda hated to think what two last-minute tickets to Alaska in July must have cost, but fortunately, she wasn't paying.

Amanda still wasn't sure coming here was the right decision. When the invitation had arrived offering to fly her and Paisley to Alaska to attend a memorial service for her great-aunt Eleanor, she'd immediately accepted. She'd only visited Eleanor and her husband, Harry, twice, once as a child with her parents and sister, and once with her own husband and daughter when Paisley was six months old. But Eleanor had stayed in touch through Christmas cards, postcards, and the occasional phone call. When Amanda's husband died eighteen months ago, Eleanor had sent a lovely letter reminding Amanda about their trip to Alaska and how much she'd enjoyed watching David land his first salmon.

Amanda wanted to be there, to honor Eleanor's life. But the invitation was for a whole week, and even though it was midsummer and past the main planting season, there was always something that needed doing at the plant nursery—mums to prune, seedlings to pot up, trees and shrubs to care for. Amanda's finances still hadn't recovered from the double hit of David's medical expenses and the loss of revenue from poor management decisions made while she and David were occupied fighting his cancer. She hated to pay hourly wages for work she could be doing. Especially since they desperately needed to replace the greenhouses, an expense far beyond her means at the moment. But this was for Eleanor. So she'd left Zia Gardens in her manager Harley's capable hands, packed a big old suitcase of David's for Paisley and herself, and gotten on the plane.

Amanda pulled out her phone and sent off a text that they'd arrived in Anchorage to her mother; her sister, Jess; and her manager, Harley. Quickly, a text from Harley popped up. Have a great trip! Wish I was there. Amanda smiled. Twenty years ago, Harley had been stationed in Alaska for two years and loved the state. He had insisted that he could handle everything at the nursery while she and Paisley took advantage of this amazing opportunity. Every day, she thanked her lucky stars that Harley had answered her help-wanted ad. Harley knew the plant business inside and out and had become something of a mentor for Amanda, as well as a friend.

Mom replied, Safe travels. A few seconds later, an emoji with its tongue sticking out arrived from Jess. Jess had received the same invitation as

Amanda, but Jess's natural habitat ran more to upscale department stores than Alaskan fishing lodges. It had taken her all of two seconds to decline. Of course, Jess had only been six when they visited Alaska, and unlike Amanda, Jess had few memories of Eleanor and Harry. She claimed all she remembered about Alaska were mosquito bites and being cold all the time.

As the people ahead of them began filing out, Amanda reached under the seat for her own small backpack. She and Paisley followed the crowd off the plane and into the terminal. Paisley fidgeted. "I need to go to the bathroom."

"Me, too." Amanda pointed to the sign. "There's one." But when they entered, they discovered they were in line behind half a dozen other women. Paisley danced from foot to foot. To distract her, Amanda said, "You're going to love Swan Lodge. It's this great big house made of logs. My great-aunt Eleanor Swan and her husband, Harry, built it a long time ago, before Swan Falls was even a town. I was just your age when my family flew up to visit."

"Will there be other kids there?" Paisley asked.

"I don't know." Amanda wasn't sure if the lodge was operating, or if not, who else might have received the same invitation to attend. "When I visited, Aunt Jess and I were the only kids, except, on the first day, there was this one boy. I was playing outside behind the lodge. Jess had gone inside for something, so I was alone, and I saw a fox. He looked right at me, and then ran into the woods, almost like he wanted me to follow. And so I did. But pretty soon, I lost him and somehow, I got turned around. I didn't know how to get back to the lodge. I was really scared."

"When you're lost, you're supposed to hug a tree," Paisley said solemnly. "That's what they said in my book."

"That's good advice," Amanda affirmed. "My parents had told me not to go into the woods, but I forgot when I saw the fox. I was afraid I would get in trouble if I didn't get back on my own, so I kept trying to find the way, but the more I tried, the more lost I got. I started crying. All of a sudden, this boy was there. He must have heard me. I told him I was lost, and he took my hand and led me back to the lodge. It turned out not to be far at all, but he didn't tease me about getting lost or crying. He was very kind."

"What was his name?" Paisley asked.

"I don't know," Amanda said. "When we got back, my mom was calling, and he left before I thought to ask. And I never saw him after that. I guess he and his family must have checked out that day."

"What did he look like?" Paisley wanted to know.

"Just an ordinary boy. About my age, maybe a year or two older, with brown hair. Nothing memorable—except he did have the nicest brown eyes." Come to think of it, maybe that was the start of Amanda's fondness for brown eyes. She'd been thrilled that Paisley was lucky enough to inherit her father's beautiful dark eyes, rather than Amanda's nondescript faded blue color. "Oh, look, it's your turn." Amanda pointed to the empty stall and Paisley rushed to it.

Once they'd finished in the bathroom, they headed down the concourse. Amanda had just paused to readjust the shoulder strap on her backpack when Paisley gasped, "It's a moose!"

Amanda looked up. Sure enough, a full-size moose with antlers wider than the compact car she had reserved posed in a glass enclosure, his glass eyes looking right toward them.

Paisley stepped closer. "It's humongous!"

"It sure is." Amanda had seen moose at a distance on both her trips, but she'd never gotten close enough to realize just how big the animals were. "Stand there, and I'll take your picture with him." She snapped the picture with her phone. "Okay, we'd better get to baggage claim and get our suitcase."

They followed the signs out of the secured area, took an escalator down a level, and found the baggage carousel where the people from their flight had gathered. Suitcases, ice chests, and heavy-duty plastic totes drifted by, and people stepped up to claim them, but Amanda didn't see any sign of the big blue suitcase she'd checked. A purple case with hibiscus stickers made a second trip past them, and then a third before a woman stepped up to pull it off the carousel. After that, a loose sock went by, followed by a gray T-shirt. Uh-oh, someone's suitcase must have come open. A few feet later, a stuffed rabbit went by, partially trapped under a black suitcase.

"That's Hopscotch!" Paisley cried.

Amanda had a sinking feeling she was right. She reached out and snagged the well-worn bunny. Yep, she and Paisley were the unlucky people with the exploded suitcase. Amanda puffed out a breath. She had chosen that one because it was bigger than any of their newer suitcases and she would only have to pay to check one bag rather than two, but she should have known better than to overstuff an old suitcase like that. She handed the rabbit to Paisley, who hugged him tight, and then collected her T-shirt and Paisley's sock and stuffed them into her backpack. The next time around, three more socks, Paisley's sparkly hairbrush, and a headband rotated by, followed by Amanda's purple bra draped over the edge of someone's duffel bag, provoking a wave of giggles from the people still waiting for luggage. Red-faced, Amanda snatched it and hid it in her pack.

Slowly the crowd collected their intact luggage and moved away while Amanda collected another half-dozen small items and waited for the case to appear. Everyone else was gone and the carousel was down to three unclaimed suitcases when an open bin came off the ramp and slid onto the carousel. Amanda recognized Paisley's Albuquerque Isotopes baseball cap on top. She snagged the tote and pawed through it. Maybe half of their stuff was there. The carousel came to a stop, and an airline employee came to collect the remaining bags. "Oh, dear." She gave Amanda a sympathetic smile. "Come with me. I'll bet we have your suitcase in the office."

Amanda shrugged on her backpack, threw the other items she'd collected into the tote, and followed her, with Paisley and her bunny right behind her. As soon as Amanda stepped inside, she spotted the old blue soft-sided suitcase in the corner. The front flap had ripped away from the zipper and was hanging loose. Amanda took a quick inventory. As far as she could see, between the bag and the tote, all their stuff was accounted for. If anything was missing, they were just going to have to cope.

The airline employee handed Amanda a roll of packing tape. Amanda stuffed the contents of the tote into the suitcase, pulled the flap back in place, and secured it with multiple wraps of tape. She thanked the woman and, after three tries, managed to extend the handle of the mummified roller bag so that she could drag it into the almost deserted baggage claim area. She took a deep calming breath and put on her optimistic mommy face. "That was nice of the airline people to gather up most of our spilled stuff, wasn't it?"

Paisley gave a noncommittal shrug. "What do we do now?"

"We get our rental car and drive to Swan Falls, the town where Swan Lodge is located." They followed the signs to the right and down the corridor until Amanda spotted the rental car company where she'd made a reservation. Only one customer was at the desk, which she supposed was the silver lining to being the last one out of baggage claim. She maneuvered her bag around the ropes and poles, but when she released the handle, the bag flopped over. She retracted the handle and pushed it out of the way, pondering what to do for a suitcase for the flight home. Maybe she could pick up something cheap at a thrift store between now and then.

"It's a red Ford Mustang," she overheard the clerk telling the man in front of her as he handed him a pen to sign the contract. "You were lucky to get here when you did. It's our last one."

Last sports car, Amanda assumed. She'd paid in advance to make sure they held her car until she arrived. A woman stepped out from the back room and nodded at Amanda while she stepped to the other end of the desk. "I can help you over here."

Amanda pulled her driver's license from her

wallet and handed it over. "I have a reservation for a compact."

"I don't know if you've heard," the woman said, not taking the license, "but there's a wildfire south of Portage that has the highway shut down from the Kenai Peninsula."

"Oh, no. Is anyone hurt?" Amanda asked her.

"No, no injuries, and they've got the fire partially under control, but I'm afraid I don't have your car. Several of our customers who were supposed to return cars last night and this morning are stuck down there on the Kenai, waiting for the road to open."

"Oh." Amanda licked her lip. "Do you have anything? A midsize, maybe? Or even a pickup?"

"No, we don't have any cars left at all."

"But I paid in advance," Amanda protested, realizing even as she spoke that it was pointless. If there were no cars, there were no cars.

"I see that," the woman said, looking at her computer screen, "and of course we'll refund the full amount. Or you can check tomorrow. If firefighters continue to make progress, they say they may be able to open the highway as early as tomorrow morning."

Amanda looked around. "Do you think any other companies—"

But before she could even finish her sentence, the woman was shaking her head. "Sorry. Everyone is in the same boat. I've got your cell phone number here. If you like, we can put you on the list to call as soon as we have a car available."

"Please do that." Swan Falls was almost forty miles from the airport. No taxi was going to take them all that way with no chance of a return fare. Amanda and Paisley would just have to spend the night in Anchorage and drive out in time to attend the service tomorrow afternoon, assuming any cars became available in time. Surely, she could find a hotel room, although it was peak tourist season, and rooms were bound to be expensive.

But at least she wasn't one of those people stranded on the other side of the wildfire, missing their planes home, she reminded herself. And fortunately, Swan Falls was north and east of Anchorage, in the opposite direction of the Kenai Peninsula.

She looked over to find the lucky man who had snagged the last car tossing the keys up and down in his hand and watching her. He must have overheard her conversation, because she detected sympathy in his soft brown eyes. "Can I drop you and your daughter somewhere on my way?"

She shook her head. She couldn't ask him to drive forty miles out of his way. Besides, she wouldn't risk riding with a stranger, even if he did have nice eyes. "Thanks, but we'll be okay."

"Do you have a reservation downtown?" he asked. "There might be a hotel shuttle."

"No, we weren't planning to stay in Anchorage.

But that's okay. We'll find a place here tonight and start our trip tomorrow."

The man looked at her and Paisley, then at the keys in his hand, and then back at Paisley again. He let out a sigh and set the keys on the counter in front of the clerk. "Give them the car."

Oh, wow. Amanda's first instinct was to refuse his gesture. After all, he'd gotten there first. But she really did need the car. "Thank you so much!"

"Are you sure?" the clerk asked.

The man nodded. "Yeah. I'll just have to figure out some other way to get to Swan Falls."

Paisley, who had been humming to her rabbit, popped her head up. "You're going to Swan Falls, too?"

"Too?" The man turned to Amanda. "Are you here for Eleanor Swan's memorial service?"

"Yes, we are," Amanda replied, studying him with fresh eyes. He was tall, long-limbed, with neatly cut brown hair to match his eyes and a tanned face. A kind face. Was he a relative? Or just a friend of Eleanor's?

"I'm Harry's great-nephew," he said, as if he'd read her mind. "Nathan Swan."

"Oh, wow. I'm Amanda Flores. Eleanor was my great-aunt. And this is my daughter, Paisley."

He inclined his head and smiled. "Glad to meet you, Paisley. Amanda. I guess we're all going to Swan Lodge, then."

The clerk cleared his throat, his fingers poised

over the keyboard. "So do you still want to cancel the car, or what?"

"I'll keep it, and we can ride together." Nathan picked up the keys and looked toward Amanda. "If that's okay with you."

"Perfect. Thank you."

"All right, then." He pocketed the keys. "Swan Falls, here we come."

CHAPTER TWO

NATHAN ROLLED HIS suitcase out of line. He looked back to see Amanda struggling to extend the handle of her canvas roller bag, which for some reason was wrapped in layers of clear packing tape. One side of the handle extended, but the other side would only come halfway out, setting the handle at a sharp angle. She pushed it down and tried again, jerking up so hard her auburn waves bounced, but with the same result.

"Let me try, Mom," Paisley offered, but she couldn't even get the handle to the halfway position.

"May I?" Nathan offered.

Amanda gestured toward the bag. "Please."

Nathan's first try produced the same result. He pushed the handles all the way in, rattled them, and this time pulled up sharply. The side that had been stuck slid smoothly past the halfway mark to its full extension, only to pop entirely out of its socket. Now the handle dangled uselessly from the other support. Nathan cast a wry smile at Amanda. "And I made it worse. Sorry."

"Don't worry about it. I don't know why I thought this suitcase was a good idea." She retracted the remaining extension pole, grasped the big bag by the padded handle on the side, and hefted it off the floor, leaning far to the left to counterbalance the bag, which probably weighed half as much as she did. She struggled a few steps forward. "Which way to the car?"

"I'll take it." Nathan reached for the bag, but Amanda shook her head.

"I'm the one who decided to use this piece of junk. I can carry it."

"Please," Nathan begged. "You can roll my bag and I'll take this one. It hurts my back just to look at you. You might get stuck and have to spend your whole life leaning. How could I live with myself then?"

She chortled. When she laughed, her whole face lit up. For a moment, he just stood there grinning, forgetting where he was and why.

"Okay, since you put it that way," Amanda set down the bag with a thump. "Thank you."

Paisley skipped over to his suitcase. "I can roll this one. Which way?"

Nathan dragged his eyes away from Amanda's face and pointed. "Right through there. There's a tunnel to the parking garage."

"Ooh, a tunnel." Using both hands, Paisley dragged his bag on ahead.

Amanda grinned and followed, leaving him

to hoist her enormous suitcase and stagger after them. At the other end of the tunnel, automatic glass doors opened, and they stepped into the dark garage, which smelled of auto fumes and damp concrete. It didn't seem to faze Amanda or Paisley, though. Paisley started to drag his suitcase on ahead, but Amanda stopped her and turned to Nathan. "Which way from here?"

He pointed to a red sports car sitting by itself under the rental sign. "That must be it."

"Cool." Paisley dragged his bag toward the car.

"Nice car," Amanda commented.

Nathan shrugged. "I reserved a midsize, but this was all they had left." He clicked the fob the attendant had given him, and the trunk of the car opened. It took some doing, but he managed to wrestle her giant suitcase inside and still make room for his. "I wonder, since we've got the last rental car, if we should wait for the others to arrive," Nathan said, "although we don't have a lot of room."

"How many are coming?" Amanda asked.

"I'm not sure. My dad has a bad sinus infection so he couldn't fly, and I know my uncle declined." Nathan shook his head. "I can't understand that. Who turns down a free trip to Alaska?" Especially when his father and uncle, Harry's nephews, were the likely heirs to the lodge, since Eleanor and Harry had no children of their own, and Eleanor's nephew passed away years ago. Personally, Nathan would never miss this last chance to honor Eleanor's memory at Swan Lodge. He'd had to take unpaid time off work to do it, but he was determined to be there. Especially since, knowing his dad and uncle, the lodge would likely be sold before the fireweed finished blooming. Despite his father having fished commercially in Alaska every summer for twenty years, he had no great fondness for the state.

Amanda shrugged. "My sister, for one. She's halfway convinced there's some hidden agenda, like those free time-share weekends where they spend the whole time hounding you into buying, but I think that's just an excuse because she's afraid of bears. All nature, really. My mom isn't coming either because her husband's family re-union is this weekend. To be fair, some people might have already made their vacation plans, and couldn't get a week off work."

"But you could?" he asked.

"I have a family business, a plant nursery in Al-buquerque, so while there's never a good time to take time off, it's my decision. Besides, I couldn't miss Eleanor's memorial service. She was special."

"She was. Is your husband holding down the fort at the nursery while you and Paisley travel?"

"No." A shadow passed briefly over her face, followed by a brave smile. "David died the winter before last. It's just me and Paisley."

Oops. The last thing he'd wanted was to make her sad. "I'm sorry for your loss."

"Thank you." And then as if to change the subject, she immediately asked, "So where did you fly in from today?"

"Phoenix," he answered, as he set his backpack in the back seat next to theirs. "One stop through Seattle."

"We went through Phoenix and Seattle." Amanda pulled sunglasses from her backpack and set them on her head. "I wonder if we were on the same planes."

"We were, at least from Seattle." He'd noticed those coppery waves bouncing against her shoulders when she and Paisley had boarded the plane ahead of him, but of course it had never occurred to him that she would have any connection with Swan Lodge. Once he might have paid more attention to such an attractive woman, but after a fiasco four years ago with his then-fiancée, he'd sworn off romance. "Why don't I give the lodge a quick call to see if we should wait for anyone? Otherwise, we'll hit the road, okay?"

"Sounds good." Amanda went to get Paisley buckled into the back seat.

Meanwhile, Nathan called the familiar number. "Hi, it's Nathan."

"Well, hello." Peggy's warm voice came through the phone speaker like an auditory hug. "I hope you're calling to tell me you're in Alaska."

"I am, and I've run into more of your guests, Amanda Flores and her daughter, Paisley. We're driving up together."

"Wonderful. I was afraid you wouldn't be able to find a rental car. I heard on the news that this fire on the Kenai has caused a car shortage. I was all set to come get you, but I wasn't sure when you were getting in."

"No need. I got the last car. Is anyone else due to fly in today who might need to ride with us?"

"No one else is coming up from the lower forty-eight. Just you and Amanda, and her little girl."

"That's too bad."

"I suppose," Peggy replied, but she didn't sound particularly heartbroken. "Drive on up. I made lasagna for dinner."

"Lasagna, huh? I'd better hang up and get on the road, see if we can make it while it's still warm."

Peggy laughed. "I'll keep it warm. See you soon."

Nathan returned to the car and climbed into the driver's seat. "Everyone ready?"

"Let's go!" Paisley called from the back seat. "I want to see a moose. A real, live one, not like the one in the airport."

"Well, you never know. Once I saw one right outside the airport, so keep your eyes open," Nathan replied, as he backed out of the parking space.

They went through the checkout and drove to the main road leading into the airport. "Look,

Paisley." Amanda waved toward the letters spelling out "Anchorage Welcomes You," rising up out of a bed of bright flowers.

"That's where I saw the moose that one time," Nathan told her. "He was eating the flowers."

"Wow," Paisley leaned closer to the window. They turned left, giving her a view of the mountains behind Anchorage. "Those mountains are so green. And they have snow spots, even though it's summer!"

"Snow lasts a long time in the Chugach Mountains in the dips and valleys," Nathan told her. "And speaking of sun, did you know the sun won't set tonight until eleven twenty?"

"Ooh, can I stay up and watch the sun set, Mommy?" Paisley asked.

Amanda laughed. "Not a chance." She turned to Nathan. "You seem to know a lot about Alaska for someone from Arizona."

"My dad was a teacher in Phoenix, but every summer we would go to Alaska for a month. He left me with Eleanor and Harry while he worked as a commercial fisherman. It was my favorite part of the year."

"Lucky you. My family visited Swan Lodge once when I was a child, and I loved it. My husband and I brought Paisley when she was just a baby. Eleanor and Harry were so much fun to be with." Amanda's face sobered. "It's hard to believe they're both gone."

"I know. But Harry lived to be eighty-nine, and Eleanor ninety-four, so I count myself lucky to have had them for so long." Nathan just wished he'd come more often in the past few years. His last visit had been summer before last, and at that time Eleanor, while not moving as quickly as she used to, still gave the impression she would go on forever.

"Paisley's right about the mountains," Amanda commented. "I'd forgotten how green and beautiful they are."

"Yes, quite different from the desert, although Albuquerque has its own kind of beauty. Did you grow up there?"

"We moved there when I was twelve. Before that, we lived near Hatch, New Mexico."

"Where they grow the green chilies?" Nathan asked.

"Yes. My dad was a chili farmer. But after he died, my mom sold the farm and we moved to Albuquerque."

Oops, he did it again. "I'm sorry." Of course, Amanda's dad would have been Eleanor's nephew. To lose both her father and her husband—that had to leave a mark. Nathan had lost his own mother when he was six, although unlike Amanda's father, his mom didn't die, just decided she didn't want to be a teacher's wife or Nathan's mother anymore. She'd stopped by for a brief visit two or three times early on, but after her marriage to a wealthy real estate developer on the East Coast, she'd vanished completely from Nathan's life. His dad had never remarried, and Nathan couldn't blame him. Why would anyone risk that kind of pain again?

"Thanks," Amanda responded. "Oh, look at the sign, Paisley. It's a moose crossing."

"Are there any mooses?" Paisley asked eagerly.

Her mother looked around. "I don't see any, but if there's a sign, they must come by here sometimes."

"Well, if we don't see one today, I'll bet we'll spot one around Swan Lodge in the next few days," Nathan predicted, glad to move on to a more cheerful topic. "They like to hang around the lake there sometimes. And I don't know if your mom told you, but there's a marsh nearby where a pair of swans come every year to nest and raise a family."

"I want to see the swans! Baby swans are called cygnets. I read it in a book." Paisley leaned forward as far as her seat belt would allow. "How long until we get there?"

Having completed the drive through Anchorage, Nathan merged onto the Glenn highway. "Not long now. Maybe fifteen minutes to the turnoff and another ten minutes to the lodge. Peggy said she made lasagna for us."

"I love lasagna. Hurry," Paisley urged. "I can't wait to see everything."

Soon they were slowing down to drive through Swan Falls. The town had grown some since the last time Amanda was there, but it was still tiny. She remembered the old diner, but now there was a store called Wildwood Wonders next door and a pizza joint across the street. The tiny post office was attached to the Swan Falls Mercantile, which as Amanda remembered sold everything from canned beans to bunny boots. Behind the post office was a park, with an open grassy area at this end and a few scattered trees toward the other. A log cabin sat alone in front of the trees, and she thought she could make out the word "Museum" on the sign out front.

Nathan turned after the park. A dozen houses lined the road for a mile or so, but soon the houses disappeared, with only the occasional drive giving a clue that anyone lived in the woods there. About five miles from town, they reached the sign for Swan Lodge. Spruce trees ran along the drive, and then opened to reveal the towering log-and-stone building with a wide front porch. Before Nathan could even stop the car in front of the lodge, the front door opened, and Peggy was hurrying down the steps to meet them.

"Oh my goodness," Peggy said as they climbed out of the car. "I can't believe you're finally here. It's been too long." Peggy enveloped Amanda in one of her famous hugs.

"It's good to see you, too." Peggy was as much a part of Swan Lodge as Eleanor. Amanda turned to her daughter, who was hanging back, sizing

Peggy up. "Paisley, this is Peggy, probably the best cook in Alaska. She's been here at the lodge for a long, long time."

Peggy laughed. "Longer than I care to admit. Paisley it's so good to see you again." Peggy bent down so they were face-to-face. "I know you don't remember me, but I remember you from when you were just a baby, and you came to see your great-great-aunt Eleanor. We had an old cat then named Agatha and you were just fascinated by that cat. You weren't walking yet but every time you saw that cat you'd start crawling just as fast as you could across the floor. I don't think Agatha ever let you catch her, but that didn't stop you from trying."

Paisley took a step closer. "Does Agatha still live here?"

"I'm afraid Agatha's been gone a long time, but we've got another lodge cat now. Her name is Shadow. She's a little shy at first, but I'm sure she'll be introducing herself to you before too long."

"Paisley loves animals." Amanda pulled her backpack strap over one shoulder and handed Paisley hers. "She is dying to see a moose."

"I haven't seen one in the past two or three days, but they do come around."

Nathan had climbed out of the car and made his way around. He grinned at Peggy. "Where's my hug?"

"It's right here," Peggy replied, laughing as she

wrapped her arms about him. "I'm so glad you're here."

"I'm sorry I didn't get here before. I didn't realize Eleanor was—"

"None of us did," Peggy told him. "We all thought Eleanor was doing just fine. She didn't seem the least bit sick or weak, until that one morning, when she just didn't wake up." Peggy blinked rapidly as though she was fighting tears, but she still smiled. "It's a blessing, really. She's with Harry now." She clapped her hands together. "All right, then. Let's get your luggage inside and get you settled in your rooms. I had the housekeeper make up the best rooms in the house for you."

"So the lodge isn't open?" Nathan asked.

"No, we've closed up for now, until everything gets settled."

Nathan nodded and pulled the suitcases from the trunk. Peggy's eyes widened when she saw the tape-wrapped canvas roller bag. "What happened here?"

"A little mishap in the airport," Amanda told her. "The zipper broke somewhere between the plane and the baggage carousel, and our things went everywhere. It took a while to collect them."

Nathan snorted. "Wait. At the baggage claim was that your purple—"

Amanda jabbed him with her elbow. "Yes, it was. Now let's never speak of it again."

Nathan made a zipping motion over his lips, but he didn't try to hide his amusement.

"We'll get you fixed up when you're ready to pack," Peggy told her. "I'm sure we have some extra suitcases in the basement. In the meantime, come on in."

Nathan picked up Amanda's suitcase, so she grabbed his, which was much lighter. They followed Peggy up the stairs to the porch, but before they stepped inside, a hoarse voice called, "Hello," from somewhere over their heads.

They all stopped and looked up. A black-and-white bird perched on the log that made up the bottom of the empty gable over the porch. "Say please," the bird said, and then fluttered its tail. "Go on, now. Shoo."

Paisley clutched Amanda's hand in excitement. "Mommy, that bird is talking!"

"Oh, that's just Maggie the Magpie," Peggy told Paisley. "Eleanor liked to have her breakfast on the back porch in nice weather, and Maggie used to hang around and try to swipe a crust or two when she wasn't looking. Eleanor would talk to the bird, and then one day, the bird started talking back."

"Shoo," the bird repeated as they went inside, Amanda tugging Paisley forward while she looked back, unable to tear her gaze away from Maggie.

But once they were indoors, there were new surprises to capture Paisley's attention. A big open room spread out in front of them. Clusters of couches and chairs were gathered around the central fireplace made of native stone that soared to the ceiling. Wide staircases on both sides led up to the second floor, where walkways with rustic wood railings on both second-story wings over-looked the room. A chandelier made of moose antlers hung over the entrance.

Beyond the fireplace was the dining area, with a dozen or so tables of varied sizes, most with a view of the back lawn and the lake behind it through a long row of windows and glass doors. The back porch held more tables and chairs.

A black shape appeared from behind the fireplace and dashed up the stairs. "Was that Shadow?" Paisley asked Peggy.

Peggy nodded. "Now you can see how she got her name." Peggy gestured toward the hallway on the right and handed over two key cards from her pocket. "Nathan, if you and Amanda will bring up your luggage on the elevator, Paisley and I will meet you upstairs." She took Paisley's hand and led her toward the stairway. "Come with me. I'll show you where Shadow likes to hide out."

Paisley was swept up the stairs in Peggy's wake. Peggy had to be in her upper fifties, but as far as Amanda could see, she hadn't slowed down at all. Amanda paused for a moment to run her fingers over the antique oak bar that served as a regis-tration desk. It smelled faintly of linseed oil and lemon, indicating a recent polish, but the paint on the beadboard front was faded. The door behind the desk, which led to Eleanor and Harry's private quarters, was closed. "It feels like if I ring this bell, Eleanor or Harry will pop out through this door to greet us."

"I was just thinking the same thing." Nathan came to stand beside her. "I can almost hear her voice. 'Now, Nathan, what have I told you about sliding down the banister?'"

"You didn't!"

"Of course I did. Look at that staircase and tell me you weren't at least tempted."

That smooth curving banister would make a great slide. "If I'd thought of it, I would have."

"Eleanor scolded me, but she was always smiling when she did." He sighed and picked up the larger suitcase. "Good memories."

"Yeah." Amanda followed him to the elevator, noticing the faded fabric on the chair cushions as she passed. Time had taken a toll on Swan Lodge, but it was still a jewel.

They got off on the second floor and Nathan called, "Peggy?"

"We're in the library," Peggy called back. "Just drop your bags in your rooms and join us. Amanda, you and Paisley are in the corner room, 207, and Nathan, you're across the hall in 206."

Amanda followed Nathan down the hallway. "I

forgot about the library. With a cat and all those books, Paisley will be in heaven."

"She's a reader, then?"

"Oh, yes. The librarians at our local branch have given her special privileges. Ordinarily, they only let children check out twelve books at a time, but they let her take as many as she wants."

"When I was her age, I loved spending time outdoors here, but I welcomed rainy days because then I'd have an excuse to curl up in the library with a good book. Still one of my favorite things." Nathan unlocked the door to Amanda's room and wrestled her suitcase onto the luggage rack there.

"Thank you," Amanda told him. "I left your bag in front of your door."

"Great." He handed her the key card to 206 and stepped into the hall.

Amanda paused for a moment to look around. The room she and David had stayed in before had been spacious, with plenty of extra room for Paisley's crib, but this one was huge. In the area near the door, a couch, chair, and desk were arranged over a worn rug with a leaf pattern. Two queen-size beds each had their own alcove with the door to the bathroom in between. Comforters with matching dust ruffles dressed the beds, in a cottage-style floral print that had been all the rage when Amanda was a girl, but now seemed overly fussy. But the furniture was high quality with classic lines, and on the far wall, heavy curtains were open to reveal sliding glass doors with an unmatchable view.

Amanda stepped outside onto the balcony. Below was a wide lawn, where she and Jess had played. Beyond, the lake spread out, cool and serene, surrounded by forest. A wooden post held a sign marking the trail that led through the forest to Swan's Marsh, where every year a pair of swans would return to nest, along with a myriad of other birds.

With a sudden flutter, a magpie landed on her balcony railing. "Hello."

Amanda smiled. "Hello, Maggie. Sorry, I don't have any treats to share with you."

The bird tilted her head to inspect Amanda for a long moment before flying across the lawn to land in one of the spruce trees near the lake. Another magpie fluttered over to perch nearby and they chattered at each other as though exchanging unflattering opinions about the new arrivals. A duck with a brown head and a striking white breast swam into view on the lake, along with his dabbled brown mate and, behind them, a line of fuzzy ducklings.

Amanda breathed in the earthy, leafy scent of forest, a smell she always associated with Eleanor and Alaska. She leaned on the railing and drank in the view until a muffled ring interrupted. She pulled out her cell phone to see her manager's name pop up. Hopefully, there wasn't already a problem at the nursery.

"Hi, Harley."

"Hi." His voice was warm, as always. "How's the trip going?"

"So far, so good. There was a slight problem with the rental car, but it all worked out and I'm here at the lodge. Is everything okay there?"

"Everything is fine. But I had an interesting conversation a little while ago, and I thought I'd better keep you in the loop."

"What kind of conversation?"

"A man dropped by looking for you. I told him you weren't available. He hemmed and hawed, but eventually told me he wants to buy this property and wanted to feel you out to see if you might be interested."

"I hope you told him no."

"Not exactly," Harley admitted. "I just said I would give you his card. I looked him up after he left. He's a local developer, has a good reputation as a home builder. He'd probably make you a worthy offer."

"The nursery isn't for sale." Amanda wanted that clear.

Harley cleared his throat. "I understand you don't want to sell, but as we've discussed, the old greenhouses aren't going to be usable much longer. The normal life of a polycarbonate greenhouse is ten to twenty years, and you're pushing twenty-two. Not to mention the HVAC system is on its last legs."

"I know." David had set up a special account for greenhouse replacement, but that money had gone to doctors, hospitals, and pharmacies instead. David never even saw most of the bills—getting through chemo had taken every ounce of energy he could muster, and it had taken most of hers to support him while caring for Paisley and juggling everything else. In the meantime, David had left his most senior employee in charge, which turned out to be a mistake.

Belinda was well-meaning but between ordering errors, missed planting schedules, and her tendency to hire her own shirttail relatives, Belinda had managed to operate the nursery at a loss for its first season ever. David never knew about that, either. Amanda told herself that they'd have time to figure out the finances after David recovered, only he never did. But David had put his heart into Zia Gardens, and that plant nursery was Paisley's heritage. Amanda couldn't let it fail. "I'll find a way to get us new greenhouses," she told Harley.

"Okay. I put his card on your desk. You can throw it away once you get back. In the meantime…" His voice grew more animated. "How is Alaska? Green?"

"So green and absolutely beautiful," Amanda told him. "Just like I remember."

"It's incredible, isn't it? I was only stationed

there for a short time, but what an experience that was. It's all so big and wild, it kind of gets into your soul, somehow."

"Yes." When Amanda had come with her family when she was a kid, Alaska had seemed like a whole different world. "I'm really glad Paisley is getting the chance to experience this place when she's old enough to remember."

"Me, too. You two have fun."

"We will, thanks. Call me if you need anything. I'll try to check in regularly."

"You can if it makes you feel better, but you don't need to do it for my sake. Better, I think, if you and Paisley just enjoy your time in Alaska, and don't worry about anything. I can handle things here. Tell the kiddo hi from me."

"I'll do that. Thanks, Harley." She hung up the phone. *Don't worry about anything.* Easy to say, but not so easy to do. The indisputable fact was that she didn't have the money to replace the greenhouses. And if they didn't have greenhouses, they didn't have a business.

The obvious solution was to borrow the money, but that wasn't so easy, either. Even after David had died, the bills had continued to arrive, and Amanda had fallen behind on their home's mortgage payments while she was attempting to get the nursery back on its feet. Selling their house had given her some breathing room, and hiring Harley was by far the best business decision she'd ever made. Thanks to him, the nursery was once again producing a decent income. The medical bills were paid off, and she and Paisley lived in a comfortable apartment not far from Paisley's school. But those late mortgage payments had done a number on her previously pristine credit score, and when she'd talked to the bank about a business loan, the interest rate they quoted made her gulp.

But if it came to that, she'd do it. Zia Gardens was Paisley's legacy from her father, and it was Amanda's duty to keep it up and running until her daughter was old enough to run it herself. Just like Amanda should be running their family chili farm now. But when Dad passed, her mother had sold the farm. She'd never asked for Amanda's opinion. In fact, the first Amanda heard about it was when Mom had brought home a bunch of packing boxes and announced they were moving to Albuquerque in a month.

When she'd protested, Mom looked surprised. "Oh, Mandy, I'm sorry, but we don't have a choice. We can't stay here. I'm no farmer."

That much was true. As a young woman, Mom had worked in an insurance office. Once she'd married Dad, she'd kept the books and handled the paperwork for the farm, much to his relief. He hated deskwork almost as much as he loved growing chilies. Farming was in his blood, he said.

Four generations had grown chilies on that farm. But now it was owned by a corporation.

When Amanda was older and knew more about business, she'd wondered why Mom hadn't considered hanging on to the land, renting it to another farmer in exchange for a share of the crop. If she had, Amanda might be there right now, and Paisley might someday be the sixth generation growing chilies. But what was done, was done. Mom had just lost her husband, and people didn't always make the best decisions while they were grieving. Now that Amanda found herself in the same situation, she had more sympathy for her mother. But she wasn't going to make the same mistake.

David would have been a wonderful farmer. There was nothing he loved more than to plant seeds and grow them into healthy plants. That's why he'd gone into the nursery business, instead. He knew exactly what plants would thrive in difficult conditions, and he had an uncanny ability to look at a sick plant and prescribe exactly what it needed to heal and grow. Someday, Paisley would do the same.

Running footsteps tip-tapped down the hall and Paisley came to a sliding stop outside Amanda's door. "Mommy, you have to see this room. Come on!"

"Coming." Amanda pocketed her phone and stepped inside, closing the glass door behind her.

Paisley ran in to grab her hand. "Hurry!" She tugged on Amanda, pulling her out the door and down the hall. Amanda grinned at her enthusiasm. Harley was right. Her money worries would still be there when she got home, but in the meantime, she was here, at Swan Lodge, with her daughter. They should enjoy this week. It might be Paisley's only opportunity to experience Alaska.

CHAPTER THREE

"I NEED TO head to the kitchen," Peggy told Nathan. "Bring everyone down to supper in about fifteen minutes."

"Will do," Nathan agreed as Peggy hurried off. He breathed in the familiar smell of books and furniture polish. The library was his favorite room at the lodge. The desk against the wall held a computer and printer for guests to use. Pine bookcases flanked both sides of a stone fireplace at this end of the long room, each shelf with a brass frame holding a paper label in Eleanor's distinctive printing that stated the category. Paperbacks mixed happily with thick leather tomes. He went to the local interest shelf, hoping the book was still there. Considering how many times he'd taken it down and flipped through it, he wouldn't be surprised if it had fallen apart by now. But there it was at the end of the row, the spine reinforced with clear packing tape. He'd just picked up the book and was thumbing through the pages when Paisley burst through the door, tugging her mother along.

"Ta-da! It's a reading tent." Paisley gestured toward the yellow-striped fabric draped over a wooden frame at the opposite end of the room. Inside, two beanbag chairs, some pillows, and a few stuffed animals were scattered over a soft fake-fur rug that spilled out of the tent beside low bookcases filled with children's books.

"That is so cool!" Amanda flashed a grin at Nathan before allowing herself to be towed to the tent and crawled inside with Paisley. "I don't re-member this being here."

"Malcolm, the handyman, and I added it about five years ago." Nathan moved past the round game table at the center of the room so that he could see Amanda and Paisley inside the tent. "It was Eleanor's idea."

"It's great. It makes the room even cozier." Amanda gestured toward a tall cabinet that matched the bookcases. "Those cabinets are full of board games and craft supplies," she told Pais-ley. "Harry used to call this the Rainy Day Room. If the weather was bad, we'd read books and play games and draw pictures. Sometimes Peggy would bring us hot chocolate. It was so much fun."

"But there's lots to see besides the library." Na-than handed Paisley the book in his hand. "Peggy has supper waiting for us right now, but tomorrow we'll visit the marsh."

"What's this?" Paisley turned a couple of pages.

"A bird identification book for south-central

Alaska. Swan's Marsh is a bird sanctuary. Oh, and we'll need these." Nathan opened the cabinet and pulled out a plastic bin. Inside was a neat stack of small notebooks and a box of pens. Nathan handed them one of each. "This is your bird list, so that you can write down every type of bird you see. Eleanor had nearly three hundred birds on her life list."

Paisley studied the notebook in her hand. "What's a life list?"

"That's all the different types of birds a birdwatcher has seen in his or her life. Some birdwatchers will travel all over the world just for a glimpse of some particularly rare bird, but you'll be amazed at how many you can see here. I've always come in the summer, but Eleanor spotted even more different kinds of birds during spring and fall migrations. According to her records, the swans have arrived during the third week of April every year but two for the last fifty years, and those years they were only off by a couple of days."

"Wow, really?" Paisley followed Nathan down the hallway toward the stairs. "I wonder how they know when to come."

"I've always wondered that, too," Amanda commented. "Do you suppose swans have a calendar app that tells them when to start migrating?"

Paisley giggled. "You're silly, Mommy. Swans don't have phones."

They were still laughing when they got to the kitchen. Peggy had a cabin of her own, but this was her domain. It was a full commercial kitchen, with an eight-burner stove, three ovens, and stainless-steel countertops, but along one side near a bay window ran a pine table set for five, with a strip of gingham down the center topped with a cast-iron trivet in the shape of a bear. Four rush-seated chairs hugged the sides and ends of the table, with the upholstered bench in the window providing seating on the other side.

The back door opened and a man about Peggy's age dressed in workpants and a plaid shirt stepped in. "Malcolm!" Nathan went to give the mainte-nance man a half hug, half shoulder bump, be-cause a full hug would have embarrassed him. "Have you met Amanda and Paisley?"

"Never had the pleasure." Malcolm smiled at them. "But I feel like I know you just from Elea-nor's stories. Glad to finally meet you in person." Malcolm shook hands with Amanda. Then he of-fered his hand to Paisley, saying, "A pleasure to meet you, miss." Paisley giggled and shook his hand.

"Let's get this dinner on the table." Peggy in-structed Malcolm to set the lasagna on the trivet, pointed Nathan toward a bowl of salad to toss, and asked Amanda to pour drinks while she finished the garlic bread.

As she carried two glasses of milk past Nathan,

Amanda asked him, "How do you know so much about Eleanor's bird records?"

"Oh, she'd tell me about it when we talked on the phone every week. She was still going to the marsh up until a couple of months ago. That should have been a clue for me that she wasn't feeling well, but I didn't catch it. I wish I had; I would have come up for one last visit." He sighed. "I knew she was in her nineties. I don't know why I didn't make time to come. Well, I do know. There was a major push to get an installation finished at work, and we've been understaffed, but still. I should have been here."

Amanda set down the milk and touched Nathan's arm. "You obviously knew Eleanor a lot better than I did, but I'm sure she didn't blame you. She called to talk with me a few times after my husband, David, died. She'd been a widow for many years, you know, and she was a strong, independent woman. She didn't like people fussing over her."

"That's true." Nathan thought back. "A few years ago, she wanted to hike up to Swan Falls. I don't know if you're familiar with the trail, but we came to a place where they've laid out the rocks to make a sort of staircase, but it's pretty steep. I offered my hand, and the look she gave me…" He laughed. "Needless to say, she scrambled up those rocks like a mountain goat."

"Amanda's right," Peggy said as she invited everyone to sit down. "Eleanor had a minor heart attack last October and they had to put in a stent, but she made me promise not to tell you about it. She didn't want you fretting."

Nathan frowned. "I never guessed—"

"Because she didn't want you to guess," Peggy continued. "Once she had that stent, she was gallivanting around the place like she was in her seventies. But the doctors knew, and she knew, that there was another partial blockage in a place where they couldn't get to without open-heart surgery, and she wasn't having that. She said she'd had a wonderful life, and more bonus years than she'd ever expected. She was ready to go anytime. And I know Harry was there to greet her on the other side."

Nathan nodded. "For sure." He glanced over at Paisley, who appeared to be engrossed in the bird book he'd given her. But from her stillness, he suspected she'd been listening to every word of their conversation. Poor kid had lost her dad, she didn't need to be listening to their gloomy talk. "What birds are you looking at, Paisley?"

"Swans." She looked up at him. "This book says trumpeter swans and tundra swans both live in Alaska. Which ones live here?"

"Albert and Alison are trumpeter swans," Peggy told her. "They come back every year in April."

"It's always the same swans?" Amanda asked.

Peggy smiled. "Always. Swans are very territorial. The original pair were Albert and Victoria. Something happened to Victoria about four years ago and Albert was left alone to take his brood south at the end of the season. Without Victoria, we were afraid Albert might not be raising any more cygnets, but he came back the next season with a new bride."

Malcolm chuckled. "I'm the one who named her."

"Why Alison?" Nathan asked.

"Because my friend in high school, Alison Wasik, played trumpet in the marching band."

Amanda smiled. "Great choice."

"Glad you like it. You'll get to see Albert and Alison and their brood tomorrow morning."

"Will we have time to visit the marsh before Eleanor's memorial service?" Nathan asked.

Peggy grinned. "Didn't I tell you? We're holding Eleanor's service at Swan's Marsh. Her favorite place in the world."

AMANDA WOKE EARLY the next morning and peeked in on Paisley, who was still fast asleep, splayed across the bed at an angle with one foot hanging from under the covers, Hopscotch half-hidden by the pillow, and a children's mystery novel from the library lying open on the floor beside the bed. After brushing her teeth, Paisley had insisted on running to the library for a new book before going to bed last night. Amanda tiptoed over to pick it up and set it on the nightstand. She crossed the room and pulled back the heavy curtains to find that the sun was already well up in the sky.

She slid open the door and stepped out, to hear a bird calling out a repeating five-note trill. She searched the tall birch outside her window for several minutes before spotting the robin, still singing his heart out. A flock of Canada geese swam across the lake, sunlight glinting on the vees in the water behind them. Only a few clouds floated in the blue sky. It was a beautiful day for a memorial service at Swan's Marsh.

A few seconds later Malcolm appeared, on a riding lawn mower. He mowed a strip next to the covered porch and then expertly traversed along the curved edge of the flagstone patio and on to the edge of the woods before turning to mow the next strip back. It wasn't until she'd been watching for a few minutes that Amanda realized she wasn't hearing any engine sound. It must be an electric mower so that he could mow before the guests came outside without disturbing their sleep. Nice. He was on his third pass when Peggy stepped out from what must be the kitchen door, lugging a tote bag. She crossed the flagstone patio to the three bird feeders and filled each of them with a different blend of seed. A minute later, Nathan stepped out and went to talk with Peggy. He must have offered to complete her chore, because then Peggy left, and Nathan finished filling the feeders.

Nathan sure seemed to feel at home here, but then he'd said he'd spent a month of every year there when he was growing up, so in a way, this was his boyhood home. He looked a bit like Harry, with a distinctive jaw and those warm brown eyes with little laugh lines at the corners. He acted a bit like Harry, too, in the gentle way he interacted with Paisley. Both of them were tall men, with broad shoulders. They could easily have been a bit intimidating, but instead they personified kindness. Maybe that was one of the reasons Peggy and Eleanor were so fond of Nathan.

"Mommy?" Paisley called.

Amanda stepped inside. "I'm right here."

"For a minute, I forgot where I was."

"I know. It's always a little odd waking up in a new place, isn't it? Did you sleep well?"

"Mmm-hmm." Paisley stretched and yawned, and then suddenly her eyes opened wide. "Have you seen Shadow?"

"No, I haven't been out of our room yet. Why?" But before Paisley could answer, something brushed against Amanda's bare foot. She yelped and jumped back from the bed. A second later, a velvety black paw reached out from under the bed skirt again, patting the floor as though feeling for that foot.

Amanda raised her eyebrows at Paisley and her daughter shrugged. "I brought her back from the library with me last night."

"I didn't see her when I tucked you in."

"She was hiding under the covers," Paisley admitted. "Shadow really wanted to stay with me."

"But Shadow isn't your cat. Peggy might be worried. You need to apologize to her for not asking for permission first."

Paisley sighed. "Okay." She put her foot down, and the velvet paws swiped across her toes. She giggled.

Amanda opened the door to the hallway. "Come on, Shadow. Better scoot." True to her name, Shadow dashed out from under the bed and was out the door so fast she was nothing but a dark blur. Amanda closed the door. "Let's get dressed and go downstairs. Peggy probably has something wonderful for us for breakfast."

She was right. When they reached the lobby, the aroma of bacon wafted across from the dining area. Against the sidewall, a divided steam tray held the bacon, scrambled eggs, and cottage fried potatoes. A basket containing several types of bread sat beside the toaster, and a small refrigerator held yogurt and butter. Peggy popped out from the kitchen, carrying a tray of strawberries, orange slices, and melon. "Good morning. You're up early."

"Not as early as you," Amanda pointed out. "How long have you been up to have already cooked all this?"

"Oh, this is nothing. When the lodge was busy,

I'd do a full spread. But I thought I'd keep it simple this morning, since we're having everyone here for lunch after the memorial service."

"You're feeding everyone? By yourself?"

"Of course not by myself. I already have it all cooked, and a few people from town volunteered to warm it up and serve for us once we get back from the marsh." A flash of movement from behind the stairs to the registration desk caught Peggy's eye. "There's that cat. I was wondering where she'd gotten herself to."

Amanda caught Paisley's eye and cleared her throat.

Paisley hung her head. "I took Shadow to bed with me last night. I'm sorry. I know I should have asked first."

"She slept with you? Well, that's a first. But it's fine with me. I'll give you a bowl so that you can make sure she has water if she wants to stay in your room at night."

Paisley beamed. "Thank you!"

"Now, you'd better get yourself some breakfast," Peggy told them. "It's going to be a big day, today."

"What time is the memorial service?" Amanda asked.

"Ten, but we'll head over to the marsh about nine thirty. Don't dress up. Just wear what you'd normally wear for a day of bird-watching. That's what Eleanor would have wanted."

Amanda figured that was probably true, considering Eleanor's usual attire was jeans and an ancient flannel shirt.

Peggy returned to the kitchen, but a second later the swinging door opened, and Nathan passed through. Amanda, who was in the process of filling her cup from the urn on the table, called, "Coffee?"

"I could use a cup."

"Cream or sugar?"

"Black for me." He sat down at the table. "Good morning, Paisley. How did you sleep?"

She tilted her head and looked at him with a puzzled frown. "In my bed."

He laughed. "That makes sense." He accepted the mug from Amanda. "Thanks. Say, once we're done eating, there's something outside I want to show you both."

"What?" Paisley demanded.

"It's a surprise. Excuse me while I fill my plate." He got up from the table as Amanda set a full plate in front of Paisley and went back to fix one for herself.

"I'm making toast," Nathan said. "Want some?"

"Sure. Whole wheat, please, for me and for Paisley."

Nathan nodded and filled the four-slice toaster. He helped himself to egg, bacon, and potatoes, and was about to sit down when the toast popped up. Using tongs, he put two pieces on his plate and two more on Amanda's.

"I'm done," Paisley announced before they could even sit down. "Can we go see the surprise now?"

"No, you need to be patient while the rest of us eat." Amanda transferred one of the pieces of toast from her plate to Paisley's. "Why don't you look through the jellies on that tray over there and bring me something good?"

"Okay." Paisley popped up and went to read the hand-written labels on several canning jars while Nathan and Amanda began eating.

Amanda looked up at the heavy beams supporting the roof. "I wonder how long Harry and Eleanor owned this place."

"They bought the land in 1962," Nathan replied without hesitation. "They moved into the old trapper's cabin on the property and built four small guest cabins that year. They opened for business the next summer. The lodge came three years later, in 1966."

"Is the trapper's cabin still here?" Amanda asked.

"No, they tore it down years ago."

"There was no town here then, right?"

"That's right. At that time, the only development in the area was a gravel parking lot at a trailhead that led to Swan Falls. Harry wanted to try to negotiate a lower price without the marsh, because what were they going to do with a marsh? Eleanor convinced him that the marsh itself would be a draw, because of the wildlife it attracted. And she was right."

Amanda chuckled. "Of course she was."

Paisley returned with a jar of of strawberry jelly and busied herself by drawing a smiley face on her toast with jelly while Amanda and Nathan continued to eat and chat, but once she'd eaten her toast, she couldn't sit any longer. "Can I go get my book from our room?"

"Sure, once you've cleared your dishes. They go in the tub over there." Once Paisley had finished, Amanda pulled the key card from her pocket and handed it over. Paisley skipped toward the stairs.

Nathan smiled as he watched her go. "She's a real reader, isn't she?"

"Yes. I'm surprised she came downstairs without a book. I usually have to physically remove it from her hands to get her to sit down and eat." Amanda loved that Paisley was a reader, but at the same time, she worried that she didn't get enough activity. She tried to schedule hikes or outings on the weekends, but weekends were their busiest time, and Amanda often put in hours working the register or the greenhouse floor.

"I was like that as a kid." Nathan set his fork on his empty plate and sipped his coffee. "But when I'd come here, Harry and Eleanor would encourage me to be outside as much as possible. They'd play lawn games or take me on hikes. Sometimes, they would give me adventure books to read, and then Harry would take me out and we'd try out some of the things in the books, like building a shelter out of spruce boughs. Once he even set up a treasure hunt for me, using compass coordinates."

"That sounds fun. What was the treasure?" Amanda asked as she finished her last bite of bacon.

"A gift certificate to the local bookstore."

"Appropriate. Is the bookstore still open? Paisley and I might have to pay it a visit."

"I think it is. The woman who owns it is a good friend of Peggy's. She'll probably be at the memorial service today."

Amanda began gathering up her dishes and silverware. "Speaking of the memorial, I'd better round up Paisley so we can get showered before the service."

"Do you have a few minutes to spare first? There really is something outside I'd like to show Paisley." Nathan nodded toward Paisley, who was descending the stairs. One hand gripped the banister, while the other held the open book she'd been reading the night before while she walked.

Amanda jumped up. "Sure, but excuse me." She hurried over to stop Paisley before she took a header down the stairs. "Honey, read or walk," she called from the foot of the stairs. "Not both at the same time."

Paisley sighed, but she closed her book and walked slowly the rest of the way. "Are you still eating?"

"No, we're finished, and Nathan says he's ready to show you his surprise." When she looked back, Nathan had bussed the table and was standing beside the back door, a pair of binoculars swinging from his hand. He gestured for them to come. "Better leave the book in here."

With a shocking lack of argument, Paisley laid her book on the table and trotted across the dining area. "I'm ready!"

"Great." Nathan ushered them out onto the covered back porch, where tables and chairs invited guests to sit and enjoy the view of the lake. Off to the side, benches surrounded a firepit on a paved patio. Nathan led them down the porch steps and across the lawn toward the lake, and then turned left to follow the trail that paralleled the lakeshore, winding in and out of the woods, until they came to a small stream that fed into the lake. A simple wooden bridge spanned the stream, but rather than cross, Nathan turned to lead them on a narrower trail beside the water. "I hope they're still out. I saw them when I was walking early this morning."

"Who?" Paisley asked.

"You'll see, at least I hope so. It's right up ahead."

He held a finger to his lips. "We need to be quiet now."

"Okay," Paisley whispered.

With exaggerated care, Nathan tiptoed farther up the path, with Paisley on his heels. Amanda followed. The creek took a bend, and on the other side, what looked like a logjam had stopped up the creek, creating a pond behind it. Nathan stepped off the trail onto a large flat rock at the edge of the pond, gestured for Paisley to stand in front of him, and pointed toward something moving in the shadows under the trees at the far edge of the pond. For a moment, Amanda thought it was a little duck, but then she realized it was an animal's head. Another wet head popped up and looked their way. Suddenly one of the animals slapped the water with a flat tail, startling Paisley, who jumped back.

Nathan caught her easily and gently set her back on her feet. "It's okay. See, they're gone. They use their tails to signal that there might be a threat, but if we're really still and quiet, maybe they'll come back up."

"What are they?" Paisley whispered.

"Beavers," Nathan whispered back. "There were three beaver kits here this morning."

Sure enough, a few seconds later, the two little heads appeared on the surface of the water, looking in their direction. Paisley watched, her eyes opened wide. After a moment, one of the beavers must have decided they didn't seem too dangerous and swam closer. Now they could see the thick fur covering its head and body, all except for the leathery flat tail that functioned as a rudder. Dark eyes like ebony beads examined them with as much curiosity as Paisley was examining the beaver, but then it turned and swam away, toward what Amanda now realized was the beaver dam. It ducked under the water and disappeared.

Paisley looked up at Nathan's face. "That's so cool."

"I thought you'd like seeing them." Nathan exchanged glances with Amanda. "We'd better head back now."

Paisley frowned. "Do we have to?"

Amanda prepared herself for negotiations, but before she could answer, Nathan replied, "Yeah, we do. I promised your mom it would only take a few minutes, and we all need to get organized for the memorial service. I probably should have waited until tomorrow to bring you here, but when I saw the kits this morning, I could hardly wait to show you." He stepped down from the rock and offered Paisley a hand.

"Is that what baby beavers are called? Kits?" Paisley asked as she took his hand and hopped down.

"Yes. Did you know they can swim when they're just a few days old? And look at this." He pointed to pointed stumps Amanda estimated to be six or eight inches in diameter. "These were the trees the beavers cut down to make their dam. They eat the bark."

"Do the babies eat it, too?" Paisley asked as they walked back the way they'd come.

"They start with milk, just like most babies, but their parents start feeding them leaves and twigs when they're just a few weeks old. I suspect that's where the parents are right now, gathering more twigs for the babies."

In the five minutes it took to return to the lodge, Paisley continued to ask questions about beavers, and Nathan patiently answered each one. Amanda had never seen her this excited over anything outside of a book. When they reached the lodge, Paisley turned to Nathan. "Thank you for taking me. Can we go again, tomorrow?"

He smiled at her. "Sure. Now, we'd better go wash up."

"Okay. See you later."

Paisley ran ahead, but Amanda held back with Nathan for a moment. "Thank you."

"For what?" he asked.

"For showing Paisley the beavers. I suspect she'll want to go see them every day we're here."

"I hope that's okay. I just wanted to share—"

"It's more than okay," she told him. "It's great. I love that she's discovering a love for the natural world."

"I'm just doing what Harry and Eleanor did for me, when I was her age, paying it forward."

"Well, Harry and Eleanor were very special people." And, Amanda was beginning to believe, so was Nathan.

CHAPTER FOUR

SINCE PEGGY HAD insisted they didn't need to dress up, Amanda skipped the black dress she'd brought, but she wasn't quite ready to go to jeans, either. Instead she wore a songbird-print top Eleanor would have liked, with black leggings, flats, and a long gray cardigan. Paisley did wear the blue dress she'd brought, but she wore pink leggings underneath. When Amanda and Paisley went downstairs, Nathan and Malcolm were already waiting, dressed almost identically in pressed jeans, button-down shirts, and light jackets. Malcolm's shirt was plaid, while Nathan's was a blue pinstripe.

"Where's Peggy?" Amanda asked.

"In the kitchen, leaving a note for her volunteers," Nathan answered. "You look nice."

"Thanks."

Peggy emerged from the kitchen, wearing her usual uniform of jeans and a long-sleeved shirt, although the shirt looked new. "Ready? Vince says he'll meet us there with the chairs." She picked up a backpack from beside the door.

"I'll take that." Nathan put the backpack onto his own back.

"Oh, I almost forgot. Nathan, turn around." Peggy unzipped the backpack and pulled out a can of insect repellent. "We don't want mosquitoes eating us alive when we get to the marsh."

They all sprayed their exposed skin and Peggy returned the can to the backpack. Nathan held the door open until everyone was through. Peggy led the way across the lawn to the Swan's Marsh trailhead. She stepped into the woods in a brisk walk, with Paisley trotting along just behind her, her head swiveling as she took in everything around her. Nathan fell in next, with Amanda and Malcolm bringing up the rear.

"Who is Vince?" Amanda asked Malcolm as they made their way along the path.

"A friend of Peggy's," Malcolm replied. "He was also Eleanor's lawyer. He's semiretired, but he has an office in town. He's a good guy."

Something rustled in the bushes beside the path, and Paisley jumped back and instinctively grabbed Nathan's hand. "What's that?"

"Probably a squirrel," Nathan said, but Amanda noticed he put himself between Paisley and the noise. "It's amazing how much noise a small animal can make in dry leaves."

But a second later, a robin hopped out of the bush, a worm dangling from his beak. He cast a suspicious eye toward the group before flying to a tree to eat his breakfast in peace.

Paisley laughed. "It was just a bird."

"An American robin," Nathan proclaimed. "You can add it to your life list once we get back home."

A few minutes later, they cleared the woods and could see the marsh up ahead. Peggy stopped and pointed to a gap in the reeds, with something white behind it. "Look right through there, Paisley. Can you see it?"

"It's a swan. Is it Albert or Alison?" Paisley asked.

"Hard to say," Peggy told her. "They look alike to me. Eleanor said she could tell them apart, but the only way I know is that Albert has a leg band and Alison doesn't. But you can't see it when they're swimming."

The swan swam past a bigger gap, giving them all a clear view, before disappearing farther into the reeds. "I'll go on ahead to help Vince," Malcolm said, but they all followed him to the large deck at the end of the trail that accessed boardwalks fanning out in three directions, zigzagging through the marsh. Someone had pulled a pickup truck into the parking lot near the deck, and a man with a thick head of snowy-white hair was unloading folding chairs from the back.

"Vince," Peggy called as they drew closer. "Thanks for picking those up. You know Nathan." She paused while the two men greeted each other.

"And this is Amanda Flores, Eleanor's great-niece, and her daughter, Paisley, from Albuquerque."

Vince offered a friendly smile. "I'm very glad to meet you both. I'm Vincent Emerson, and I'd like to offer my condolences. Eleanor was a special person. She'll be missed."

"Yes, she was," Amanda replied. "Thank you."

"Now," Vince said, turning to Peggy, "tell me how you want everything set up."

The whole group pitched in, and under Peggy's direction they soon had the folding chairs arranged in rows facing out toward Swan's Marsh. Ten rows of ten chairs, with an aisle down the middle. Considering the size of the town, it was hard for Amanda to imagine a hundred people showing up at Swan's Marsh for a memorial service, but presumably Peggy knew what she was doing. Vince carried a card table to the front and set it up. Peggy, retrieving the backpack from Nathan, took out two cans of mosquito spray and set them on the rail posts at the entrance to the deck. Next, she unpacked a green tablecloth, which she spread over the table and anchored with clips. And finally, she pulled out a beeswax candle with a hurricane shade, a vase made from polished birch, and two framed photos, which she set up on the table. The first picture was of Eleanor, gray curls blowing away from her face and Swan's Marsh in the background. Sunlight caused her to squint and highlighted the wrinkles in her face, but there was nothing but joy in her smile. A mallard who had just taken off from the water was visible over her shoulder. The other picture was of Eleanor and Harry, when they were probably in their sixties, together on the porch of the lodge. His arm was around her, and she was leaning her head against his shoulder. Their gentle smiles spoke of a forever love.

Peggy put the vase in between the two photos. It took a second for Amanda to recognize it as an urn, presumably the one holding Eleanor's ashes. That's when it hit her—Eleanor was truly gone. Tears pushed against the backs of her eyes. It might seem strange that she could miss someone she'd only spent a few days with in her entire life, but Eleanor had found a home in her heart. When Amanda's dad died, Eleanor had come to the funeral, and for years afterward, every so often Amanda would receive a picture postcard with a brief note that always ended, "Love, Aunt Eleanor and Uncle Harry." Eleanor was the only relative on her dad's side of the family that had really kept in touch, and those postcards had meant a lot to Amanda. Eleanor would call, too, every once in a while, and for some reason Amanda, who was normally a reserved child, would find herself telling Eleanor every little thing going on in her life. And Eleanor had listened as though Amanda was the most fascinating person on earth.

Someone touched her back and she turned to see Nathan's warm brown eyes looking at her with concern. "You okay?"

"Yeah. It just hit me, you know. That I'll never see her again."

"I know. Especially here, I keep expecting to turn around and see her standing on one of the boardwalks with binoculars. Or motioning me over to point out some little duck and reciting its entire migration path."

"Yeah, she really did love birds. My dad said when he was a kid and she was a young adult, she could identify almost any bird just from its call."

"That's right, your dad was Eleanor's nephew. So I guess they grew up on that farm in Hatch, New Mexico, you told me about."

"Yes." Amanda was surprised he remembered the details. "I wonder how she and Harry ended up here."

"You'll find out soon," Peggy told them, as two or three cars pulled into the parking lot. "We'll begin in about fifteen minutes. Nathan, you still want to say a few words?"

He nodded. "If it's okay with you." He turned to Amanda. "But she's your blood relative. Would you like to speak?"

"I—I haven't prepared anything." Maybe she should have. She was Eleanor's only relative present.

"It's very informal," Peggy told her. "Everyone

will have a chance to share if they want to. Just do whatever feels right."

The first people from the parking lot made their way to the deck, chatting together as they selected chairs. A man who looked to be about in his mid-forties, dressed casually in jeans and a Henley, came forward and was talking with Peggy. More people arrived, several stopping to use the insect repellent Peggy had set out. Within minutes, most of the chairs had filled. Nathan touched Amanda's elbow. "We'd better sit down. Malcolm is saving us seats up front."

Amanda nodded and looked around for Paisley. She found her leaning on the rail in the corner of the deck, gazing out across the marsh. Amanda examined the tall reeds and water plants, but she didn't spot anything to merit Paisley's fascination. "What do you see out there?"

"It's kinda like an ocean, isn't it?" Paisley answered. "The way the grass moves whenever the wind blows, it looks like waves."

"It does." It was soothing somehow, the undulating pattern of the marsh grasses swaying. "Eleanor loved it here." She gave Paisley's shoulders a squeeze. "Come on. We need to find our seats. We're about to start."

Paisley followed, but she kept looking back at the marsh. "If Aunt Eleanor was my aunt, why didn't she ever come over to visit, like Aunt Jess?"

"Well, for one thing, she lived here in Alaska,

and would have had to fly to come visit. And besides, she wasn't as close a relative as Jess. Aunt Jess is my sister, and Aunt Eleanor was my grandfather's sister, my great-aunt." Amanda wasn't sure now was the best time for this discussion, but Paisley wouldn't be satisfied until she understood. "Which makes her your great-great-aunt."

Paisley thought about that for a second. "Was she old?" she asked, as they settled in the two chairs between Malcolm and Nathan.

The man who had been talking with Peggy moved to the front of the deck to stand beside the table, and the low buzz of conversation began to drop off. "She was ninety-four," Amanda whispered to Paisley.

"Ninety-four! That's really old!" Paisley's comments rung out just as everyone else grew quiet.

Laughter bubbled through the crowd, and the man at the front grinned. "She's right, you know. Ninety-four years is old, although somehow when you talked with Eleanor, you tended to forget her age." He smiled and gave a little nod toward Amanda and Paisley. "I'm Dan William, pastor at Swan Falls Community Church, and Eleanor was one of the first people to greet me and my family when we moved here six years ago. Since that time, she and I have spent quite a bit of time together, and she's told me lots of stories. As you can imagine, in ninety-four years of life, Eleanor was witness to many changes. The farmhouse in

New Mexico where she was born didn't even have electricity until she was six years old, and yet Peggy tells me that the day before Eleanor passed away, she was adding new photos taken with her digital camera to the lodge's website."

He consulted a note card in his hand. "She had almost four hundred birds on her life list, and considering there are only five hundred forty-something species of birds in Alaska, and she seldom left the state, that's pretty amazing. Just this past May, she spotted a surf scoter and a harlequin duck right here at Swan's Marsh, on the same day!" From the oohs and aahs from some of the people there, Amanda gathered those must be rare birds. The pastor continued. "Eleanor loved this marsh, and she loved sharing it with other people. That's why she wanted her memorial service here. So that you could all enjoy the scenery while we share our memories of Eleanor. But before we do that, Vince has an announcement."

The man who had brought the chairs stood and moved to the front of the deck. "Hello. For those who may not know me, I'm Vincent Emerson, and I was privileged to work with Eleanor. For various reasons, I can't give you all the details yet, but I do want you to know that Eleanor's will states that ownership of the property containing Swan's Marsh will be transferred to a trust. It will remain a bird sanctuary in perpetuity, so that we and future residents and visitors to Swan Falls will be able to enjoy the wildlife and birds, just as Eleanor did."

As everyone applauded, Peggy came forward again. "Thank you, Vince. Now at this time, if anyone would like to share something about Eleanor, we'll take turns. Nathan, let's start with you."

Nathan stood and went to the front. "Hi. I know some of you, but for those who don't know me, I'm Nathan Swan, Harry's great-nephew. I grew up in Phoenix, but every summer my dad would work in Alaska and I would come here, to Swan Lodge. That month was the best part of every year for me, and not only because in July, Phoenix is basically the temperature of molten lava. It was awfully nice to be able to go outside without my shoes melting to the sidewalk." He paused while the group laughed. "But the main reason I loved coming is because of Harry and Eleanor." He took a long breath. "My dad loved me, but you know, being a single parent isn't easy. Sometimes, it felt like I was just one more chore on his list of things to do. But Harry and Eleanor always made me feel like I was special. They would take me hiking and fishing and bird-watching. They kept in touch when we were apart as well. Sometimes Eleanor would find out what book I was reading, and she'd get a copy to read at the same time so we could discuss it. She didn't ever stop doing that, even after Harry died. Sort of a mini book club, I guess. Anyway, she's always been special to me, and I know she was to you, too, so I'll stop talking and let someone else have a chance." He nodded toward the photo. "Love you, Eleanor. We'll miss you."

One after another, people came forward to share their stories. Amanda was amazed at how many people Eleanor had touched in her lifetime. Many shared how she had helped them in a time of need, or lent encouragement at just the right moment, or sometimes how having her around had made them smile.

After a while, Amanda took her turn. "I'm Amanda Flores, Eleanor's great-niece. I was ten the first time I met Eleanor. She and Harry had a standing invitation for family to come up to Alaska for a visit. My dad was a farmer, and it was hard to get away, but we finally came up for a week one August, and it was like nothing I had ever experienced. It rained a lot—" she had to pause while the crowd laughed. "Yeah, Harry told us later that rain was pretty much a given in August, but the rain didn't matter, it was still beautiful. So green and fresh. Harry and Eleanor took us to the state fair to see the animals and all the giant vegetables. Even my sister, who isn't exactly an outdoorsy person, agreed that musk ox calves have to be in the running for cutest babies ever. But my favorite part was when Eleanor brought me here, to Swan's Marsh, and told me about the swans and other birds who call this home. It was almost like she was introducing me to her friends."

Amanda felt a tear well up and waited to take a breath. "The next time I saw her was two years later when my father died. She traveled down to the funeral. I don't remember a lot of details about that time, but I do remember how kind she was to my sister and me, answering our questions and just being around to comfort us. And it didn't stop there, she continued to keep tabs on us, calling and sending birthday cards. I always intended to come back to visit her, but that didn't happen until eight years ago, when I flew up with my husband and baby daughter. I was a little afraid the Alaska magic would be gone, but it almost felt like I'd never left. Harry and Eleanor were twenty years older, and yet they seemed the same, as energetic as ever." Amanda thought about telling them how supportive Eleanor had been when David died, but that felt too private to share. "Eleanor always made me feel valued and loved." She looked up at the sky. "Goodbye, Aunt Eleanor. We love you."

The tears overflowed as she returned to her seat. Nathan patted her shoulder and handed her a tissue. She gave him a little smile. If she missed Eleanor this much, she could only imagine how Nathan felt.

Malcolm got up and stepped to the front. "Before I met Eleanor, I'd been going through a rough patch. I was living in Anchorage then. My two kids had grown and moved down to the lower forty-eight, and my wife decided she didn't want to be married to me anymore. Then the company I'd been working for for twenty-three years went bankrupt, leaving me without a job. So, all my plans were out the window. Luckily for me, I happened to see an ad for someone to handle outdoor maintenance at Swan Lodge and thought that might be interesting. Before that, the only thing I knew about Swan Falls was that there was an exit sign on the highway. But when I drove through and saw the mercantile with the hanging baskets out front, and the diner, and the people hanging out at the park, it felt like a good place. And then I got to the lodge and met Eleanor. She gave the particulars of the job and pay and all, but she didn't ask about my experience, or why a man my age was looking for a new job, or anything like that. She took me to the shed and pointed to about a dozen assorted lawn mower parts scattered across a workbench and asked me if I could put it back together. So I said, 'Yes, ma'am.'"

"'Good,' she says, 'because my husband took this stupid thing apart to overhaul it last winter, and then went and died on me.' Then, she gave me that look—you might know the one I mean. Where you got the feeling she could see right into your soul?" Murmurs of agreement swept through the crowd. "And then Eleanor says, 'I miss that man something fierce, and sometimes I'm so mad he left me behind that I could just spit. But nobody gets through life without hurts and losses, so I figure we walking wounded can help each other keep going. You want to be part of that?' and I told her I did."

Malcolm looked out over the marsh. "Eleanor loved this spot. It's been an honor for me to build this deck and extend the boardwalks the way she wanted so that more people could enjoy the birds like she did. I'm proud to have been able to call Eleanor Swan my employer and my friend. To be honest, I'm a little annoyed at her for leaving. But even though I never knew Harry, I'm glad they're together again. Fly free, Eleanor!"

From the reeds in the marsh behind him, a gray-and-white bird with a black cap suddenly took flight. The long sharp wings and fanned tail with longer feathers on each end marked it as an arctic tern. Amanda remembered Eleanor telling her all about their long journey each year, following the sun from their birthplace near the Arctic Circle all the way to the Antarctic Circle in the Southern Hemisphere, and then back home again.

The bird made a sudden swerve and flew directly toward them. People gasped. It circled the deck and then spiraled upward into the air before, with a sudden flip of its tail, it turned and flew across the marsh. They all watched, wordless, until it had disappeared into the cottonwood trees on the far bank.

The minister stood and Malcolm took his seat again. He stared out over the water at the path the bird had taken. "Wow. I was going to say a few more words about Eleanor, but nothing I could say would be a more appropriate goodbye. Thank you for coming, everyone, and the family has asked that I let you know you're all invited to a light lunch reception at the lodge." He offered a final prayer and then looked out over the marsh. "Godspeed."

CHAPTER FIVE

NATHAN HELPED HIMSELF to a lemon bar as he listened to yet another story about Eleanor, this one from a young woman who had introduced herself as Melisa Englund, the local fourth-grade teacher. "Ms. Eleanor didn't even have kids, but she came to every school play and concert and basketball game. I remember when I was in sixth grade, which would have made me eleven, we were putting on a play, and I had the role of Mary Poppins. We'd practiced and practiced, but when the time came for me to sing the first song, the words just went right out of my head. I froze. But then I looked over and there was Ms. Eleanor, right in the front row. She started singing 'A Spoonful of Sugar' just loud enough for me to hear, and once I started, the words all came back. And after the show, she made a point of coming to tell me what a wonderful job I did."

"That sounds like Eleanor," Nathan agreed. "She always encouraged me, too."

Peggy came from behind him and put a hand

on his arm. "So glad you could come, Melissa. Excuse me, but I need to steal Nathan away for a few minutes."

"Of course."

Peggy motioned for Nathan to follow her. "Vince says he needs you in the library."

"What for?" Nathan asked. He glanced around the room. Paisley was in a chair near the fire, holding a book on her lap and talking to another girl about her age, but he didn't see Amanda anywhere.

"I'm not sure. He just asked me to round up you and Amanda and Malcolm. They're already up there."

"Hmm." Since Vincent had been Eleanor's lawyer, maybe he was going to offer family members and longtime staff some sort of memento. Nathan wouldn't mind having something to remember Harry and Eleanor by, perhaps a copy of that photo of the two of them on the porch of the lodge the first year it was built.

Presumably, Eleanor had left the lodge to Nathan's father and uncle, since they were Harry's closest relatives, and they would no doubt put it on the market as soon as possible. Uncle Mick had never shown any interest in Alaska. Dad had been fond of Harry and Eleanor, but his summer pilgrimages to Alaska had been about earning money, not enjoying nature. Commercial fishing meant long days of hard labor, but Dad had earned enough extra to be able to invest in Arizona real estate during the housing bust, which had paid off very well. He was presently shopping for a comfortable retirement home on a golf course. Operating a lodge in Alaska would be the last thing he'd want to do.

It would be a shame if Swan Lodge were bought by some big corporation and became just another property in a chain. Maybe Nathan could convince his father and uncle to let him have a go at operating the lodge. He had no experience, other than what he'd observed by shadowing Harry and Eleanor, but he could learn. He liked his current job in IT well enough, but it was just a job, not a calling. He'd never experienced the sort of satisfaction that he'd observed in Harry and Eleanor, their love for this place shining through in the way they shared it with their guests. But Dad and Uncle Mick probably wouldn't go for it. They had both recently retired and neither of them would want to take on a new project, even if Nathan was willing to manage it.

Besides, Eleanor might just as well have left it to a charity, perhaps to finance the Swan's Marsh wildlife refuge. Either way, this week would probably be Nathan's last chance to say goodbye to the place that had meant so much to him. Nathan followed Peggy up the stairs and into the library. Amanda and Malcolm stood near the window, in conversation with Vince.

"Ah, good, we're all here. Let's take a seat."

Vince pulled out a chair from the round table, and everyone else followed suit. Vince took a pair of reading glasses from his pocket and put them on, and then opened the folder in front of him. After a dramatic pause, he cleared his throat. "Despite what you might have seen in movies, we generally don't do any kind of official 'reading of the will' these days. However, as Eleanor herself was a fan of old movies, and since you all happen to be here today, I thought it might be appropriate to have an informal gathering."

"This won't take too long, will it?" Peggy asked. "We have guests."

"I'm sure they can manage without you for a few minutes." Vince tapped the papers on the desk. "I am named in Eleanor's will as executor, so it will be my responsibility to carry out the terms. I don't know if she talked with any of you about what was in the will…?" Vince let his voice trail off, but everyone shook their heads except Peggy.

"We talked about the pros and cons of certain ideas," Peggy told him, "but she wouldn't tell me what she decided, except about putting the marsh in a trust."

"Yes, the marsh. Let's start with that. The Swan's Marsh Wildlife Refuge is to be held in trust, overseen by a board of directors. There is a sum of money attached, which will produce income for maintenance. If everyone agrees, she wanted the board made up of myself; Lars Johanson, the current mayor of Swan Falls; Marissa Allen, a wildlife researcher and a good friend of Eleanor's; and two family members: specifically Nathan Swan and Amanda Flores." He looked toward Amanda, then turned to Nathan. "Would you both agree to serve on the committee?"

"Of course, if that's what Eleanor wanted," Nathan responded. It would be a chance to repay Eleanor for all the years of hospitality and love.

"Um, I'm not sure. Since I live in Albuquerque—" Amanda started to say, but Vince interrupted.

"Don't worry about that. The board will generally meet once a year, and there's no reason it can't be done remotely. Eleanor left an endowment to pay for upkeep, so it's not as though anyone expects you to fly up to Alaska to replace a cracked board in the boardwalk."

"In that case," Amanda said, "I'd be honored."

"Excellent. I'll contact Ms. Allen and Lars to make sure they're willing to serve."

"I'm sure Marissa will agree," Peggy interjected. "She used to come to Swan's Marsh two or three times a year to take pictures, and to get Eleanor's help on a book she's writing about Alaskan ducks and geese. She called yesterday to let me know that her son has a stomach bug. Otherwise she would be here."

"Sounds like Swan's Marsh will be in good hands." He turned the page. "There's also a provision in the will to provide playground equipment for the park in Swan Falls, and while Eleanor didn't specifically ask it in the will, I know she would be pleased if Nathan and Amanda would work with me to choose the equipment." He smiled. "Perhaps Paisley could act as a consultant on that. I was talking with her earlier, and she strikes me as a highly intelligent young lady."

Amanda laughed. "I'm sure she'd be happy to give her opinions."

He patted his briefcase. "I brought a catalog with me today. I'll leave it with you, along with the budget. Once you've chosen, let me know and I'll get them ordered and coordinate with the mayor about site preparation." He turned a page. "Another minor provision—should the Deanna Somers bronze sculpture entitled *Swan Trio* ever be recovered, it is to go to the Swan Falls museum for display."

Nathan's heart sank. The loss of that sculpture was one of his biggest regrets. Both Harry and Eleanor had assured him it wasn't his fault, but he still felt responsible for the loss.

"Deanna Somers. Isn't she the artist that made the famous seagulls sculpture in Seattle a few years ago?" Amanda asked.

"Yes," Vince answered. "*Swan Trio* is much smaller, of course. I don't know all the details, just that it was stolen from Swan Lodge."

"Deanna Somers stayed here one summer in the

1960s," Peggy explained. "She had a commission from the Swanson hotel chain for a swan fountain sculpture for their flagship hotel in Las Vegas, but she was having trouble coming up with a concept. Somebody told her about Swan Lodge, and she came here to watch and learn about the swans. She spent most of the summer in one of the cabins and would spend hours at the marsh almost every day, watching the swans and talking with Eleanor. After she went home, she created several smaller sculptures, working out all the details before she zeroed in on the final seven-swan design that she used to make the huge fountain for the Vegas hotel. She sent one of the small ones to Eleanor and Harry, as a thank-you for helping her 'recover her muse.' It was gorgeous—a swimming swan and two others taking off from a base with reeds and cattails."

"Oh, I remember that sculpture from when I came here as a child," Amanda said. "It used to sit on the end of the reception desk, right? It was beautiful. What happened?"

Nathan took up the story. "I was staffing the front desk that day—"

"Now, Nathan, don't go blaming yourself," Peggy interjected. "It could have happened to anyone."

"Maybe, but I was supposed to be at the desk, not roaming around the building. Except there was a large party checking in and the guy who was supposed to be handling the luggage wasn't anywhere to be found," he explained, "so I took all their luggage upstairs myself. It took several trips, and I probably left the desk unattended for a good twenty or thirty minutes total. After I'd finished, I went back to the desk and another couple was waiting to check in. I didn't notice the swans were missing until the man asked for a map. We always kept the maps on a shelf under the end of the desk where the swans sat. So the sculpture had to have been stolen while I was upstairs."

"And they never caught the thief?" Amanda asked.

"No. The state troopers talked with everyone who was around Swan Lodge at the time," Nathan answered, "but as far as I know, they came up blank."

"Harry wondered if one of the summer employees might have had something to do with it," Peggy mentioned. "We used to get summer help then, usually college students. The sculpture theft happened in the last half of August, just before most of them went home. But it's not like they could have just slipped it into their luggage and taken it—the sculpture was about three feet tall and must have weighed fifty or sixty pounds. Harry always drove them and their luggage to the airport, so it would have been pretty obvious if any of them were carrying around a crate that size. If any of them were guilty, they must have been working with somebody local."

"Or shipped it in advance," Malcolm pointed out. "I wonder if the troopers checked everyone's whereabouts for the next few days."

Vince cleared his throat. "If the troopers couldn't find any clues at the time, I doubt we're going to solve anything now. Interesting as this is, we should probably return to the business at hand." He reached into the back of his folder and took out two envelopes. "Peggy and Malcolm, I know you both have retirement accounts, but Eleanor also set aside a sum to provide each of you with an annuity. The details are here."

"Aw, there was no need for her to do that," Malcolm said. "She's been nothing but generous."

"She told me she wants to thank you both for your years of loyalty, and most of all for your friendship." Vince turned another page and gave a little pause, as though waiting for his audience to focus their attention, although they were all gazing at him.

"And finally," he said, "we come to the residual of the estate. Except for the funds mentioned in the other bequests, including the Swan's Marsh Trust, Eleanor and Harry had invested most of their retirement savings into a joint and survivor annuity, which ceased payment upon Eleanor's death, so, with the exception of personal property and her vehicles, the residual of the estate consists of the real property here including this lodge, the cabins, the various outbuildings, and a relatively modest cash savings account that she used for payroll, operating expenses, and maintenance."

He glanced at Nathan, and then at Amanda, before dropping his gaze to the paper in front of him, and read aloud, "The residual of my property, real and personal, I leave in equal shares to my husband's great-nephew Nathan Alexander Swan and to my great-niece Amanda Renee Clemente Flores."

AMANDA STARED AT the lawyer. Eleanor had left half of this lodge to her? Why would she have done that?

Voices swirled around her, but Amanda couldn't focus. Her time spent with Eleanor amounted to a matter of days. It wasn't as though they were really close. Not like Nathan, who had apparently talked to Eleanor on a weekly basis. And yet, for some reason, Eleanor had left them equal shares of Swan Lodge.

"Does anyone have questions?" Vince asked. Amanda had dozens, but she couldn't seem to put any of them into words. Everyone else at the table looked as shocked as she was. Vince gave a kind smile. "I'm sure you will, once you've had time to think." He pulled out a stack of business cards, passing one to each of them. "I'll be contacting each of you soon, but in the meantime if you need me, feel free to give me a call. Now, I've kept you away from your guests for long enough. We'd better head downstairs."

Everyone pushed their chairs back and stood. Amanda followed suit, still in a daze. Peggy and Malcolm slipped out the door, but Nathan and Vince held back. Nathan touched her elbow. "Are you okay?"

"I—I'm fine. I just…" She paused.

"I know." Nathan shook his head slowly. "It's a lot to take in. I never expected this."

"Well, for you, it makes sense. For me, I just don't understand it. Could it be some kind of mistake?"

"No mistake," Vince assured her. "Eleanor made this will a little over a year ago. She was quite definite about what she wanted."

"But why me? She had other relatives—my sister for one." Jess was not going to be happy to learn Eleanor had put Amanda in the will and left her out. "And Nathan's father, and didn't you mention cousins?" Amanda asked Nathan.

"Yeah, Harry had five other great-nieces and nephews besides me, and their father, Harry's nephew, is still living. As far as I know, none of my cousins has ever met Eleanor, though."

"Well, there you go. Eleanor must have felt like they were strangers, but you and Nathan were family." Vince pulled another book from his briefcase. "Here's that playground equipment catalog I mentioned. I'd like to get that ordered while you're still in Alaska. Are you both planning to stay for the entire week?"

Amanda and Nathan both nodded.

"Splendid. Give me a call and we'll set something up." He went into the hallway.

Nathan started to follow, but he looked back. "Are you coming?"

"In a minute. You go ahead." Amanda waited until he'd left to walk to the window and stare out at the lake. In the surrounding woods, she caught an occasional glimpse of the brown metal roofs on the cabins. This was hers, well, hers and Nathan's. Eleanor had given it to them.

And that's when it hit her. This solved everything! That's why Eleanor changed her will a year ago, not all that long after David's death. Amanda hadn't told her about the medical bills and aging greenhouses, but somehow Eleanor had known, and wanted to help.

Amanda had no idea how much one half of an Alaskan lodge would bring, but it had to be more than the cost of two new greenhouses. With the money from the sale, she could rescue the nursery so that Paisley could one day take over her father's business. There should even be enough left over to start a college fund for Paisley. Maybe she would major in horticulture or get a business degree. Either one would teach her what she needed to know to make a success of Zia Gardens someday. Yes, thanks to Aunt Eleanor, everything was going to be all right.

CHAPTER SIX

THE NEXT MORNING, Nathan found Peggy and Malcolm at the kitchen table. "Good morning."

"Morning. Want some coffee?" Peggy started to get up, but Nathan held up a hand to stop her.

"Sit. I can pour my own." He did and took a chair at the table.

Malcolm's eyes crinkled up in the corners. "Good morning, boss."

Nathan laughed. "That doesn't sound quite right."

"But it's true," Peggy insisted. "Unless you're passing out pink slips, we're working for you now. But don't think just because you own the place that you can boss me around in my own kitchen."

"I wouldn't dream of it," Nathan assured her.

Peggy laughed, but then her face sobered. "Seriously, though, what are your plans? You're not going to sell to some big hotel conglomerate, are you?"

"Actually," Nathan replied, "I'm thinking of running it."

Peggy pointed at Malcolm. "Ha! Told you."

"Fine," he grumbled. "I owe you a chore."

Peggy turned her beaming face to Nathan. "I told Eleanor you were the only one in the family who wouldn't sell. She fretted over it for a long time, about what would happen to the lodge once she wasn't around any longer."

"So you knew she was going to do this?"

"Not for sure. She told me she'd left it to you in the will she wrote after Harry died, but early last year, she said she was going to talk with Vince about updating the details and she refused to tell me what she was changing. I figured it was about the marsh and the trust she was setting up. I never thought about her leaving half to Amanda, though. If I'd have known—"

"You would have pressured her to change her mind," Malcolm said. "Which, no doubt, is why she didn't tell you."

Nathan looked at Peggy in surprise. "I thought you liked Amanda."

"I do. She was a sweetheart when she first came here as a girl, and she still is. Her sister, on the other hand—well, let's not get into that. Amanda is a good mother, too—you can tell, the way she interacts with Paisley. But she doesn't have roots in this place. And Vince didn't mention it, but the date on that will was not long after Amanda's husband died. Makes me wonder."

"Wonder what?" Nathan asked. "Are you saying Amanda might have played on Eleanor's sympathy to get herself added to the will?" From what he'd seen of Amanda, she didn't seem like the type. On the other hand, he didn't think his ex-fiancée was the type to take advantage of a situation either, so obviously he wasn't a great judge of character.

Peggy shrugged. "Eleanor didn't feel up to traveling at that time, but I know she talked on the phone to Amanda several times after her husband passed. Amanda might have dropped a hint or two."

Malcolm raised his eyebrows. "Are we talking about the same Eleanor? Peggy, you said yourself you were terrified of her the first couple of months you worked for her. Yes, Eleanor had a big heart, but she wasn't some feeble-minded ninny who would fall for a sob story, and she still had her wits about her." Malcolm nodded decisively. "So don't go thinking Amanda somehow pulled the wool over Eleanor's eyes. If Eleanor left her half this place, it's because she wanted her to have it."

"I guess you're right," Peggy admitted. "But it still worries me. Amanda never lived here. She doesn't have the same affection for this place Nathan does."

Nathan thought about it. "That could be a good thing. I want to stay and manage the lodge, get the cabins fixed up and opened, run it the same way Harry and Eleanor did. If Amanda doesn't have any sentimental ties to this place, she's more likely to leave the day-to-day operations in my hands."

"Maybe." Peggy's voice was doubtful. "But even if Eleanor wanted to leave a little something to Amanda, I wish she would have left you the majority share, rather than half-and-half. That way you'd be in control."

"Well, she didn't," Malcolm replied. "And I think you're selling Amanda short. She's been running that plant nursery since her husband died. Maybe she knows things about running a business that the rest of us don't. Could be she should be the one worried about working with an inexperienced partner. Not that I'm saying you're not going to do an excellent job, Nathan," he hastened to add. "I know Eleanor had faith in your abilities, and living here every summer, you're bound to have absorbed a lot of practical knowledge. I'm just saying you should look at it from Amanda's point of view."

"Point taken," Nathan said. "But just so we're clear, are you both still willing to stay on and help me get this place up and running again?"

"Absolutely," Peggy stated.

"Me, too," Malcolm assured him. "I put a new coat of sealer on the cabin logs last summer and did a few repairs, but Eleanor wouldn't let me touch anything on the interiors."

"That's because she saw what you'd done with your own cabin." Peggy turned to Nathan. "Can you believe he painted his living room walls acid green?"

Malcolm gave a sheepish grin. "There was a can of mis-mixed paint on the clearance rack at the hardware store. I admit, the color turned out to be a little brighter than it looked on the little patch on the lid. I repainted it off-white a few months later."

"Too late. Eleanor had already made up her mind that you should stick to outdoor repairs and maintenance. You're lucky she even let you inside the lodge to eat."

Malcolm huffed. "Be that as it may, the result was that the roofs and walls are in good repair, but other than a yearly cleaning, nobody's done anything to the insides of the cabin in five years or so. They're going to need paint and updates before they're ready to rent out again."

Nathan nodded. "The lodge could use some fresh paint as well, and the lamp in my room needs a new switch. I suspect the pros are already booked through the summer, so I'd like to do as much as we can ourselves. I'll talk with Amanda—"

"Good morning," Amanda called as she came through the swinging door to the kitchen.

"Oh, my goodness. I didn't realize you were up and about." Peggy jumped up from the table. "I'm a little behind this morning, but I'll have the breakfast buffet ready in twenty minutes or so. In the meantime, let me pour you some coffee. Or I can put a kettle on for tea if you prefer. Where's Paisley?"

"She'll be down soon. She finished her book last night and wanted to exchange it for a new one before she came down. Coffee sounds great, but I can pour my own. Peggy, please don't go to all the trouble to set up a breakfast buffet every morning just for us. Paisley and I are perfectly happy with cereal at the kitchen table."

Peggy sniffed. "You're welcome to eat in the kitchen if that's what you want, but I can certainly do better than cereal. I've got a French toast casserole in the oven, and I was going to make scrambled eggs and sausage."

Nathan's mouth watered. It had been a few years, but Peggy's French toast wasn't something one forgot. "The French toast with the caramel sauce?"

"That's the one."

"That sounds fabulous," Amanda told her. "But we couldn't possibly eat that and eggs and sausage."

"Same here," Nathan told Peggy. "Unless you or Malcolm want them."

Malcolm shook his head.

"All right, then." Peggy sat back down and picked up her mug. "But I feel like I'm not earning my keep."

"Are you kidding? We eat like kings around here," Nathan declared, before turning to Amanda. "Malcolm and I were just talking about repairs around the inn and cabins. For starters, the lobby area could use a fresh coat of paint."

"Agreed." Amanda sat down and took a sip from her cup. "I'm a decent painter if you want to save some money over hiring a pro."

"Exactly what I was thinking. How about if after breakfast, we do a walk-through and make a list of what needs doing, and then we can go into Wasilla for paint and equipment?"

"Sounds good, although I also want to make time to check out the catalog Vince gave us and choose the new playground equipment. Paisley's pretty excited about the idea."

"Get that order in soon," Malcolm advised. "If you wait too long, you'll have to let the ground thaw next summer to install it."

Nathan nodded in satisfaction. "Sounds like we have a plan."

AMANDA RAN HER finger over the strip of blue painter's tape she'd just applied to the top of a built-in bookcase, pressing it tight against the wall. It would be a crime to get paint on that gorgeous wood. As she stepped back, she noticed a Bluetooth speaker on one of the shelves. That's what they needed—music. She plugged in the speaker, paired it with her phone, and started the upbeat playlist she liked to listen to when she was cleaning.

Nathan, who had been spreading a drop cloth

across the floor on the other side of the lobby, gave her a thumbs-up. Even Malcolm looked up from his job filling dents and holes with spackle to grin at her. Paisley, however, didn't even lift her eyes from her book. Amanda knew from experience that when Paisley was caught up in an exciting chapter, the world around her ceased to exist.

Amanda moved to the next section of wall and applied tape to the baseboards there. They were stained the same reddish-gold as the floor, although both the floors and baseboards had a few scratches. She made a mental note to add matching stain to the list for their next trip to the hardware store.

The morning had been surprisingly productive. A walk through the lodge and cabins had revealed the need for fresh paint throughout the public areas and cabins, new flooring in two of the cabins, a new microwave in one, and a myriad of loose screws, burned-out light bulbs, missing kitchen utensils, and other minor tasks, each of which Nathan had dutifully noted on his phone. Then they'd sat down with Paisley, the catalog, and Vince's budget sheet to choose playground equipment that suited a variety of ages, from a mini-cabin playhouse for preschoolers to a climbing bar set where older kids and even adults could practice their chin-ups and brachiation, which was the proper word for swinging from rung to rung overhead using one's arms, according to Paisley.

Amanda smiled to herself. Sometimes it was a little humbling to be the mother of a kid like Paisley. A slide, four swings, a rope-net tunnel, and moose on a spring with a saddle for riding rounded out the fun. The three of them had then dropped the list by Vince's house. He'd been pleased with their choices and assured them he would arrange for new equipment right away, along with a load of rubber mulch for the playground.

Afterward, they'd driven to Wasilla to choose paint. Nathan's pick was a creamy neutral labeled "Vanilla Custard," not far from the dingy white currently on the walls, but Amanda's vote was for a muted sage green. "The green will make the warm reddish tones in the wood pop. Here, let me show you." She'd picked up a stain sample in a similar color to the log walls and floor of the lodge and held it next to the paint chip.

Nathan looked doubtful. "That does look good together, but it's a big room. Is there such a thing as too much popping? It's supposed to be a restful place. If we paint the whole room that color, it might be like a visual string of firecrackers in there."

Amanda laughed. "Okay. If you're not comfortable with that much color, how about if we paint the walls of the dining room and open area this cream color, and only use the sage on the walls in the alcove behind the reception desk." She picked up another swatch that was a darker shade of green, more of an olive. "We could even use this for the beadboard on the front of the desk." She sandwiched the stain sample between the two paint swatches to simulate the way the wooden desktop would break them up. "See?"

Paisley, who had been leaning against a wall and reading her book, looked up to examine Amanda's sample. "That's pretty," she volunteered.

"It is," Nathan admitted. "Okay, let's go with that. Now, what color for the walls of the cabins?" He drew in a breath as though he was girding himself.

Amanda took pity on him. "The cabins are too small for a lot of visual clutter. Let's keep it simple and go with the cream." She'd almost laughed at the look of relief on his face.

"Great. I'll find someone to mix it for us."

While the clerk got their paint order ready, they'd collected brushes, rollers, and drop cloths. "I'm getting hungry," Paisley said.

"Me, too," Nathan told her. "How do you feel about pizza?"

"I love pizza! Pepperoni?" Paisley suggested.

"Sure," he told Paisley. "Let me check with Peggy and Malcolm to see what they want on their pizza, and I'll call in an order. We can pick it up from Raven's Nest Pizza on the way home."

Home. Funny how easily the word had fallen from his lips. But then, Amanda supposed this place really was home to Nathan. After all, he'd spent one-twelfth of his childhood here at the lodge. As she applied a stripe of fresh paint onto the wall above the baseboard, she had to admit, she felt at home as well. It would be sad, selling the place. Even though she'd had no specific plans, she'd always felt like Eleanor and the lodge would be there forever, ready to welcome her and Paisley back some day. But Eleanor was gone, and soon the lodge would be as well.

After finishing that section of baseboard, Amanda stood and stretched. Across the room, Nathan was covering a section of wall with the new paint, his roller action keeping time to the beat. He was right, the soft creamy paint was a nice backdrop for the natural wood. It was probably a good thing he had convinced her not to use too much color on the walls, since she'd read that homes decorated in neutrals sold better than those with more color. Hopefully, a bit of green in the reception area wouldn't be enough to turn off any potential buyers.

"Hello!" a female voice called from near the front door.

Amanda looked over to see a woman with two suitcases on the floor near her feet. Between the music and concentrating on her painting, Amanda hadn't noticed anyone coming in. The woman was gazing around the half-painted lobby, a bemused expression on her face. Several gray-streaked wisps of hair escaped the messy bun on the top of her head and fell to the shoulders of her baggy cotton sweater. A streak of yellow stained the ribbing at the wrist.

"Hi." Amanda used her phone to stop the music. "Can I help you?"

"Yes. I'm Yolanda Harrison, and you are…"

"Amanda Flores."

"Ah, Amanda. You must be new. It's nice to meet you. I'm ready to check in, and I would sell my soul for a cup of tea. Is Eleanor around?"

"Um, no. I'm afraid—"

"Ms. Harrison." Nathan had put down his roller and come to join them. "I don't know if you remember me. I'm Nathan Swan."

"Nathan! Oh, my goodness. I haven't seen you since you were in high school." Immediately, the woman wrapped her arms around him in a hug. Nathan reacted with a chuckle and patted her on the back. After a moment, she stepped away and beamed up at him. "Eleanor must be thrilled to have you here with her."

Nathan shook his head. "I'm afraid Eleanor passed away about a month ago."

"Oh, no!" She pressed a hand to her chest. "I'm so sorry to hear that. I knew she was getting up there, but when I was here last summer, she still seemed so vibrant." She shook her head. "The world has lost a great lady."

"Yes," Nathan agreed.

"Well, I shall certainly miss her company." She

sighed, but after a moment, she straightened and rested a hand on the handle of her suitcase. "Is room number 102 available? That's where Eleanor always put me, so I didn't have to deal with stairs."

"Oh, um." Nathan shifted his weight to the other foot. "After Eleanor passed away, Peggy canceled all the outstanding reservations. I gather you didn't get the email."

"No, I didn't. Oh, dear. I've been traveling, you see, and I lost my cell phone for a while. When I finally got a replacement there was so much email and so many messages, I wasn't able to read them all. I do think I remember seeing something from Swan Lodge, but I just assumed it was confirmation. After all, I've been coming here for more than thirty years."

Malcolm must have alerted Peggy because she came rushing from the kitchen. "Yolanda!"

"Peggy!" The women hugged. "I just heard the news. I suppose I've missed Eleanor's memorial service."

Peggy nodded. "It was yesterday, at the marsh."

"Oh! Eleanor would have loved that."

"It was her favorite place."

"Mine, too." Yolanda gave her a sad smile. "So," she took a breath. "Nathan tells me you tried to cancel my reservation, but I must have missed the email. I don't suppose…" She gestured toward the hallway, let her voice trail off, and gazed at Nathan with wide eyes. Amanda waited for him or

Peggy to tell the woman they weren't prepared for guests. There would be paint and dust and noise for the next several days while they tried to get as much as possible done before Amanda headed home. But Peggy was silent.

"Well, we're kind of in the middle of some renovations, as you can see." Nathan gestured toward the half-painted wall he'd been working on.

"I don't mind that," Yolanda declared.

Nathan looked toward Amanda. "What do you think?"

Yolanda turned soft doe eyes toward Amanda, who felt herself weakening. "You would be the only guest. Wouldn't you be lonely?"

"Not at all. I spend most of my days at the marsh anyway. I'm a plein air painter, you see. And I never eat breakfast, just tea and maybe toast or a pastry, so I won't be any bother."

Amanda glanced toward Peggy to see if she had any objections. Peggy gave a little nod. "All right, then." Amanda gestured toward the glass doors at the rear of the lobby. "Why don't you and Peggy sit down with a cup of tea on the back porch, while I get room 102 ready for you?"

"Lovely." Abandoning her luggage, Yolanda sailed across the lobby, stepping around drop cloths and painting equipment. Peggy followed.

"I'll run a card key," Nathan offered, "And then I'll come help you fix up the room."

"Great. I'll get the linens and a cleaning cart."

Fortunately, yesterday's inspection had included the linen closet and laundry room at the end of the hall, which was also where cleaning supplies were stored. Amanda started for the hall, but she paused when she saw Yolanda stopping at the chair where Paisley was curled up with her book.

The older woman smiled at her. "Hello there. I'm Yolanda Harrison. What's your name?"

Paisley looked up, blinking, as though she was surprised to find herself there rather than in the world she'd been reading about. "Paisley Flores," she answered after a moment.

"It's nice to meet you, Paisley. What are you reading?"

"A book," Paisley replied, matter-of-factly.

Yolanda laughed. "I see that. What's the title?"

"*Treasure Island.* I found it in the library this morning and just started reading."

Yolanda's smile grew. "A classic."

"Have you read it?"

Yolanda shook her head. "I never have. Maybe I should, once you're done with it. Is it good?"

"I think it will be. It's hard to read, though, because it was in olden times and people talk weird." Paisley slipped in a bookmark and closed the book. "It's about a boy named Jim who lives at an inn kinda like this one, and they have this mean old guy staying there. He drinks rum, and sings, and he might be a pirate. And look." Paisley flipped to the end to show her something on the inside back cover. "It has a map."

"Is it a treasure map?" Yolanda asked, but when she saw it, she frowned. "Oh, dear. It looks like someone drew their own map in the book."

"Yeah, you're not supposed to draw in books."

Yolanda tsked. "At least they didn't damage the pages." Yolanda shifted the strap of her bag on her shoulder. "Well, I'll let you resume your reading."

Paisley took her at her word and immediately opened the book up again. Yolanda went through the glass door and settled at a table on the back porch, and Amanda went to gather what she'd need for the guest room. She returned with a cleaning cart and parked it outside the open door of room 102. Nathan was inside, pushing the curtains aside and cranking open the window to let in fresh air. Dust motes floated in the sunlight streaming in. Amanda grabbed a microfiber cloth from the cart and began wiping down the chest of drawers.

"Has she really been coming here for thirty years?" she asked Nathan.

"Sounds about right. She used to come with her husband and two sons." Nathan stripped the bed and carried the old sheets to the cart, returning with a fresh stack. "They were a few years older than me. Really nice people," he said as he snapped a sheet open and tucked it around the mattress with neat hospital corners. "Later, the husband stopped coming, divorce, I think. By the time I was in high school, Yolanda was coming by herself, and she'd stay for a month or more."

"Oh. I guess I should have asked how long she planned to stay before I agreed."

Nathan shrugged. "It doesn't matter. We are a lodge, after all. The whole point of this place is to have guests. And if she doesn't mind smelling paint and putting up with a certain amount of noise, I don't see a downside. We should give her a break on the price, though."

"Agreed." Amanda grabbed window cleaner and a squeegee and went to work on the mirror.

Working together, they had the room and adjoining bathroom sparkling within twenty minutes. Amanda filled a basket with an assortment of tea bags, while Nathan stocked the bathroom with fresh towels and toilet paper. He came out of the bath and gave the room one more visual inspection. "Everything looks good." He held up a hand and Amanda slapped him a high five.

"We make a good team."

CHAPTER SEVEN

NATHAN FINISHED A last swipe with his roller and stepped back away from the wall to look for any spots he might have missed, but all he saw was a clean, creamy surface. Thanks to Amanda's skill in taping and hand-painting the edges, they'd managed to finish the lobby walls in less than two days. He looked toward the reception area, where Amanda was currently applying a second coat of sage-colored paint she'd chosen to the wall behind the desk. She was right, the color looked good against the wood trim, giving the front desk a welcoming, woodsy vibe. Maybe having a partner was a good thing.

Amanda finished her wall, set her roller in the tray, and came to stand in front of the desk, where a guest would stand when checking in. The effect must have pleased her, based on her smile. Her hair, a few shades darker than the cedar trim on the door behind the desk, contrasted with the streak of green paint smeared across one cheek. And yet, despite the paint, despite having her hair tied in a tight ponytail, despite the old gray sweatshirt that Peggy had loaned her for painting, Amanda was beautiful.

Nathan blinked. Where had that thought come from? Sure, the first moment he saw her at the airport, he'd noticed she was pretty. But today, with color in her cheeks from her hard work and that happy smile on her face, she was a step beyond attractive. And that was a problem.

Nathan had terrible taste in women. That was just a fact. He'd had three serious-ish romantic relationships in his life. He'd dated a woman in college for five months, only to discover she was using him to get closer to his roommate, who happened to be the son of a software magnate. She succeeded, although Nathan heard the marriage only lasted a year. His second serious girlfriend was always taking him to the weddings, reunions, and holiday celebrations her large extended family held. He'd felt like they were moving toward something permanent, until he found out she was just using Nathan until someone better came along. But it was his third girlfriend, Priscilla, who had been the final straw.

Priscilla. Fun, supportive, pretty, she seemed like the perfect girlfriend. Well, maybe not perfect. Looking back there were signs. Like the way she expected Nathan to pay for all the meals and outings, even though they had comparable incomes. Sometimes when they would go out, she'd mention she was out of coffee and needed to stop by the store, only to collect a cart full of groceries and then stand back and wait for Nathan to run his credit card. But, he'd rationalized, he got a steady salary while her income was commission-based, so it was harder for her to budget. He wasn't quite sure he'd ever made a conscious decision to become engaged, but somehow, he found himself paying for an ostentatious diamond ring, and next thing he knew, they were choosing a wedding date.

Funny thing was, he'd been happy about it. He looked forward to married life. But none of it was real, as he'd discovered when he returned home from an overseas assignment to discover Priscilla was gone, along with almost everything he owned, including his good credit. And on that date, he'd declared himself perpetually single. No more romantic entanglements. He was done.

So, he had no business noticing how Amanda's cheeks were the color of rosy ripe peaches, or the way her smile could light the darkest Alaskan night. Not that he believed Amanda was anything like Priscilla, but he needed to keep this relationship professional. He could do that.

Really, he could have done a lot worse in a professional partner. Amanda had skills, not just a vision for decorating but her ability to communicate her ideas, and she wasn't afraid to compromise. Not to mention her stamina—yesterday they'd worked all day and into the evening with only a few breaks, and much of that time Amanda had been crawling along the floor to tape off baseboards, or on a ladder hand-painting around archways. At the same time, she'd been attentive to her daughter, occasionally asking her to hand up a tool or give an opinion.

Earlier this afternoon, Amanda had suggested a quick trip to see the beavers, which Paisley enthusiastically accepted. When they returned, Peggy mentioned that she was baking cookies and wondered if Paisley could give her a hand. Judging from the mouthwatering smells coming from the kitchen, the cookies were almost done.

Malcolm walked in the front door, carrying a stack of mail he'd picked up at the post office when he was in town, which he deposited into the basket on the end of the reception desk, next to the wall where incoming mail had always gone. He stopped to inspect Amanda's work. "I like it."

"Thanks." Amanda beamed at him. "I'm going to paint the front of the desk a deeper shade, but before I change colors, I need to paint this little piece of wall on the side here. Does this desk move, or is it built in?"

"You know, I'm not sure," Malcolm replied. "Let's find out."

Nathan crossed the floor to join the inspection. "I always thought it was built in. See this line of paint?"

"That doesn't necessarily mean it's attached," Malcolm said, "just that the painters decided it was easier to paint around it than to move it. There's a little gap between the beadboard and the wall. Amanda, could you hand me that letter opener?"

Amanda picked up the tool from the shelf behind the desk and gave it to Malcolm. He pushed the thin blade into the space between the desk and the wall and ran it up and down. "I don't feel any supports or attachments. I think it's freestanding."

"Then let's see if we can move it so I can paint the whole wall." Amanda gathered up the tray of mail, the call bell, and the brochure rack from the top of the desk and moved them to a console table on the other side of the entryway. Nathan and Malcolm positioned themselves behind the desk. Amanda went to join them.

"On three," Nathan said. "One. Two. Three." With a grunt he pushed, and a half second later, so did Malcolm and Amanda. With a groan, the desk slid forward.

Once they'd built up some momentum, it moved easily. Something fell to the floor on Nathan's right, but he didn't slow down to see what it was until Amanda called, "Stop. That gives me enough room to work. Thanks for your help."

"Anytime," Malcolm told her.

Nathan reached down to pick up the envelope lying on the floor. "This fell when we moved the desk. It must have been between the desk and the wall. Doesn't look like it's ever been opened. I hope it's not something important." The address was a small label preprinted with Eleanor's name and address, with a picture of a flower on the left edge. It looked like the sort of thing charities would enclose as a small gift to potential donors. Eleanor and Harry used to have a whole drawer full of them under the reception desk. Probably still did. The postage stamp read, "Greetings from Alaska," in the retro style of a vintage souvenir postcard. "Look at that—a thirty-seven-cent postage stamp. That's been a while."

Amanda came to look over his shoulder. "Weird that there's no return address. What does the postmark say?"

"Looks like Seattle." Nathan held the blurred image closer to his eye. "I think it says August 19, 2002."

"Wow, twenty-two years ago."

"Well, are you going to open it or not?" Malcolm asked.

Amanda frowned. "Can we? Or are we supposed to turn it over to the executor of the estate?"

"I'll ask." Nathan pulled out his cell phone and texted Vince.

While he waited for an answer, Paisley came from the kitchen, carrying a plate of cookies. Peggy followed behind her, with a tray holding glasses, napkins, and a pitcher of lemonade. "Ready for a

break?" she asked as she set her tray on the desktop. "Say, I love that color."

"Thanks." Amanda smirked at Nathan, before
taking one of the chunky cookies studded with
nuts and chocolate chips from Paisley's offered
tray. "These look yummy. What kind are they?"

"Cowboy cookies," Paisley told her. "Peggy
showed me how to make them. She has a special
scoop like for ice cream but littler so that all the
cookies come out the same size. Nathan, do you
want some?"

"Yes, please." Nathan took two and bit into one.
"These are great."

"Mr. Malcolm, do you want a cookie?"

"Thank you, Miss Paisley." Malcolm relieved
her of another cookie, but then winked and reached
for two more. Paisley grinned at him.

As though she'd been summoned, Yolanda came
strolling in through the back door. "Do I smell
cookies?" she called as she crossed through the
main lobby.

"Yes, ma'am," Paisley answered and offered
her the tray.

Peggy handed her a napkin. "Let me get you a
plate." She turned toward the kitchen.

"No, this is fine, thank you." Yolanda selected
a cookie and set it on the napkin.

Nathan's phone chimed and he checked the text.
"Vince says go ahead and open it."

"Open what?" Peggy asked as she filled a glass with lemonade and passed it to Yolanda.

Nathan waved the letter. "This. We found it between the desk and the wall. It must have slipped out of the basket and fallen in there twenty-two years ago."

Amanda handed him the letter opener from the back of the desk, and he slit the top of the envelope, removed the page inside, and opened the first fold to reveal a message formed from letters clipped from newspapers and flyers. Something stiff was contained in the bottom fold of the paper. "What in the world?"

"Is it an advertising gimmick?" Amanda asked, peering at the letters.

"I don't think so." Nathan pulled out the insert, which proved to be a photo print of something lit by dappled sunlight on the forest floor. His heart beat faster as he recognized the image. It was the Deanna Somers sculpture that had graced the reception desk for so long! He set the photo and envelope on the desk, finished unfolding the page, and read the message aloud. "'SenD $5000 to bANk to REceiVe LOcaTION OF the SwaNS.' And then at the bottom is the name of a bank in Belize and some numbers. Account numbers, I guess?"

Amanda stared at the paper. "A ransom note?"

"Apparently," Nathan replied.

Yolanda picked up the photo he'd set on the

desk. "Is that the swan sculpture that went missing? I remember that."

"Put it down," Peggy ordered. "There might be fingerprints."

Yolanda dropped the picture as though it had scalded her. "Sorry. I didn't think."

"I'd already touched it anyway," Nathan assured her. "Besides, even if fingerprints last that long, I can't imagine anyone who went to all the trouble to cut out letters wouldn't have worn gloves."

"Would Harry and Eleanor have paid that much to get the sculpture back?" Amanda asked. "And wasn't it insured?"

"Actually, it wasn't," Peggy said. "Harry and Eleanor assumed it would be, but it turns out standard policies have a limit on jewelry and art. You have to take out a special rider, and they didn't. Since it was a gift, they didn't think to look into that."

"How much was it worth?" Yolanda asked. "If you don't mind me asking."

An old pang of guilt flashed through Nathan's chest. "When they contacted the artist after the theft, she estimated it was worth about twenty thousand. Probably more now, since she's done other notable public art. How could he have been so careless as to lose something so valuable?"

Amanda nodded toward the envelope. "Since it was sealed, I assume that Harry and Eleanor never saw the letter."

"So it seems," Nathan agreed.

Yolanda shook her head. "Surely if the first letter got no response, the thief would have sent another."

"They didn't," Peggy declared. "I would have known. I'll bet this letter was a hoax. Somebody who heard about the theft trying to take advantage."

"Maybe," Amanda said. "But you said the theft happened just before the summer employees left." She turned to Nathan. "Do you remember the date?"

"August 16th." That date would be burned into Nathan's memory forever.

"That means this letter was mailed from Seattle only three days later," Amanda said. "How widely publicized was the theft?"

"It was in the Anchorage newspaper, and because of the artist's name, other newspapers around the country picked it up." Peggy looked toward the ceiling and tapped her finger against her jaw. "But as I remember, the story was in the Sunday paper, and the theft happened on a weekday—"

"Wednesday," Nathan supplied.

"If the 16th was a Wednesday, this letter was mailed on Saturday," Amanda pointed out. "Maybe by someone passing through the Seattle airport on their way home? Someone did say Harry suspected one of the summer employees might be involved."

Nathan thought about that. "But we know they couldn't have taken the sculpture to the airport with them without Harry knowing. He assumed they had a local accomplice. Since they had no response to their ransom note, the accomplice probably just sold the sculpture."

"But the ransom note says 'location of the swans.'" Amanda was almost quivering with excitement. "Maybe the thief didn't have an accomplice. Maybe he or she hid the sculpture somewhere and was going to disclose where after they'd received the ransom payment."

Nathan gasped. "But that would mean—"

"Yes." Amanda grinned. "The sculpture might be hidden right here, somewhere on the grounds of Swan Lodge!"

AMANDA DABBED HER paintbrush over a missed spot in a gap on the beadboard covering the front of the reception desk. Done. Now she just needed to wash out her brushes and rollers, put away the equipment, and allow the wall and desk to dry thoroughly before recruiting Malcolm and Nathan to help her move everything back into position, everything, that is, except the mail basket. That needed to go farther from the wall to prevent any other letters from falling into the gap.

What a strange coincidence that the ransom letter would be the one that was lost, so many years ago. What if Harry and Eleanor had opened it?

Would they have paid the ransom and recovered the swans? Would that have soothed Nathan's conscience? Probably not. He seemed determined to blame himself for the loss. And why? Harry and Eleanor had chosen to leave the sculpture on the desk, and it wasn't as though they never left it unattended. There was a reason the call bell sat conveniently in the center of the desk. But from what Amanda could see, Nathan was one of those overachievers when it came to shouldering the blame.

Maybe it came from his childhood. He'd said his father was a single dad, so Nathan had probably taken on more responsibility than other children his age. As a single parent herself, Amanda knew how easy it was to fall into the trap of treating your child like a small adult instead of letting them be a child, especially with an introverted and thoughtful child like Paisley. Not that teaching responsibility was a bad thing. Nathan wouldn't be the man he was today if he'd had a different childhood, and she had to admit, she liked the man he was.

She appreciated how he encouraged Paisley to put down her book and get outside while still validating her reading. How he deferred to Peggy, holding doors and listening to her advice, even though she was technically his employee now. Amanda's employee, too, she guessed—hard as that was to grasp. But it seemed quite natural to think of Nathan in charge here, welcoming people from all over the world to experience a little slice of Alaska, just like Eleanor and Harry had for decades. Too bad they were going to have to sell.

But in the meantime, maybe she could help, not only to fix up the place before putting it on the market, but possibly to help Nathan find the sculpture. Once she'd cleaned up her paint tools, Amanda went to check on Paisley, who was once again with Peggy. She found them at the kitchen table, rolling a meat mixture into balls. The aroma of tomatoes, garlic, and basil hung in the air.

"Hi, Mommy. We're making my favorite for dinner, spaghetti and meatballs. Did you know you can make meatballs at home, and you don't have to buy frozen ones? Peggy showed me how."

Amanda laughed. "I did know that, actually, but I haven't done it in a long time."

Peggy got up and went to the stove to raise the lid on the stockpot there and give it a stir. "Paisley's a good cook. She's been a big help."

"I'm glad," Amanda said, trying not to reveal her amazement. Paisley had never shown much interest in culinary arts. "Do you know where Nathan is?"

"Last I saw he was heading toward the east wing, carrying a toolbox. If you find him, tell him dinner will be ready in about an hour."

"I'll pass it on. Thanks."

Amanda headed off. She followed the sound of banging that led to an open doorway. Inside the room, she spotted Nathan lying under the sink, doing something with the plumbing. She went inside. "Hey."

Nathan dropped the wrench, which landed with a thud an inch from his face. "Aargh."

"Oops." Amanda bent down to look at him. "Sorry, I didn't mean to startle you."

He shook his head. "It wasn't you. I had the wrong size wrench. Could you please hand me the one and a quarter?"

Amanda searched the box of wrenches until she found the one he'd requested. "Here you go."

He fit the wrench to the nut and tightened it. "Better." He slid out from under the sink. Amanda offered him a hand, and he took it to pull himself up. "Thanks."

"No problem. Just a wobbly sink?"

"Yeah." He grasped the edges of the sink and tested it. "Seems tight now." He put a check next to a task on his phone. "There we go. One more down. Just a hundred or so to go."

"But look at all those checkmarks," she said. "We've made a lot of progress in the past two days. I finished painting the desk, by the way. Once it's dry, we can move it back."

"Great. What's Paisley up to?"

"She's helping Peggy make meatballs. Peggy says dinner's in an hour. I could start taping off the trim in the library, but I was thinking…" She paused.

"About what?"

"About that letter we found. I feel like that sculpture has to be somewhere nearby."

Nathan looked skeptical. "Really?"

"Well, the letter said it would give the sculpture's 'whereabouts' for five thousand dollars. If the thief planned to cut-and-paste a second letter with directions, it would need to be an easy-to-explain hiding place. And if it was one of the summer employees, that would explain how they planned to make money off the sculpture even though they didn't take it with them."

"Harry thought they probably had a local accomplice."

"Possibly, but the letter only asked for five thousand dollars. Sure, that's a substantial amount of money, especially twenty-two years ago, but I would have to guess there are expenses involved in getting money wired to an anonymous offshore banking account, and if the thief had to split the proceeds with an accomplice, it doesn't seem like it would be worth the risk of getting caught."

"Maybe the accomplice sold the sculpture, but the thief sent the letter, too, to try and milk a little more out of the theft. If someone is willing to steal a sculpture, I doubt they'd have a moral objection to lying on a ransom note."

"I can't argue with your logic, but I have another theory. Suppose one of the summer employees, or possibly a guest, stole it and hid it somewhere, figuring if they got caught in the act, they could pass it all off as a prank. Then, once they were safely out of town, they mailed the letter."

"That does make sense. Harry and Eleanor always liked to give people the benefit of the doubt. If someone claimed it was an elaborate joke, there's no way they would have pressed charges." Nathan returned the wrenches he'd been using to their proper slots. "But even if you're right, where does that leave us? The sculpture isn't just tucked away in a corner of the attic somewhere, or someone would have stumbled across it in the past twenty-two years."

"There's an attic?" That hadn't been included in their inspection tour.

"No," Nathan said as he picked up his toolkit and walked toward the hall. "I was speaking figuratively. Although…" He stopped so abruptly Amanda almost ran into him.

"Although, what?"

"The lodge does have a basement."

"Does it?"

Nathan shut the door behind them. "Maybe, since we have an hour before dinner, we should have a look around."

Amanda grinned. "Lead the way."

CHAPTER EIGHT

"The door to the basement is at the back of the pantry in the kitchen," Nathan told Amanda as they walked down the hallway, carrying his tools. He adjusted the weight in his hand. So many projects. Did they really have time for what was most likely a wild-goose chase? But if there was any chance they could recover the sculpture… "We need to check out the basement anyway," he said aloud. "Make sure the boiler is in good shape. We forgot to inspect it during our initial walk-through."

"Right." The corners of Amanda's lips twitched, as though she was secretly amused at his rationalization.

He dropped off the toolbox in the closet at the end of the hall before heading for the kitchen. Paisley and Peggy were standing with their heads together, arranging something onto a parchment-covered baking tray.

"Hi, Nathan," Paisley said. "I made meatballs for the spaghetti."

"I see that. Good job."

Peggy picked up the tray and slid it into a hot oven. "We'll just bake these for twenty minutes and then I'll add them to the sauce to simmer," she told Paisley. "Thank you for your help."

"Nathan and I are going to check out the basement," Amanda told her daughter. "Want to come?"

"Yes!" Paisley scurried toward them, but then she stopped and turned to Peggy. "If you don't need me anymore."

"I can handle it from here," Peggy assured her. "You go on ahead, but wash your hands first."

"Okay." Paisley ran to the sink.

"Use soap," Amanda called, before leaning closer to Peggy. "Thanks for letting her hang out with you."

"She's always welcome in my kitchen," Peggy assured her. "Paisley is a delight."

Amanda's smile lit the room. Paisley came skipping back. "I'm ready."

Nathan took them through the huge pantry, lined on both sides with neatly labeled shelves of food and kitchen gear. A dozen aprons hanging from hooks on the back of the basement door almost obscured it from sight, but Nathan pushed them out of the way, found the knob, and opened the door, exposing a small landing and a flight of stairs that disappeared into the darkness. Gingerly, he felt along the wall beside the door for a light switch, mindful that basements were a favorite hangout for spiders. Fortunately, his fingers found the switch before encountering any cobwebs, and the basement was flooded with light.

He led the way down the steps, with Paisley and Amanda right behind him. To his relief, the basement was neat and tidy, with nary a spider web in sight. The boiler and assorted attachments took up the area to the right of the stairs, while the space on the left was filled with rows of storage shelves and an open area with various pieces of old furniture. Nathan stepped to the right and stared at the huge hot water tank. Amanda came to stand beside him. "Is it in good shape?"

"Um…" Nathan ran his eyes over the pipes and ductwork. There didn't seem to be any steam coming out, or water dripping anywhere, and there had been no shortage of hot water since they'd arrived. "It looks fine to me."

"Me, too." Amanda clapped her hands together. "So since the inspection is done, we have until dinner for the treasure hunt."

Paisley poked her head out from behind one of the tall shelving units. "What treasure hunt? Is this about that letter you found with the stuff glued on it?"

"Yes," Amanda told her. "Somebody stole a swan sculpture, and we think they might have hidden it around here somewhere."

"Do you think it's in one of these boxes?" Paisley pointed toward the nearest shelves, which were stacked with cardboard banker's cartons.

Nathan shook his head. "No, the sculpture was about this tall." He held his hand about three feet off the ground. "It's too big to fit in one of those boxes."

"What is stored in all these boxes?" Amanda went to read a few random labels. "Employee records 1975–1979. Taxes 1980–1985. Guest books 1966–1978. What is a guest book?"

"You know, those impressive-looking books hotels used to have on top of the desk for the guests to sign when they check in," Nathan explained.

"Oh, yeah. I think I've seen that in old movies." Amanda opened the box and took out the top book, bound in red leather with the name "Swan Lodge" inscribed in gold. "Ooh, fancy. Why don't hotels have these anymore?"

Nathan shrugged. "I guess they eventually decided it was an invasion of privacy for everyone who came into a hotel to be able to see exactly who stayed there and when."

"Good point." Amanda opened the book to the first page, where people had signed and written their home addresses. There were two from Texas, one from Idaho, another from Buffalo, New York, and two with addresses from Deutschland. Amanda remembered a German-speaking couple staying here when she'd visited as a child. Wonder how they'd ever even heard of Swan Falls, Alaska.

Paisley came to look at the cover. "It's pretty."

"It really is." Amanda flipped to the center of the book and showed Paisley. "Even the names are fancy. People then must have practiced their signatures until they were just right." They made a pretty picture with their heads close together over the book, Paisley's dark curls pressed against Amanda's mahogany-colored waves. After a few moments, Amanda looked up and saw Nathan watching. She gave a sheepish smile and closed the book. "Oops, didn't mean to get sidetracked." She returned the book to the box and the box to the shelf. "Let's keep checking."

Amanda and Paisley took the next row and Nathan the one after that, carefully inspecting each item on the shelves and opening any box that might be big enough to hold the sculpture. They uncovered everything from old bedsheets to photo albums, but no sign of the swans. Next, they searched the pile of broken and damaged furniture, opening drawers and peering into chests, but with no luck.

"Dinner's ready!" Peggy shouted.

"Coming!" Amanda called up the stairs. She met Nathan's eyes and shrugged. "It was worth a try. And I definitely want to take a look at those old photo albums when I get a minute."

"I'll carry the box up," Nathan volunteered.

Malcolm and Yolanda were already sitting at the table when they got to the kitchen. He put the box out of the way and went with Amanda and Paisley to wash his hands, while Peggy set a big bowl of pasta in the center of the table. Once they'd joined the others, Yolanda asked, "Peggy said you were searching for the sculpture in the basement. Did you find anything?"

"Nothing pertaining to *Swan Trio*," Nathan said.

"Oh. I saw the box—"

"It's photo albums," Amanda told her. "I thought it might be fun to look through them after dinner."

"What a good idea." Yolanda nodded her thanks as Peggy handed her a plate of spaghetti and meatballs.

Paisley passed her a bowl of shredded Parmesan. "Here's some cheese, too."

"Thank you." Yolanda smiled at the girl and sprinkled a generous portion over her pasta. "A little bird told me you made the meatballs."

Paisley's eyes widened. "Maggie the Magpie told you?"

Yolanda laughed. "No, it wasn't really a bird, that's just a silly expression. Peggy told me. She said you're going to be a wonderful cook someday."

"I like cooking," Paisley declared. "Maybe I'll have my own restaurant."

Nathan didn't miss the brief look of incredulity that passed over Amanda's face, which made him suspect Paisley hadn't shown a lot of interest in cooking before landing at Swan Lodge. But he understood, because Peggy had also taught him to cook, back in the day. There was something about working with Peggy in her kitchen that could make something as simple as peeling potatoes fun. Maybe it was the way she would ask questions while they worked, not the usual canned questions people asked children about what grade they were in or what they wanted to be when you grew up, but opinions, like whether carrots or green beans would be better with pork chops, or if they liked big dogs or small dogs the most. And then she would listen seriously to their answers, as though their opinion really mattered. At least, that's how it had been with Nathan, and to a boy with no mother and an overworked father, that gentle give-and-take had been a revelation.

"You know," Peggy said as she passed around a salad bowl, "if one of the summer employees really did hide the sculpture and write the letter, they might have thought better about it over the years. I don't know what the statute of limitations would be on something like that, but if you two—" she pointed to Nathan and Amanda "—were to contact them and say you didn't intend to press charges, maybe they would tell you where they hid it."

"Not a bad idea," Amanda said slowly. "But do you remember everyone who was here at the time?"

"No. I remember most of the kids, but years

kind of run together," Peggy admitted. "Was that the year we had a Kristin and a Krista?"

Nathan thought back. "Krista. Short with dark hair, liked to belt out songs from musicals while she cleaned?"

Peggy chuckled. "That's her. She worked here for three summers, I think."

"I don't remember Kristin, though," Nathan said.

"Tall girl, with a Southern accent." Peggy tipped her head to one side. "Now that I think about it, I believe it was the next summer when she and Krista were here together, after you graduated and stopped coming up."

"If you were the thief, would you have returned the next summer?" Amanda wondered aloud.

"Probably not," Nathan said. "Besides, Krista was tiny. I don't think she could have picked up the sculpture by herself. Who else? Oh, Hector was here that summer."

Peggy smiled. "Hector was a hard worker. I think he singlehandedly split enough wood for the entire season. Good thing, because that other boy—can't think of his name—he was so lazy. You'd tell him to mow or clean something, and next time you looked up he'd not only be goofing off, but he'd be flirting with the girls, keeping them from their work."

Yolanda laughed. "I remember him. Good-looking young man, always at hand to load up luggage and collect tips when someone checked out, but hard to find any other time. What was his name… Dirk? Dick?"

"Derrick." Nathan remembered him now. "Seems like everybody liked him, at least at first."

"Yeah, until they got tired of doing his work for him." Peggy pressed her lips together and frowned.

"Do you remember your kitchen assistants that summer?" Nathan asked Peggy.

"I don't, but maybe if I look at those photo albums after dinner, it will jog my memory."

"Did you have any local people working for you that summer, or going in and out?" Amanda asked.

"Yes, we always have local housekeepers who work year-round. Ava Burke is our current housekeeper. Her mother, Anita, used to work here when she was a teenager, but I'm not sure what years it would have been."

Nathan set down his fork. "I'm sure somewhere in those boxes in the basement there have to be employment records with names and addresses for all the employees. I doubt most of them would still be at the same address two decades later, but we could try contacting them."

"If they used their parents' address while they were in college, they might still be there," Amanda pointed out. "And we might be able to find them online. Let's take a look after dinner and see what we can find out."

Was it possible that they would be able to recover the sculpture after all this time? It would be a big load off Nathan's conscience if they did. But Amanda was half owner of the lodge. Was it fair to ask her to make the effort to search for this sculpture when she could be fixing up the lodge so that it could begin making money for her? "Are you sure you want to take the time?" he asked her. "It's probably hopeless. And even if we did find *Swan Trio*, it goes to the museum."

"Yes, but Eleanor wanted it to go there, and I feel like we owe it to her to try to respect her wishes. Besides—" Amanda grinned "—do you have any idea how many times I've stayed up reading past my bedtime to find out the answer to a mystery? Let's at least take a crack at solving this one."

If she was willing, so was he. "Okay, Sherlock. You're on."

CHAPTER NINE

AMANDA GATHERED SPACKLE, a putty knife, and a few rolls of masking tape after breakfast the next morning. The library was next on their list of rooms to paint. Paisley and Nathan were already there, Paisley to read her book and Nathan to work on the letter they planned to send to the summer employees that were here at the time *Swan Trio* was stolen. Wouldn't it be something if they were able to find that lost sculpture?

Before Amanda could head up to the library, her phone rang. She answered, "Hi, Harley. Everything okay?"

"Everything is fine. You picked a good time to be in Alaska; the high temps here have been close to a hundred every day this week, so we've been doing some extra irrigation on the outdoor container plants. The cacti are loving it, though."

"How's business?" Amanda wasn't sure what she wanted to hear. If they were inundated with customers, she'd feel bad for leaving them short-handed. If they weren't, she'd worry about income.

Except, that didn't really matter so much now, did it? The money from the sale of the lodge would take care of everything.

"It's about the same as this time last year," Harley told her. "We're in that usual August lull right now, but it always picks up again right after Labor Day. We got the last of the mums potted on, so they'll be filled out and ready when fall hits. I'd like to schedule an autumn container-gardening class for mid-September, but I wanted to okay it with you before I put it in the newsletter."

"Great idea." Those classes, where they demonstrated how to combine different plants to create interesting arrangements in containers, always brought in a good crowd, and the participants often returned to buy more plants later. "How are the ornamental chili peppers coming along?" The bright red, yellow, and purple peppers were a favorite for containers.

"They're thriving, although I've had to use more supplemental lighting than I like."

"I know." The plastics that made up the greenhouse roof and walls slowly became less translucent over time, and they'd had to bring in artificial lighting to keep their seedlings compact and healthy. "With any luck, the lodge here will sell in time to replace those greenhouses before the start of the growing season next spring."

"That would be great."

"We've been working on sprucing the lodge up

before we put it on the market. Painting, mostly, and minor repairs. I'm playing with the idea of staying a little longer, just to keep things moving forward." After all, the sooner they finished, the sooner they could list the lodge for sale. "Would that be a problem?"

"Not for me. We're good here. Hang on a sec." She could hear a muffled conversation directing a customer to the ground covers. "Okay, I'm back. What does Paisley think of Alaska?"

"She's really into it. There's a pond nearby with a beaver dam, and she likes us to go there pretty much every day. She loves seeing the beaver kits."

"I'll bet she does. Tell her I said hi. I'll put that class together for the second Saturday of September. In the meantime, feel free to stay in Alaska as long as you like."

"Thanks, Harley. I'll look into it and email you our new plans." She pocketed the phone and gathered up her equipment, glad to know Harley wasn't missing her too much. She was enjoying fixing up the lodge, and she would love to be able to solve the mystery of the missing sculpture, but most importantly, she wanted to make this a memorable trip for Paisley. After all, this might well be their last visit to Alaska. If it weren't for Nathan, Paisley might have spent her entire time indoors, reading books. Amanda needed to be more intentional about sharing experiences with Paisley.

Maybe this afternoon, once she'd finished preparing the library for paint, she'd plan an outing.

She found Nathan in front of the computer in the library, staring at the screen. They'd located the employment records easily enough for Krista, Hector, Derrick, and the two kitchen aids, Heidi and Jasmine. Meanwhile, Peggy and Yolanda had dug through the photo albums until they found the one for that year, with a picture of the entire staff on the front porch. Harry, Eleanor, Peggy, the six summer employees including Nathan, plus two locals. One of them, Bethany Coleman, now ran the local ice cream shop, according to Peggy. They'd all agreed that since Nathan had worked with these people, they would be more receptive if the letter came from him, but judging by his frown, he wasn't having an easy time composing it.

"Hi." She smiled at Nathan as she passed on her way to peek into the reading tent, where she found Paisley sprawled against a stack of pillows, the cat stretched out across her stomach and a book propped up on her chest. "You look comfortable."

"I am." Paisley grinned and stroked the cat. "I love it here."

"Me, too. Let's plan to do something this afternoon. Maybe we could walk to the marsh."

"Maybe," Paisley murmured, already transported back into the world inside her book.

Amanda took her tools to the window, where

she began taping off the woodwork, trying to be as quiet as possible so as not to disturb Nathan's concentration. But she'd only gotten one side of the window done when Nathan spun his chair around to face her. "Want to trade jobs?"

She could see the frustration on his face. "Are you having trouble writing the letter?"

"Yeah. I mean, what do I say? 'Hey, remember me from Alaska two decades ago? Just out of curiosity, did you happen to commit a felony while you were working here that summer?'"

Amanda laughed. "Maybe not quite so direct. What have you got so far?"

He turned back to the computer. "Dear Blank. I'm writing because you worked at Swan Lodge the summer of 2002." He looked over. "That's it."

Amanda tried to imagine how she would react to this letter. "You could start by letting them know about Eleanor's passing. I'm sure they all remember her fondly. Although…" Amanda paused. "Letters might not be the best way to go about this. I mean, other than a birthday card or something, the only thing I ever get in the mail is bills or solicitations. Even if our letter managed to get forwarded to their current mailing address, the former employees are likely just to dump it in the trash with the other junk mail. Maybe social media would be a better way to reach them." She came to read over Nathan's shoulder. "I know

Swan Lodge has a website. Does it have a social media presence?"

"I don't know. I'm not really on social media," he admitted.

Amanda tilted her head. "Don't you work in IT?"

"I do, and that's probably why I don't do social media. I get enough screen time at work."

"That makes sense. Let me check, then." Amanda pulled her phone from her pocket and did a quick search. "Here it is. Swan Lodge has a page with almost three thousand followers. What do you bet that at least some of the employees we're looking for are following?"

Nathan leaned forward. "That's a thought."

Amanda tried to pull up the list of followers, but it wasn't available. "Looks like the followers aren't public on this page. We'd need to sign in as administrator to see them. I don't suppose you have the password."

"I'll bet Peggy does," Nathan said. "I'll ask her."

"I'll come with you. Paisley, I'll be downstairs if you need me."

"Hmm," came the voice from the tent.

They found Peggy on the patio, pouring a large sack of seed into one of the bird feeders.

Nathan went to help. "Let me—"

"Thanks, but I've got it," Peggy told him as she shook the last few seeds into the feeder. "This is our last sack. I need to pick up more at the mercantile later."

"I can get it," Nathan offered. "I need to run into town for a couple of things anyway. Say, we were wondering if you have the passwords for Swan Lodge social media stuff."

"No." Peggy made a face. "Computers and I don't get along. I eventually mastered email and reservations on the website, but I stay away from social media. That was Eleanor's job."

"Huh." Nathan frowned. "I wonder if she kept a list of passwords somewhere."

"You might check the desk in her room."

"I'll take a look. Thanks." He and Amanda went back inside. Amanda picked up the staff photo from the album before joining Nathan at the door behind the reception desk that led to Harry and Eleanor's private suite.

Nathan took out the master ring of keys and sorted through them until he found one marked with fuchsia nail polish in the shape of a heart. He opened the door and held it for Amanda to step inside. When they'd done the tour through the hotel and cabins, they hadn't come in here. Now Amanda wondered why.

Light filtered through the blinds on the window facing the front of the inn. In the corner nearby, a computer monitor sat on top of a wooden desk, with a pullout drawer for the keyboard. A light layer of dust covered the surface. A pottery bowl in the corner of the desk held wrapped candies.

"I'd forgotten about these." Amanda picked up one of the candies. "Eleanor used to carry butterscotch in her pockets. We'd go out to the boardwalk in the marsh and we'd each have one to suck on while we watched the birds. Whenever I smell butterscotch, it makes me think of Eleanor. It always felt like such a special treat when she would share her candy."

"She had a way of making everyday things seem special," Nathan agreed, as he looked around the room, a wistful expression on his face. "So many memories in here."

"I'll bet."

He gave his head a little shake and opened the desk drawer. "Bingo. Here's a list of usernames and passwords." He sighed. "It drives IT guys like me nuts, the way people write down their passwords and keep them right next to the computer. This time, though, it works in our favor."

Amanda gave a rueful laugh. "There may or may not be several sticky notes with frequently used passwords on the bottom of my computer screen at home." She reached under the desk to push the power button on the computer.

Nathan tsk-tsked, but he was smiling. While they waited for the computer to start up, Nathan wandered around the moss-green couch and past Harry's leather recliner and Eleanor's cozy wing chair to examine the items in the bookcase near the kitchen door. Stacks of books kept company with photographs, a fat beeswax candle, a vase filled with different bird feathers, and various other small items. He picked up a rock about two inches across. "I remember this. I was probably about ten when I found it."

"What is it?" Amanda asked.

"An ammonoid." He passed her the rock, which she could now see was shaped like a snail's shell. "It's from the Cretaceous period. We read all about it. I gave it to Eleanor on her birthday." He chuckled. "I'd forgotten all about it."

"She didn't, though." Amanda turned the stone over in her hand. "She kept it all these years."

"She was sentimental, although she'd never admit it."

The computer's main screen showed up and Amanda typed in the password from the sheet. "We're in," Amanda told him. She clicked a few more keys. "Okay, I'm on the Swan Lodge page. There's a Krista Richards and a Krista Hollis following this page."

"Krista's last name was Torres." Nathan came to look, resting a warm hand on her shoulder as he did. He leaned closer, and Amanda breathed in the woodsy scent of his aftershave. "Do you have a picture?" he asked.

"Yes," Amanda replied. "The top post is an anniversary celebration, so she probably goes by her married name." Amanda clicked on the profile of Krista Richards. A photo of a smiling couple popped up.

"That's our Krista," Nathan confirmed, lifting his hand to point, and leaving her shoulder feeling neglected. "Her hair is longer than she wore it in college, but otherwise she hasn't changed much."

"Great. Then we can message her. Here, you do it since she knows you." Amanda got up quickly to let Nathan take her place. "Just tell her who you are, and let her know that Eleanor has passed away, and maybe that we're trying to find the people who worked here when she did. Let's wait to ask about the sculpture until she responds."

"Good idea." Nathan typed in the message Amanda had suggested. "How's that?"

"Looks good. Send it."

Nathan pressed the send button. "Based on your experience, how long until we'll hear back, do you think?"

"That all depends on how often she checks in. Somewhere between immediately and never. Let's look for those other employees." They found one follower that might be Heidi, but she also had a different last name. "I'm just not sure," Nathan said, comparing the profile photo with the one in the album taken twenty-two years earlier. "The pink hair is throwing me off."

"Yeah, and her face is in profile in the group photo," Amanda pointed out. "Let's wait and see what Krista says. Maybe she's kept up with some of the others."

"Okay." Nathan signed out of the computer. "In the meantime, I need to run into town. Is there anything you need?"

"Masking tape," she said immediately. "The stuff I have isn't wide enough to cover the molding on the edge of the bookcases. Will they have it here, or will I need to go to Wasilla?"

"They might. The mercantile carries a lot of things besides groceries. Why don't you and Paisley come with me? We could stop by Glacier Scoops for ice cream and show Paisley the town."

"Great idea. I was thinking I should get her out doing something today. And while we're getting ice cream, we could ask Bethany Coleman a few questions about the sculpture."

Nathan nodded. "You're reading my mind."

Amanda powered the computer off. "I'll get Paisley and we'll meet you out front." She went upstairs and poked her head into the library. "Paisley, we're going into town with Nathan."

Paisley groaned. "Aw, I just got to a good part, where he sneaked onto the island, and he hears somebody in the trees. Can I stay with Peggy?"

"You could," Amanda told her, "but then you'd miss out on the ice cream."

"Ice cream?" Paisley poked her head out of the tent. "What kind?"

"I don't know. We'll have to see what they have at the ice cream shop."

"I'll come." Paisley crawled out and stretched. The cat followed and rubbed against her ankles. She reached down to stroke the cat's head. "Sorry, Shadow. I'll be back later."

CHAPTER TEN

NATHAN WAS WAITING beside the rental car when they went outside. He waved a piece of paper. "I've got Peggy's list. Are you excited to explore the metropolis of Swan Falls?"

"What's a metropolis?" Paisley asked as she climbed into the back seat.

"Nathan is joking," Amanda told her daughter. "A metropolis is a big city, bigger than Albuquerque. Swan Falls is a tiny little town."

In less than ten minutes, Nathan was turning off Lodge Road onto Knik Avenue. A block later, he made another left turn and parked in the lot at the end of Main Street, between an old black pickup truck and a camper van. He grabbed a stack of reusable shopping bags he must have gotten from Peggy, while Amanda and Paisley got out and looked around. Across the street to the east, a gray-bearded man on a riding mower made a final pass down the edge of the park and pulled up under a carport behind the buildings.

Paisley pointed toward a peach-colored store

with a covered patio on the north side of their parking lot. The sign out front read "Glacier Scoops Ice Creamery" in old-fashioned letters. "Is that the ice cream place?"

"Yes," Amanda told her. "They have this incredible flavor with currants in it that I've never had anywhere else. At least they did when you were a baby."

Nathan locked the car and joined them.

"Ice cream or shopping first?" Amanda asked.

"Ice cream!" Paisley and Nathan shouted in unison.

Nathan laughed. "We've got to keep our priorities straight. Right, Paisley?"

"Right!" Paisley giggled and skipped along beside Nathan toward the shop. Amanda chuckled and followed. Inside, a dark-haired woman Amanda recognized from the memorial service was taking orders from a family of four. She looked to be about Nathan's age. Presumably, this was Bethany Coleman, who used to work at the lodge. While she was scooping ice cream for the family, Nathan, Amanda, and Paisley studied the flavors written in colored chalk on the blackboard on the wall behind the counter. A brief description followed each flavor.

"What's Moose Tracks?" Paisley whispered to Nathan.

"Caramel swirl with little bits of chocolate and toffee," he told her. "It's one of my favorites."

"I love toffee," Paisley declared.

"Me, too," Nathan told her. "Blueberry Goldmine says it has toffee, too, and a blueberry swirl. I might have to try it."

The family paid and took their cones outside, and the woman behind the counter turned her attention toward them. "Hello. Good to see all of you. I couldn't stay for the reception after the memorial service, so I never got a chance to tell you I'm so sorry about Eleanor."

"Thanks, Bethany," Nathan said. "It's good to see you, too."

"You're Eleanor's niece Amanda, right?" Bethany asked.

"Yes—well, great-niece. This is my daughter, Paisley."

"Welcome to Swan Falls." Bethany smiled at Paisley, who was peering into the freezer tubs, her bottom lip caught between her teeth. "Are there any flavors you'd like to sample before you make up your mind?"

"Can I?" Paisley asked. "Because I can't decide between Moose Tracks, Marshmallow Swan Fudge, or Very Berry."

"Then by all means, let's do a taste test." Bethany scooped up samples in tiny wooden spoons and passed them to Paisley.

Paisley tried each with the solemn expression of a connoisseur, letting the ice cream melt on her tongue before swallowing. After the third sample, she sighed. "They're all sooo good, it's hard to choose."

"Well, while she's thinking, I'd like a scoop of Caramel Currant on a sugar cone, please," Amanda said.

"Blueberry Goldmine for me," Nathan said.

"One scoop or two?" Bethany asked.

"One," Nathan replied. "I have to pace myself. Peggy's making strawberry-rhubarb pie for dessert tonight."

"You lucky ducks. I won one of Peggy's strawberry-rhubarb pies at the auction last year. I think it cost me eighty bucks." Bethany pulled a scoop from the tray and a cone from the rack.

Amanda blinked. "For one pie?"

"For one of Peggy's pies. Even people from Anchorage and Wasilla know about Peggy's cooking. The pie auction takes place during the Feather Festival so there are lots of extra people bidding. It's a big fundraiser for the school." She handed Amanda her cone and started on Nathan's. "When I used to work for the lodge, I'd pop by the kitchen after I finished cleaning rooms and ask if Peggy needed any help, but instead of putting me to work, she'd almost always be trying out some recipe she wanted me to 'sample.' She and Eleanor used to brainstorm flavor combinations with me." She handed Nathan the blueberry-streaked cone. "I think it was Eleanor who invented this one."

Nathan took a taste. "I like it."

"One of my bestsellers," Bethany told him. She turned to Paisley. "Have you decided what you want?"

"I can't choose between the Marshmallow and the Moose Tracks."

"How about if I put a half scoop of each on a cone for you?"

"That would be awesome," Paisley agreed. She accepted the cone and happily carried it outside while Amanda held the door.

Once Paisley was settled at a picnic table, Amanda turned, intending to pay for the ice cream, but Nathan was just pulling out his wallet.

"Let me get this," Amanda said, but he waved her away.

"I've got it." He handed Bethany some bills and dropped the change in a tip jar. "We were showing Amanda some of the old albums at the lodge," he said to Bethany before pausing to lick his cone. "Do you remember that summer when the swan sculpture went missing?"

"You bet I do," Bethany answered, leaning back against the wall and crossing her arms. "I was afraid I might lose my job over it."

"Why is that?" Amanda asked. "Did someone accuse you?"

"Not exactly, but the police were asking me to account for my whereabouts. See, I'd already gone home for the day," Bethany explained, "but my folks were off in Anchorage for a doctor's appointment, so I didn't have an alibi. I was afraid they might believe I'd stolen the sculpture, especially since my mom had some health issues going on and money was tight right then. But it was fine. Nobody accused me, and when Eleanor heard about my mom, she gave me extra hours and raised my pay. Later on, Eleanor and Peggy organized a spaghetti feed to raise extra money for Mom's treatment."

"Is your mom—" Amanda started to ask, but stopped herself, not wanting to make things awkward.

But Bethany smiled. "Mom is fine, still in remission. My parents retired and moved to Idaho."

"That's great," Nathan said. "I always liked your mom." He turned to Amanda. "Bethany's mom was the postmistress here for years and years. She was so nice, a smile and a good word for everybody who came in."

"That was my mom," Bethany agreed. "We don't have local delivery, so everybody in town stopped in to collect their mail and chat."

"What was the local gossip at the time of the theft?" Amanda asked. "Did people have any theories about who did steal the sculpture?"

"Lots of theories. International art rings. Kleptomaniacs. Space aliens, even." Bethany looked toward Nathan. "One of them was about you. One of the summer employees was pushing the concept that you were an ungrateful relative who resented having to work under the same pay and working conditions as everyone else, so you stole the sculpture out of spite."

Nathan blinked. "Wow. I had no idea."

"Nobody believed it," Bethany assured Nathan. "The people here have known you since you were a little kid. They never took him seriously."

"Which employee was it?" Amanda asked.

"It was that one guy from the Midwest. Derrick something. Cute guy, seemed nice at first, but he was always ditching what he was supposed to be doing." Bethany paused for a moment. "Looking back, I wonder if he wasn't spreading rumors to deflect attention away from himself."

"That's a good point." Amanda looked at Nathan. "Maybe we take a closer look at him."

"Why, after all this time?" Bethany asked.

"We were just trying to piece it all together," Nathan answered before Amanda could mention the letter they'd found. He must not have wanted that information out there.

Amanda caught a drop of melted ice cream with her tongue before it could fall. "This currant flavor is amazing. I'm sure we'll be back soon. It was good to meet you, Bethany."

"You, too. Thanks for stopping by."

Outside, the family that had preceded them had finished their cones and were tossing their napkins in the trash can. Paisley sat at one of the small round tables, licking her cone and staring toward a nearby tree. Amanda went to sit beside her. "What are you looking at?"

"That bird." Paisley pointed toward a blue bird with a tall crown. He hopped to a different branch of the tree, and the dark iridescent feathers on his head and shoulders glistened in the sun. "He's staring at me."

"That's a Steller's jay." Nathan dropped into the third chair at the table. "They're notorious camp robbers. He's probably hoping you'll accidentally drop some food so he can swoop in and steal it."

"Do birds like ice cream?" Paisley asked.

"From what I've seen, jays like everything."

As though to prove his point, the jay suddenly swooped to the trash and snatched up the broken bottom of a sugar cone, carrying it to the top of the tree. From out of nowhere, another jay appeared and landed on a nearby branch, squawking and reaching toward the cone. The first bird pulled away and flew off, with the second in hot pursuit.

Paisley laughed. "They're not very good at sharing."

"No," Nathan agreed, just as one of the jays returned to the tree and fixed beady eyes on them. Nathan broke off an edge from his waffle cone and tossed it to the ground. The jay instantly dropped from the tree, grabbed his offering, and whisked it away. "But they are good at finding opportunities."

"Mom, can you hold this for a minute?" Paisley handed her cone to Amanda and pulled her notebook and a stub of a pencil from her pocket. "How do you spell Steller?" Eleanor would have been so proud.

Once they'd all finished their ice cream, Amanda said, "We can get everything on the list at the mercantile, right?"

"Right," Nathan said. "It's that way." They crossed the street to a small park with a long, narrow log cabin in the middle. A sign in front labeled it Swan Lake Museum of History and Art. A grand name for a small building.

"This is new," Amanda said. "It was just a park last time I was here."

"Actually, the cabin is old, but it used to be in the woods not far from the falls. As far as anyone knows, it was the first home in this area. By the time Swan Lodge was built, though, it was seldom used. The family that owned it donated it to the town and had it moved here about five years ago. Eleanor told me all about it."

"Can we go inside?" Paisley asked.

"Let's find out," Nathan replied. They walked closer, but the front door was padlocked shut. A sign on the door said more information was available at the post office.

"Where's the post office?" Amanda asked.

"Right there." Nathan pointed toward the building that backed up to the park with the mower parked behind it. "It shares a wall with the mercantile. Let's go see what they say about the cabin."

About a dozen people were inside the post office, chatting as they checked their boxes or sorted through their mail. One woman was at the customer window, choosing between several stamp designs. A young man with a reddish beard waited patiently until she'd made her decision and then rang up the sale. "Thanks, Ted." She attached one of the new stamps to a blue envelope and handed it to him. "Will you take that for me? It needs to be in Wisconsin by next Thursday for my cousin's birthday."

"No problem. Thanks, Janice." He turned his attention to Nathan and Amanda. "Can I help you?"

"We were wondering about the cabin museum in the park. When is it open?"

"Except during the Feather Festival, it's usually by appointment, you know, for class trips and things like that. But hang on." He looked over at four men standing near a table beside the post office boxes, and called, "Lars, got a minute? These people are asking about the museum."

A friendly-looking man with glasses and a slight paunch came their way. "Hello, I'm Lars Johanson, mayor of Swan Falls. I'm so glad you're taking an interest in the history of the town. Come with me." He led them around to the side of the building so that the cabin came into view. He stopped then and pulled out a ring with multiple keys. After sorting through them for a few moments, he located the one he wanted and worked it off the ring. "Here you go." He handed the key to Amanda. "Be sure to lock up when you're done. You can leave the key with Ted at the post office."

Amanda blinked. "You're just giving us the key? You don't even know who we are."

"Of course I do. I know Nathan, and you're Amanda Flores. And if I'm not mistaken—" he bent lower and smiled at Paisley "—you are Eleanor's great-great-niece. Sorry, I don't remember your first name."

"Paisley," she told him.

"What a pretty name. Peggy told me about you, says you're quite the reader. You should drop by Birdsong Books while you're in town. Here." He took a pen and card from his shirt pocket and scribbled something on the back. "Give this to Helen at the bookstore, and she'll give you ten percent off." He winked. "Mayoral discount."

"Thank you," Paisley whispered as she accepted the card.

"You're welcome." He straightened. "I'm sorry I wasn't able to attend the memorial for Eleanor. Long-standing appointment I couldn't get out of. But I do look forward to working with you on Swan's Marsh Board of Directors. Enjoy the museum." He glanced at his watch. "I'd show you around, but I'm meeting with the Feather Festival Committee in ten minutes. See you soon." He smiled and was gone, walking briskly across the street toward the diner.

Amanda watched him go. "Wasn't that the same man who was mowing the grass at the park?"

Nathan chuckled. "Probably. In a town as small as Swan Falls, people often have to do double duty. Ready to go see the museum?"

"I am!" Paisley shouted.

Nathan grinned at her. "Race you."

"Go!" Paisley dashed toward the cabin, giggling. Nathan took off at a lope, letting her get a good lead before closing in behind her. Amanda followed at a slower pace, smiling as she listened to Paisley's delighted laughter upon reaching the cabin first. She pointed to a nearby tree and said something to Nathan. He lifted Paisley to sit on his shoulders and walked closer to the tree, where they both peered up at something hidden in the leaves.

Something deep in Amanda's chest warmed to see them having such fun together. She caught up to them. "What are you looking at?"

"There's a birdhouse up there," Paisley told her. "I think I hear baby birds inside."

Amanda followed their eyes to a plain cedar box with a sloping lid and a hole in the front. A second later, a tiny bird swooped in and disappeared through the hole. A raucous round of cheeping followed.

"They're swallows," Nathan told them. "They eat a lot of mosquitoes. That's probably why someone put nesting boxes in the trees in the park, to encourage them."

A small sign was posted near the base of the tree. Amanda read aloud, "'Nesting boxes provided by Swan Falls Fourth Grade Class.' What a fun project."

"I wish my school did projects like that," Paisley said. "Is it hard to build a birdhouse?"

"No, these are easy," Nathan told her. "We can build one together back at the lodge this afternoon if you want. I'm sure there's some scrap wood lying around we can use."

"Really?"

"Sure." Nathan swung Paisley down and set her on the ground.

"Ready to go inside the museum?" Amanda asked, holding up the key.

Nathan nodded. "I'm curious to see how they can combine history and art into one small log cabin."

They got their answer as soon as Amanda opened the door, and they stepped inside into a square room. The front wall was logs, but the other three sides were white plaster walls with paintings hung every couple of feet. In the very center of the back wall, between two windows, was a large painting of Swan Falls in the autumn. Yellow, gold, and orange foliage lined the sides of the creek, with the falls rising majestically above.

A stained-glass panel featuring a swan swimming among grasses hung in front of one of the windows, with an abstract stained-glass pattern on the other one.

Amanda went closer to read the plaques on the wall. The stained glass had been made by an artist in Anchorage, commissioned and donated by Patti and Tomas Johanson, presumably relatives of the mayor. A local artist, Mary Youngblood, had donated the painting. A quick glance around the room showed three smaller paintings in the same style hung on the left wall, two at Swan's Marsh, and a lovely one of Swan Lodge. In between, a doorway with a velvet rope across it gave a view into a typical cabin kitchen layout, with a woodstove and a heavy table and two simple chairs. A rocking chair sat next to the stove. Wall shelves held crockery, cast-iron skillets, and kitchen tools.

Paisley ran to the door. "Can I go in?"

"No, these things are for looking at, not touching," Amanda told her as she came up behind her. "That's why the rope is there."

"What's that thing?" Paisley pointed toward a cast-iron cylinder clamped to the edge of the table with a funnel-shaped top and a crank on the end.

An informational sign rested on an easel just inside the door. "It's a sausage grinder," Amanda answered. "Like the sausage we get at Tia Elena's." The green chili and cheese sausage links they bought at a local butcher shop were one of Paisley's favorites.

"Why did they want to grind it up?" Paisley asked. "Instead of eating it on a bun?"

Nathan covered a laugh, while Amanda explained, "No, it's not for grinding the sausage. It's to grind the meat to make the sausage. See, they would put pieces of meat in the top, then turn the crank and grind it into little pieces that come out the other end. Then they could mix the pieces with seasonings, like Tia Elena's green chilies and cheese. That thing behind the sausage grinder is a sausage stuffer. It pushes the ground-up sausage into a tube, which is where sausage gets it shape."

Paisley considered that for a minute. "Sausage is made of meat?"

"Yes. Tia Elena's sausage is made of pork, but that's probably not what people in Alaska used."

"The people here mostly used moose," Nathan said. "But that green chili and cheese sausage sounds amazing."

"If you come to visit us in Albuquerque, we can make it for you," Paisley offered. "Can't we, Mommy?"

"Sure," Amanda agreed. Not that Nathan would ever be coming to Albuquerque. The thought made her sad. She would miss him. So would Paisley.

Paisley lost interest in the kitchen diorama. "Let's go see the next room." This doorway looked into a room with a simple bed covered with a pile of faded quilts. A bearded mannequin sat on the bed, dressed in heavy canvas pants and a loose homespun shirt. He wore one leather boot and was bent down to pull on the other one. A floppy-brimmed hat rested beside him. Across the room, a female mannequin sat in a rocking chair. She wore a brown dress with a high collar and a full skirt, covered with a white apron. In her lap was a mukluk sown halfway up the seam, as though she was in the process of repairing it. Its mate sat on the floor at her feet. On the wall behind her hung a gorgeous parka, trimmed with a blue-and-gold diamond pattern along the hem, sleeves, and front pocket, which curved upward along the front. A wide band of fur edged the bottom and hood.

"Look, Paisley, the plaque says Eleanor donated this parka," Amanda pointed out. "It was hand-sewn for her by Sonya Anouchka, who was a well-known Yupik designer in the 1950s and '60s. It says it's based on traditional designs, with the fur on the inside for better insulation."

"It's pretty," Paisley commented. "I guess it gets real cold here in the winter."

"Colder than we're used to, for sure," Nathan said. "But Harry always said, 'There's no bad weather, only bad clothes.' That parka would keep you warm."

Amanda had stepped back to examine the art on this wall. These were smaller pictures, clustered together. The set to the left of the doorway were photographs of Alaskan birds and animals. Several were clearly taken at Swan's Marsh, and two were signed to Eleanor, from the photographer.

"Here's the story of Swan Lodge," Nathan said, pointing to a display on the wall next to the door.

Amanda and Paisley went to join him. A black-and-white photo of Harry and Eleanor holding hands on the front porch headed the display. Below, it told their story, beginning with the grubstake they acquired by winning the Nenana Ice Classic.

"What's the Nenana Ice Classic?" Amanda asked Nathan.

"It's a pool where people try to guess exactly what time the ice will break on the Tanana River at Nenana," Nathan answered. "It's a fundraiser for lots of nonprofits. Have you never heard that story?"

Amanda shook her head.

"I'm surprised. Harry loved to tell it. Shortly after they married, Harry and Eleanor moved to Alaska, where Harry got a job working for the railroad in track maintenance, and Eleanor as a secretary for a law firm in Anchorage. Only trouble was that Harry's job meant a lot of travel, and they didn't get to spend as much time together as they would have liked. They had dreams of starting a business of their own, where they could be together every day. They were saving up, but it was going to take a lot of years before they'd put away enough for a down payment on a lodge or motel somewhere. Then Harry heard about the Nenana Ice Classic, and he says he had a good feeling about it. He wanted to put everything they'd saved so far into it, but Eleanor was not about to let him gamble away their life savings. So he bought a single ticket—I don't remember how much it cost, something like a dollar—and his guess was that the ice would go out on their anniversary of May 8, and for the time he choose 4:22, which was his best guess as to when he and Eleanor had been pronounced husband and wife."

"How sweet. And that was the winning ticket?"

"It was indeed, although actually, their anniversary was May 9—Harry had it wrong. Eleanor never let him live that down."

Amanda laughed. "I can only imagine. Then what happened?"

"One day they went to see a place way out on the Glenn Highway past Sutton. It wasn't exactly what they wanted, but it was the closest they'd found, and they were considering putting in an offer. But on the way home, Eleanor was looking at the map and the name Swan Falls caught her eye, so they decided to stop and see it. There was a gravel road about halfway in those days. They parked and intended to hike to the falls, but they saw a for-sale sign and followed that trail toward the marsh, instead. And when they saw the swans nesting there, they decided this area would be the perfect place for Swan Lodge."

"Wow."

"They got a big swath of land cheap, which was good because it cost them a ton to bring in electricity and water. Then they used the rest, along with a bank loan, to build the cabins and the lodge. Once it was up and running, other people wanted to move to the area, so they ended up selling off the lots here, which grew into the town of Swan Falls. I think it was pretty haphazard at first, until the Johanson family moved in and started the mercantile. They were the force behind laying out the town in a grid pattern and eventually getting it incorporated."

"Johanson, like the mayor?"

"Yes. His parents run the mercantile. You met his sister, Bethany, at the ice cream shop."

"I thought her name was Coleman."

"That's her married name. Her husband works on the North Slope two weeks of every four, so it works for them to live here in Swan Falls. There's a whole bunch of Johanson brothers and sisters, but as far as I know, Bethany and Lars are the only ones who still live here."

"How do you keep up with all this?" Amanda asked.

"Bethany is the youngest sibling. All her siblings, except Lars, had already gone off when I knew Bethany as a teenager." Nathan checked his watch and looked at Paisley, who was studying the animal photos. "Have you seen everything?"

She nodded and skipped over to him. "It's neat how everything here is named Swan, and so are you."

"Yeah, but you're part of the Swan Family, too, even if it's not your name. Let's go do Peggy's shopping."

They locked up the museum, dropped off the key in the post office, and went next door to the mercantile. It was a large building by Swan Falls standards. Most of the store was taken up by groceries, but one wall had a low row of cubbyholes filled with jeans and work pants for men, women, and children. Shirts, jackets, and fishing vests hung above. Hats, both sunhats and winter beanies, were stacked on a shelf nearby. A curtained changing room was shoehorned into the corner. The display rack opposite the clothes held tools, everything from axes to shovels to screwdrivers. Amanda found the masking tape she was looking for at the end of that row. The next row featured school supplies, fishing tackle, and Alaska souvenirs, followed by pet food, birdseed, and dog beds.

Paisley stared in awe. "They have everything."

Amanda couldn't disagree. She picked up an item from the pet section. "It's a hummingbird feeder kit you can make with a mason jar. Want to hang it on our balcony at the lodge?"

"Yeah!"

Nathan came around the corner, pushing a small shopping cart. He loaded two bags of birdseed onto the bottom rack. "Did you find what you needed?"

Amanda held up the masking tape and feeder. "And more."

A woman who looked like an older version of Bethany was staffing the register. When they got to the front, she told Amanda, "I'm so sorry about your aunt. Swan Falls just won't be the same without Eleanor. She was a great lady."

"Yes, she was," Amanda agreed. "Thank you." Amanda stepped to the side to let Nathan check out. A cardboard display there read, "Vote for Feather Festival King and Queen," and it had a pocket full of handouts with a QR code explaining where to vote online. There were six headshots of people on the sign, including one of Peggy.

The cashier saw her reading the display. "Take a paper. It tells you how to cast your vote."

Amanda shook her head. "Oh, I'm not a resident—"

"You're Eleanor's family. That makes you one of us. And I never saw any rule that said you had to be a resident to vote. We used to do it with paper ballots, but now they've moved it onto the internet. Easier to count, I guess."

Maybe she should go online and vote for Peggy. But when Amanda looked closer, Peggy's name had a line through it and a handwritten notation next to it said, "Ineligible."

"Look at this," Amanda said to Nathan. "Why is Peggy ineligible?"

"Oh, that," the lady at the register replied. "The first two years we held the Swan Parade, Harry and Eleanor got, like, ninety percent of the votes for Swan King and Queen. After that, Eleanor pushed through a rule that said nobody could be chosen more than twice. The people on the nominating committee knew Peggy was Queen three years ago, but they didn't realize she'd done it once before, until after they'd printed up the posters."

"Too bad," Amanda said. "Peggy sure seems to be involved in the community."

"Oh, my yes." The woman scanned a jar of mustard. "If you got more than two people together to work on any sort of community event, you could bet at least one of them would be Peggy or Eleanor. That's why they nominated her, but Peggy was the one who pointed out she'd already done her two stints as Swan Queen." She scanned the last of Nathan's purchases and packed everything into the shopping bags. Nathan grabbed the heaviest one and the birdseed. Amanda took the other three and handed the lightest one to Paisley. "There are eggs in there, so be careful."

They stepped outside and Amanda started toward the car, but Paisley called, "Wait. The bookstore is across the street. The one the mayor told us about."

Amanda looked toward Nathan. "Do we have time?"

"Sure," he said. "Give me the groceries, and I'll stash them in the car while you and Paisley look around." He effortlessly added their three bags to his load and took off toward the parking lot.

Amanda and Paisley crossed the street to the blue A-frame with the Birdsong Books sign in the front. On either side of the front door, window boxes overflowed with pansies and geraniums. Behind the glass, books lined the windowsills. An orange-striped cat with a white chest slept on a blue-and-yellow cushion on a wicker chair in the corner of the porch. Paisley immediately went to investigate. "Hello, kitty."

The cat lifted its head and blinked at her. The front door opened, and Yolanda stepped out, carrying a big bag of books. "Oh, hello there. Are you here for Peggy's special order? I picked it up already when I did my shopping."

"No," Amanda told her. "We just wanted to do a little browsing."

Yolanda laughed and hoisted the bag. "I was just going to do a little browsing, too, but as you can see, several books decided to go home with me." A woman with silver glasses and tight white curls stepped onto the porch. Yolanda waved at her. "Thanks, Helen. See you later." She walked off toward the parking lot.

The bookstore proprietor looked at Paisley, who was reaching tentatively toward the cat. "That's Hobbs. He's a bookstore cat. He likes to be tickled under his chin."

Paisley stroked the cat's throat. "He's purring!"

"He does that a lot."

"He's not like Shadow," Paisley told her mother. "He likes people."

"The funny thing," the bookstore owner said, "is that he and Shadow are from the same litter. Their mother belongs to the mayor."

Paisley looked up. "You know Shadow?"

"Of course. I go out to Swan Lodge all the time. Peggy and some other ladies are in a book club together with me, and we often meet at the lodge. I'm Helen McCall, by the way. I was there the other day for Eleanor's funeral reception, but you probably didn't see me. I was mostly helping out in the kitchen."

"Thank you," Amanda said. "That was so kind of you."

Helen waved away her thanks. "It's the least I could do after all Eleanor has done for this community over the years."

Paisley reached into her jeans pocket and pulled out the mayor's business card. "A man gave me this and told me to give it to you."

Helen read the card, shook her head, and handed

it back. "Lars was just showing off. I give first-time customers a ten percent discount, and people staying at the lodge always get fifteen percent off. The people at Swan Lodge have been some of my best customers. Want to come in and pick out a book?"

"Yes!" Paisley hurried to the door. The cat, apparently not having had its fill of petting, jumped down from the chair and followed her. Amanda dutifully held the door for the cat before going in.

Inside, golden-hued wooden bookshelves filled the space, with hand-lettered signs denoting the several types of books available. A circular staircase in the middle of the room led up to a loft where, according to the sign, biographies and history were to be found. In the back was a children's corner, and Helen and Paisley made a beeline toward it. There, a comical moose cut from plywood with a hole in the face for a photo opportunity stood on one corner of a yellow-and-green rug, with two child-size chairs and a rocker taking up the rest of the rug. Bookcases had been arranged in a square to divide this portion off from the rest of the store. Hobbs walked back and forth along the top of one of the bookcases under Paisley's outstretched hand.

"What book are you reading now?" Helen asked Paisley.

"*Treasure Island*. I like it, but it's taking a long

time to read because it's, like, super old, so I have to look up a bunch of words in the dictionary."

"Yes, that's the only problem with reading classics," Helen agreed. "Styles have changed in the past hundred and something years. But a good story is a good story. Say, I happen to have a rather valuable early copy of *Treasure Island*." She looked over at Amanda. "Would you both like to see it?"

"Yes, please," Paisley said, giving the cat one last pat.

Helen took them to the other side of the store, to a bookcase with glass doors. A small padlock secured the hinged metal fastener in the center. She pulled a key from her pocket. "I hate doing this, but sadly I had a spate of shoplifting many years ago, so I started locking up my more valuable books." After jiggling the key for a second, she turned the lock and opened the door. She selected a faded blue leather book from the shelf and opened it to the middle. "It's an illustrated copy from more than a hundred years ago."

"That's Jim." Paisley pointed to a boy in the woodcut-style illustration. "And that's the *Hispaniola*, the ship they sailed to the island." She turned the page. "That's Captain Flint. He's a parrot. He sits on Long John Silver's shoulder. Long John Silver has a peg leg."

"You've been reading, all right," Helen observed

with approval as Paisley leafed through the rest of the pages.

"My book doesn't have pictures," Paisley told her, "except that somebody drew in the back."

"I hope it wasn't a rare copy," Helen said as she returned the book to its place in the cabinet.

The front door jingled, and Nathan walked in. "Hi, Helen."

"Nathan, hello. Yolanda already took Peggy's book, if that's why you're here."

"No, I'm just hanging with Paisley and Amanda today."

"Peggy was showing us an antique copy of *Treasure Island*," Amanda told him.

"Neat. When did you get that locking bookcase?" he asked. "I don't remember it."

"Years ago. I kept having books go missing that summer until finally, I got some glass doors and one of the summer employees at the lodge helped me attach them to the bookshelf and added the lock. It was the same summer the swan sculpture went missing from the lodge. Biggest crime wave in Swan Falls history, probably," she said with a rueful smile. "Oh, well. Come with me, Paisley, and we'll find you something good to read. Do you like mysteries?"

The two of them drifted over to the children's section, leaving Amanda and Nathan alone. Nathan was staring at the glass case.

"What are you thinking?" Amanda asked.

"I was just wondering if all those thefts are just a coincidence. What if whoever stole the sculpture was also the book thief? All the summer employees used to come here a lot. After all, there are only so many places to hang around in Swan Falls."

Amanda moved closer to the children's section. "Helen, do you remember the name of the person who helped you build the locking bookcase?"

"A young man. Sometimes he'd read books here instead of buying them, but I didn't mind as long as he didn't damage the books. I figured helping me with that bookcase was his way of saying thank you. Let's see—what was his name?" She tapped a finger against her cheek.

"Hector?" Nathan suggested.

"No, I remember Hector. It was that other boy. He was an English major, like me, and liked to discuss literature. Not too many people are interested in the classics."

"Was his name Derrick?" Amanda asked.

"Yes. That's it. Derrick."

Amanda exchanged glances with Nathan. "If we assume the same person who stole the books also took the sculpture, does helping Helen rule him out?" she asked in a low voice. "Or could it have been a way of diverting suspicion, like the way he started rumors about you."

He shrugged. "Or maybe one has nothing to do with the other. I suspect we'll never know."

CHAPTER ELEVEN

THAT EVENING, Nathan picked up his new book on how to run a bed-and-breakfast. Not that the lodge was exactly a B&B, but close enough that he figured he could get some useful information. All those years of visiting Eleanor and Harry should have taught him most of what he needed to know, but it had never occurred to him that he might someday be in charge.

He'd intended to sit in the lobby, but deep evening light shining low across the water drew him outside. Amanda stood on the patio, her face turned upward to watch a flock of ducks overhead, the older ducks quacking encouragement to the youngsters who were just learning to fly. The sun brought a warm glow to her skin and reflected the fire in her coppery waves. The entire flock dipped low and settled onto the water in the middle of the lake, breaking up the smooth plane of the sunlit surface like so many pieces of stained glass.

He went to stand beside Amanda, and she turned

to give him a smile. "I don't think I could ever get tired of this view."

"No," he agreed. "It's always different, and yet always the same, too. Is Paisley in bed?"

"Yes. She said she wanted to read, but before I even left the room, her eyelids were drooping, and the book was falling from her hands. Busy day today."

"It was." After returning from town, they'd gone to visit the beaver kits, and then he'd helped Paisley build a birdhouse, and installed it for her in a tree near the lake. After dinner, they'd filled the hummingbird feeder and mounted it on a bracket on the balcony. Then Yolanda had rounded Paisley, Amanda, and Nathan up for a game of badminton before bedtime. Amanda turned out to be almost comically bad at it, but she didn't let that stop her, laughing whenever her racquet missed the shuttlecock and cheering everyone else's successes.

"I appreciate you being so patient in town, today," Amanda said. "Paisley loved spending all that time at the museum and bookstore. Sorry we didn't get any painting done."

"Painting will be there tomorrow. What's the point of being here in one of the most beautiful places in the world, if we don't take the time to enjoy it?" He looked out at the lake. "Want to walk a bit, or did you get in enough steps today?"

"A walk sounds nice." They wandered to the

edge of the lake, and then turned to follow the shoreline. When they reached a rocky spot where they had to climb, he offered a hand up to Amanda. She didn't immediately drop his hand once they were back on level ground. Instead they walked along, fingers clasped. They came to a high point that jutted into the water and stopped to take in the view. The sun was lower now, and the trees cast a shadow across their part of the lake. Swallows darted here and there. A trout chased a bug from the water, landing with a splash.

"Beautiful," Amanda murmured.

"I've always loved this place," Nathan said. "All year long, I'd look forward to coming, and I hated to leave. I remember once getting in trouble with my dad, because I disappeared just before it was time to go and made us late to the airport. We didn't miss our flight, but it was close."

"That doesn't sound like you," Amanda told him. "I got the impression you were a responsible kid."

"Usually I was, but that day, even though I knew we were supposed to be leaving right away, I had this strong urge for one more walk through the woods. Like you said, that was totally out of character for me. It was a good thing, though, because I found a girl, one of the guests at the lodge, lost in the woods. I'm sure she would have found her way back eventually, but she was scared, and I showed her—" He paused when Amanda's mouth dropped open. "Why are you looking at me like that?"

"That was me!" Amanda gasped. "I was lost in the woods that day, and you were the boy that helped me. I've never forgotten that moment of kindness. In fact, I was telling Paisley about it in the airport."

"Wow." Nathan should have put it together. That little girl, her red hair in two braids hanging down her back. The look of trust she'd given him when he took her hand to lead her home.

"The first time I saw you, something about you seemed familiar." She took a step closer. "I wrote it off, figuring it was because you're related to Harry, but I think it was your eyes." She touched his face. "They look the same as they did then. Gentle and kind."

Her own eyes sparkled, blue gray at first glance, but with an indigo starburst around the pupil hinting at hidden depths. His gaze fell to her rosy lips. They parted as she took a quick breath. And then he was reaching for her, even as she wrapped a hand behind his neck and pulled him closer. When their lips touched, every coherent thought went out of his head. He closed his eyes and reveled in the feel of her soft lips moving against his mouth. Her scent filled his nose, a clean citrus aroma overlying something warm and cozy. His fingers tangled in the soft waves of her hair. Birds sang, ducks quacked, and squirrels chattered all around them in a natural symphony.

When they finally broke the kiss, he rested his forehead against hers. "Wow."

"Agreed." She chuckled softly. "I looked for you, you know. After that day when you found me in the woods and brought me home, I kept hoping to find you again, but I never did." She stroked his cheek. "Until now."

"Until now," he repeated. Somehow it felt like, without knowing it, he'd been looking for her his whole life, too.

AMANDA PEELED THE last piece of masking tape from the molding at the edge of the window, and carefully wiped away a tiny drip of paint that had squeezed under the tape. Last night had been— unexpected. Yes, she'd felt an attraction to Nathan from the beginning, but she'd never allowed herself to consider acting upon it. But holding his hand out there at the lakeside had felt only natural. And then when she'd discovered he was the boy she remembered from so long ago, that kiss seemed inevitable, and the only thing that mattered was that magnetic pull between them. But in the morning light, she'd come face-to-face with reality, and realized that a romantic relationship with Nathan was out of the question.

As if she'd summoned him, Nathan appeared at the door, carrying his toolbox in one hand and a desk lamp in the other. He'd spent the morning tightening screws, touching up scratches, and dealing with other items on the checklist, while Amanda painted the library. He inspected the wall. "I really like that sage color you chose. It feels peaceful in here, like in the woods."

"Thanks." Amanda's cheeks grew warm. She wasn't sure if she'd ever think of a walk in the woods as peaceful again. Not after the way his kiss had stirred up that emotional tornado inside her. That kiss hadn't felt like a casual flirtation; it felt like a promise. So very right—and yet so wrong. They couldn't be making promises to one another. He had a life in Phoenix. Hers was in Albuquerque. She was a single mom, heading up a demanding business. She had far too many responsibilities to allow herself to be distracted by kisses, no matter how incredible. She struggled to keep her voice casual. "How are the repairs coming along?"

"So far, so good. I've replaced washers in all the leaky faucets, changed the burnt-out light bulbs, and tightened the loose doorknobs. I think this lamp just needs a new switch. I'm taking it to Malcolm's workshop to get him to show me how to fix it. He's good with electrical things." He bent to peer into the reading tent. "Is Paisley around?"

"No, she's reading on the balcony today so that she can keep an eye on the new hummingbird feeder. According to her last report, she's had at least three hummers visiting already."

"Good for her." He set his load on the floor and stepped closer, those warm brown eyes of his studying her face as though he were memorizing every feature, just the way he had in the woods last night. His gaze dropped to her mouth, and she knew he was thinking of kissing her again. But before he could, Amanda turned away and picked up a rubber mallet, which she used to tap the lid tighter onto the paint can.

"Amanda?" He touched her shoulder. "Is something wrong?"

"No, of course not. I just—" She turned to face him. "I think maybe we got a little carried away yesterday. The kiss—I mean it was nice…" She trailed off.

"Very nice." Once again, his gaze flickered to her lips, and then back to her eyes.

"But I don't think…" Again, she paused.

Nathan rubbed the back of his neck. "You don't want me to kiss you anymore?"

She swallowed. "It's not that I don't want it—"

"But…?"

"But I—I don't know." She walked toward the open window, allowing a fresh breeze to cool her face. After a moment, she turned back to him. "Obviously, I'm confused. Can we just table this discussion for now?"

"If that's what you want."

"It is." It wasn't. What she wanted was for him to take her into his arms and pull her close and kiss her until her knees went weak, but as she'd told her daughter a million times, what someone wanted wasn't necessarily what was best for them.

He met her gaze before answering. "Let me know when you're ready to talk about it."

She wasn't sure she would ever be ready. Better to focus on practical matters. "I'm done painting this room. I know we still have the hallways to paint, but maybe it would be a good idea to get a real estate agent in now and ask their opinion about what more we need to do before we place the lodge for sale."

Nathan's head jerked back. "You want to sell?"

"Well, yeah," Amanda answered. "Don't you?"

"No."

"But how—"

"The whole point," Nathan broke in, "of Eleanor's leaving the lodge to us rather than other relatives was so that it would stay in the family. Otherwise, she would have just instructed Vince to sell and divide up the money. At least, that's what I think."

"But I can't stay here," Amanda protested. "I have a business in New Mexico to run."

"I thought—" He stopped.

"What?"

Nathan shook his head. "Never mind. There's no reason for you to stay. I can operate the lodge."

"But what about your job in Phoenix?" she asked.

"I'll resign. Running Swan Lodge is what I want to do. I've been reading up, and I have some ideas for marketing. It might take a year or so to get profitable again, but once we are, you and I can split the profits."

"I'm sorry, Nathan, but that won't work." Much as Amanda would have liked to keep the lodge in the family, she needed to sell, to pay for the new greenhouses. "I need that cash up front."

Those brown eyes, usually so warm, suddenly chilled. "It's already August, so we don't have much tourist season left, but if I can get the place up and running within a couple of weeks, I can bring in a little cash this season and spend the winter getting ready for a big reopening next summer. If I defer some of the upgrades I want to make, I should be able to turn a profit by then."

"Next summer isn't soon enough," Amanda insisted. She needed to get the greenhouses installed before spring planting. "I need the money now."

Nathan glared, and then snapped, "I thought you were different."

Amanda drew back. "What are you talking about? Different than who?" she demanded, but he spun on his heel and marched out the door, leaving the toolbox and lamp abandoned on the floor.

"Wait!" she called. "Where are you going?"

"Outside, to cool off," he said without slowing. "But this conversation isn't over."

CHAPTER TWELVE

NATHAN KEPT WALKING until he reached the end of the trail and found himself staring out across the marsh. This was exactly the reason he'd sworn off romance, and yet, here he was again. How was it that he kept falling for women who were just in it for the money? Amanda had seemed so real. She seemed to find joy in simple things like humming-birds, and beaver ponds, and ice cream. She'd even helped Nathan attempt to find out more about the lost sculpture and clear his name. But all her hard work and encouragement were about the quick payoff, not about Swan Lodge. Not about Harry and Eleanor's legacy. Not about him.

Was that kiss yesterday just part of a scheme? Maybe Amanda hoped she could charm him into giving her what she wanted. But if that was her plan, it wasn't going to work. He'd fallen for it once. It wasn't going to happen again.

He paced along the boardwalk, catching glimpses of birds and ducks between the reeds. A small flock of Canada geese dabbled nearby, tipping themselves bottoms up so that they could graze on aquatic plants. A purplish dragonfly, its lacy wings shot through with silver, darted past him and landed on a post.

By the time he reached the last of the boardwalk, he was feeling calmer. He looked toward the forest and the mountains beyond the marsh. Quite possibly one of the most beautiful places on earth. At least Swan's Marsh was safe, locked in a trust and dedicated to preservation of the birds that called it home. Amanda couldn't sell it to the highest bidder. If only that were true of Swan Lodge.

Could Amanda force him to sell? He suspected the answer was yes. They each owned a half interest in the property, and Amanda might well have the legal right to demand it be sold and divided. He'd have to ask Vince how that worked.

As he turned and retraced his steps along the boardwalk, listening to the chirps and quacks and hums of nature, doubts began to surface. Had he overreacted? Just because Amanda wanted to sell didn't necessarily make her a terrible person. She was widowed recently, and she had Paisley to support. Maybe she just craved the security of money in the bank, rather than invested in a lodge so far away from her. He'd tried to explain that the lodge could provide a good income for her in the long run, but maybe he needed to show her that the lodge was a worthwhile investment. Put together some projections. But would she listen to him, after he'd stormed out of the room like that?

He thought back to the way she'd grimaced, when he'd snapped that he thought she was different, and the regrets came flooding in. In truth, he'd been lashing out at Priscilla and her manipulations, but Amanda had borne the brunt of it. That wasn't fair. Amanda had done nothing to deserve his anger. He owed her an apology and a fair hearing.

Just before he reached the dock, the kazoo-like "oh-oh" of the trumpeter swans drew him. He followed the boardwalk around a corner and spotted them, scratching at the bottom of the marsh with their webbed feet before dabbling to eat the plants and rhizomes they'd uprooted. All the while Albert, Alison, and the young cygnets called back and forth, keeping tabs on one another. Caring for one another.

He took the trail back toward the lodge. At a sunny bend, he spotted three salmonberries, ripe and bursting with juice. He picked them and carried them back to the lodge. Peggy was away from the kitchen, for once. He washed the berries and dropped them into a blue teacup. Then he went in search of Amanda.

She wasn't in the lobby or the library. He knocked on the door of her room, but there was no answer. No sign of Paisley, either. He went out front, where he found Peggy and Malcolm, Malcolm raking the gravel of the drive smooth, and Peggy pulling a few stray weeds.

Peggy brushed back a loose strand of hair with her garden glove, leaving a faint streak of dirt on her forehead. "Hello, Nathan. Are you ready for lunch? I have chicken salad for sandwiches."

"Not quite yet. Have you seen Amanda?" he asked.

"She said she was taking Paisley to see the beavers," Malcolm said. "Seemed a little upset. I asked why, but she didn't want to talk about it."

"Thanks. I'll find her." He turned to go.

"Nathan," Peggy's voice stopped him. "Maybe you should leave them for now. Give them a little time alone."

"No, it's my fault that she's upset," Nathan told her. "I need to fix it."

He found Amanda and Paisley halfway home on the trail to the beaver pond. Paisley, at least, seemed to be her normal self, skipping ahead on the trail. "Hi, Nathan. We saw three babies today, and one of them was eating a stick that was floating in the water. He was so cute. I helped Peggy make chicken salad and oatmeal cookies this morning and she said we could pack lunches and go for a picnic beside the lake."

"That sounds fun," he told her. "You're getting to be quite a cook."

"Yeah, I know. It's fun."

Amanda caught up with them. "Paisley, why

don't you go on ahead and wash up? Nathan and I need to talk for a few minutes before lunch."

"Okay." Paisley flashed a mischievous smile. "But don't take too long, or I might eat your cookies."

"You'd better not," Nathan answered with a grin and pretended to be sneaking up on her. Paisley shrieked happily and ran down the path toward the lodge. Nathan turned to face Amanda.

She watched him with wary eyes. Not that he blamed her after his outburst. He opened his mouth to apologize, but before he could she blurted out, "Do you want me to go?"

"What?"

"I'd planned to stick around for another week to get all the painting done on the lodge and to take Paisley to the Feather Festival, but clearly you don't trust me. Maybe it would be better if Paisley and I get back to Albuquerque, and we can work some kind of agreement through Vince."

"No, this is your place just as much as it is mine. I'm sorry I spoke to you the way I did. You didn't deserve that."

She pinned him with her gaze. "It was pretty intense."

"You're right. It won't happen again," Nathan promised and held up the cup. "I brought you a peace offering."

Amanda eyed the golden-pink fruits. "What are they?"

"Wild salmonberries. Try one."

She popped one into her mouth. "Mmm. They taste like raspberries, but more subtle." She ate another one.

"I'm glad you like them. I do think we need to talk through our plans. I promise to keep an open mind if you will."

"All right." She took the last berry. "I'd like to understand a little bit about why you got upset. After you'd gone, I realized I hadn't explained about why I need money right away." She returned the cup to him.

"You see," she continued, "my husband started Zia Gardens Greenhouse and Nursery seven years before we married. He got a small business loan to buy the land and build the greenhouses. Within ten years, he'd paid off all the loans and everything was going well. Greenhouses only have a life of fifteen to twenty years, so once the loans were paid off, he was building a fund to replace them when the time came. But then he got sick, and we didn't have the greatest insurance plan." She shrugged. "We'd both always been healthy, so it didn't seem that important."

"So you had to spend the greenhouse savings on medical bills." Nathan was starting to see where this was going.

"Yes. To make matters worse, when David couldn't work, he left his most senior employee in charge, but it turns out she wasn't much of a manager, and the business started losing money. He got very sick, very quickly, and I was so caught up in taking care of him that I didn't realize how bad it had gotten until after he was gone."

"I'm so sorry." He touched her arm. "That had to have been horrible for you and Paisley."

"It was hard, but we're doing better now. I've got a great manager in place, and we're operating in the black. But we desperately need to replace the two greenhouses, and I don't have enough cash on hand to do it. That's what I meant when I said I need the cash up front."

"I understand." Maybe he could find a way to accelerate the cash flow. "How long can you put off replacing the greenhouses?"

"According to Harley, my manager, it should have already happened. The panels become opaquer over time, and we've had to use too much supplemental lighting, which gets expensive, besides which, the panels get brittle and crack with age. He says we can't last for another year." She touched Nathan's arm. "But I understand why you want to keep Swan Lodge and operate it like Harry and Eleanor did. I do think you could make a success of it. So why don't you just buy me out? I'm sure you could borrow the money."

"Actually, I don't think I can," Nathan confessed.

"Why? With this property for collateral, I would

think any bank would be eager to give you a mortgage for half the value."

"You'd think so, wouldn't you." He looked out over the lake. Was he really going to tell Amanda his most embarrassing secret? But she'd shared her problems. It was only fair that he was honest with her. "You're not the only one with financial problems. I filed for Chapter Seven bankruptcy three years ago." He looked at her face, expecting to see disgust and judgment, but he only saw concern.

"Why? What happened?"

"It goes back to a year and a half before that. I met this woman through work, and we started seeing each other. Her name was Priscilla Snook. She seemed great."

"I gather she wasn't?"

"No, but it took me a long time to figure that out. We'd been dating a while when I was given an assignment that would take me out of the country for a few months. Before I left, I bought a ring and we got engaged. We started looking at houses, but inventory was low, and they were going fast. We agreed that she would make all the wedding plans and find us a house to buy while I was overseas. I'd been gone less than a week when she emailed photos of this perfect house at a great price, but she lost the chance to bid on it because I wasn't there to sign the offer. So to keep that from happening again, she said the real estate agent had suggested I give her my power of attorney."

"Uh-oh."

"Exactly. So she sent the document for me to sign and notarize. I should have been suspicious that it gave her authority to handle all my property, but I thought that was just the standard language. I'm sure you can guess the rest. When I came home, there was no wedding, no house, no fiancée. She'd cleaned out all my accounts, borrowed a huge amount of money in my name, and disappeared."

"Wow. I'm so sorry."

He frowned. "It changed me. I used to trust people, but now—"

"Now I understand what you meant when you said you thought I was different."

"And that was entirely unfair." He held out his hands, palms up. "You are nothing like Priscilla. But just for a moment there, I was having flashbacks—"

"Got it. So, what are our options? I would love for you to be able to keep the lodge and run it just like Eleanor and Harry did, but I can't afford to wait. There must be some way for us both to get what we want."

He considered the problem. "Can't you borrow the money for your greenhouses? After all, you said that's what your husband did the first time around."

"I've looked into it, but I'm kind of in the same situation as you. David was able to take advantage of some special programs for new businesses and got a low rate on a small business loan, but those aren't available for an existing business. And when I was juggling finances, I missed some mortgage payments. It all got paid off when I sold the house, but that bank isn't in any hurry to loan me more money. So far, I've only found one bank that will, and with the interest rate they're offering, the payments are too high for the nursery to carry."

"What were you going to do before you found out Eleanor had left you half?"

"I'm not sure. The nursery is in a prime location. I've had offers to buy the land. Possibly, I would have had to sell and move the nursery to a different spot with cheaper real estate and build the new greenhouses there. I'd hate to, because our convenient location gets us a lot of local traffic, but it might have come to that. I just know that one way or another, I'm going to keep Zia Gardens going until Paisley can grow up and take over. When Vince called us in and told us we'd inherited, it felt like the answer to a prayer. It still does."

Nathan nodded. "What if Paisley doesn't want to take over the nursery? What if she'd rather become an animal trainer, or a chef?"

"Zia Gardens is her heritage." Amanda stood up a little straighter and pushed her shoulders back.

"And if she chooses something else, well, at least she had the choice."

"I understand." And he did, hard as it was to accept.

"Look, I don't know every banking rule and regulation, but is it possible you could get a loan even after a bankruptcy?" Amanda asked. "After all, you'd only be asking for half the value of the lodge, and you could explain the circumstances."

"It's possible," Nathan said. "I was told bankruptcy will be on my credit history for six years. I assumed that meant I wouldn't be eligible until then, but maybe I'm wrong. I'll give Vince a call tomorrow and see what he advises. And in the meantime, please don't go." He gave a wry grin. "And not just because you're a gifted painter. Your home may be in Albuquerque, but when I was growing up, I learned you can have more than one home. As long as it's still in our names, Swan Lodge is home for you and Paisley, too."

CHAPTER THIRTEEN

LATER THAT DAY, Nathan stood on the edge of the lake, looking out over the water. After consulting with Vince, Nathan had filled out a loan application with a local bank in Wasilla. The loan officer had promised to get back to him once she ran it by a committee, but from her body language, Nathan wasn't hopeful. Still, there had to be some way to get Amanda the money she needed for those greenhouses while allowing him to keep the lodge and run it. Eleanor always said she did her best thinking outside, surrounded by nature, but so far it hadn't inspired any solutions.

At least Amanda was talking to him. After he'd blown up like that, he was lucky she hadn't demanded an immediate liquidation of the property. According to Vince, as co-owner, she did have that right. She was willing to give him time to find an answer, but she wasn't going to wait forever. He needed to come up with a plan.

At the sound of footsteps on the path behind him, he turned to find Peggy walking his way.

She put her hands on her hips. "Saw you out here, standing like you're holding up the weight of the world on your shoulders. Is this something to do with Amanda?"

"Why would you say that?" Nathan asked.

Peggy snorted. "I've seen the way you look at her. And Malcolm mentioned he saw you two holding hands next to the lake yesterday evening."

"Malcolm needs to mind his own business," Nathan muttered, but Peggy just laughed.

"Malcolm is a romantic, but over the years, I've seen plenty of these little vacation flirtations. They don't necessarily mean anything. Is that the problem? That she's going home in a week?"

"More than that," Nathan admitted. "She wants to sell the lodge."

"Oh." Peggy frowned, but after a moment she nodded. "I suppose we shouldn't be surprised. She doesn't have the connections here that you have. Did you explain that you'll run it and take care of everything, and all she has to do is wait for the money to roll in?"

"It's the waiting that's the problem. She needs an inflow of cash for new greenhouses to keep her other business going."

Peggy sniffed. "If that's the case, it sounds to me that that's the business that should go, not this one. Harry and Eleanor made a good living here, and Swan Falls depends on Swan Lodge for its very existence. If you were to sell out to some big corporation, what would become of the town?"

He hadn't really considered that. "Would it make any difference to the town who runs the lodge?"

"It could make an enormous difference. Take my friend Helen, for instance. She runs Birdsong Books. Now, how many towns the size of Swan Falls have an independent bookstore? Not many, I'd wager. But she makes a go of it because of the business from the lodge. Eleanor ordered most of the books in the library upstairs through her shop. And when people check into the lodge, we'd give them a whole package of coupons and flyers for all the local businesses—the diner, the pizza place, the craft co-op, Swan Falls Mercantile, the Wednesday farmers market. Is a corporation going to do that? Maybe, but I doubt it."

"Amanda seems adamant."

"Maybe she doesn't realize just how important Swan Lodge is to Swan Falls. If she got to know the people here—" Peggy snapped her fingers. "That's what you need to do. Get her involved. The Feather Festival is coming up, and we always need volunteers. Amanda is a hard worker. If she pitches in, she'll see for herself how much it would damage the community if the lodge goes out of the family."

"When I was talking with Vince today, he did mention that the playground equipment we ordered will be arriving this afternoon. We could recruit volunteers to install it with us."

"Great. Check the weather forecast and pick a day. I'll make some calls and a picnic lunch for everyone."

"Sounds fun."

"We'll make sure it is. Almost everyone who spends time here falls in love with Swan Falls. We just need to make sure that happens with Amanda, too. And once she's invested in the town, she'll understand that Swan Lodge needs to stay in the family, no matter what it takes."

"THOSE OATMEAL COOKIES you made were awesome," Amanda told her daughter as they brushed their teeth after lunch. "Did Peggy give you the recipe so we can make them at home?"

"No, but I'll ask her. When are we going back to Albuquerque?" she mumbled around the toothbrush.

"I moved our flight back a week, to after the Feather Festival. Why, are you homesick?"

Paisley shook her head and rinsed the toothbrush. "I like it here. There're the beavers, and the swans, and Shadow, and Maggie the Magpie, and the reading tent. I wish we could live here forever."

"But what about your friends? Wouldn't you miss them?" Although come to think of it, Paisley hadn't spent a lot of time with friends this summer. She could only remember one or two play-dates and one sleepover back in early June.

Paisley shrugged. "Lucy moved to Texas anyway, and I don't think Kennedy likes me that much. She was really Lucy's friend."

"I'm sorry." How could Amanda not have known about this? "You didn't tell me Lucy's family was moving. When did that happen?"

"A long time ago. The sleepover at her house was her goodbye party."

"Oh." Was she the world's worst mother, or what? Granted, June had been a zoo at the nursery, but how could she have let all this time go by without questioning why Paisley hadn't wanted to get together with Lucy. "Well, school starts two weeks after we're due home and you'll be in the fourth grade this year. I'll bet you'll find some great new friends in your class."

"Maybe." Paisley seemed to have more immediate things on her mind. "I'm going to find Malcolm. He said he'd teach me how to make a bird feeder."

"Okay. Put the cap on the toothpaste first."

Paisley stuck the lid on and scurried out. Once she was gone, Amanda sat down and took a moment to take stock. Her daughter would be starting a new school year without the support of her best friend, and Amanda hadn't even realized it. The business her late husband had founded and nurtured into a success was on its last legs unless she could find a way to replace the greenhouses. And the only way she could see to do that was to sell Swan Lodge, which would displace Peggy and Malcolm and break Nathan's heart. Tears of frustration stung her eyes. How could she be letting down everyone she cared about all at once?

Because she did care. She cared about Harry and Eleanor, and she hated to disappoint them, if indeed Nathan was right, and the reason Eleanor left the lodge to the two of them was so that it would stay in the family. She cared about Peggy and Malcolm, who had worked here so many years and called it home. They were both in their fifties, late to be finding a new job, but not yet ready for retirement. She cared about Nathan, probably more than she should. She genuinely liked him, and after hearing what he'd been through with his fiancée, she was even more impressed with his kindness and generous spirit. Not to mention, she found him unsettlingly attractive—not that anything could come of that.

Because, bottom line, she was Paisley's mother, and she loved that girl to the depths of her soul. She didn't want to disappoint anyone, but if it came to a choice between what they wanted and what was best for Paisley, Paisley would win every time. When Amanda had lost her father, she'd also lost her birthright, her chance to take over the chili farm that had been in her family for generations. Paisley had lost her father, too, but she wasn't going to lose Zia Gardens. Somehow, Amanda would see to that.

Could Amanda find a way to make everyone happy? She had another week to find out. In the meantime, maybe she could at least help Nathan reach one of his goals. She went down the hall to the library and used that computer to sign on to the Swan Lodge page on social media. One message was waiting.

She opened the message from Krista, which looked to be several paragraphs long. Krista sent her condolences and shared several fond memories of the two summers she'd spent at Swan Lodge. She said she would let her summer co-workers know about Eleanor's passing. "We lost track of Derrick after he got expelled from college, but everyone else kept in touch," she wrote. "Those summers at Swan Lodge had an enormous impact on my life, and I'm sure the others will say the same. Eleanor was a special person, and the world was better because of her. If Peggy is still there, send hugs from me.—Krista."

Amanda found Nathan and Peggy on the patio refilling the bird feeders. Yolanda sat at a table nearby, sipping a cup of tea and reading. Peggy hung up the last feeder and turned. "Amanda. Just the person I needed to see. The playground equipment is here, and Nathan and I are trying to put together a work party. Would tomorrow work for you?"

"Tomorrow's fine, but what do you mean by a work party? Isn't it being professionally installed?"

"No, the townspeople will want to be involved," Peggy assured her. "I'll make a few calls." She picked up an empty birdseed bag and started for the house.

"Before you go," Amanda said, "Krista responded to the message on social media."

"What did she say?" Peggy asked.

"Lots of wonderful things about Eleanor and about her time working here. She specifically said to give you a hug," Amanda told the older woman.

Peggy smiled. "That sounds like her."

"She also mentioned that she would pass on the news about Eleanor. Apparently, she's kept up with the other summer employees she worked with here—"

"That doesn't surprise me," Peggy said.

"Except," Amanda continued, "for Derrick. She says she lost touch with him when he was expelled from college."

Nathan looked up. "Interesting. Did she say why he was expelled?"

"No, but what are the most common reasons? Cheating, violating drug policy, absenteeism, crime..." Amanda ticked them off on her fingers.

"Crime." Nathan repeated.

"If he'd gotten away with stealing a valuable art object, that might have emboldened him to try it again," Amanda pointed out.

"Okay, but if it was Derrick who stole the sculpture, does that help us? We don't know where he is. And you didn't find him on social media."

"That's true, but I could still try contacting him through the information on his work application," Amanda said. "Maybe he's feeling guilty. If the statute of limitations has passed, he might want to get it off his chest."

Peggy snorted. "Not likely."

"She's right," Yolanda piped up. "The Derrick I remember was not the sort to let his conscience get in the way. When I checked in, he gave me this story about how hard he was working to put himself through college because his parents couldn't afford to send him. Later, I heard him telling one of the girls that he had a trust fund set up by his grandparents that covered everything. I called him on it, but he had this way of grinning to make you feel like you were in on the joke."

"He was a charmer," Peggy agreed. "My friend Helen at the bookstore thought he hung the moon because he would discuss classic literature with her. She's always given Swan Lodge employees a discount, but she would slip him books for free."

"She told us he helped her make a bookcase to protect her more valuable books after some were stolen," Amanda told her.

"Locking the barn after the horse ran away maybe?" Yolanda mused.

"Could be," Peggy said. "Anyway, I'd better get to those calls if you're going to get any help with that playground tomorrow. Ten o'clock, okay?"

"Fine with me," Amanda said.

"Me, too," Nathan agreed. "The weather should be fine."

Nathan and Amanda stepped inside. "Do you actually know how to install playground equipment?" she asked him.

"Vince assures me that it comes with all the anchors and connectors and everything we need," Nathan told her. "And he's trying to round up someone with experience. He's also lined up a delivery of rubber mulch late tomorrow, which we'll need to spread under the equipment."

"Sounds like a plan. Do you think it's okay to bring Paisley?"

"Absolutely," Nathan told her. "I'll bet there will be other kids there for her to play with."

"That would be great. Okay, I'll see what contact information I can find in Derrick's employment file, and we can go from there."

"Thank you." He paused to look straight at her, those brown eyes soft and kind once again. "Not just for all the effort to find the lost sculpture, but for the work you've put into fixing up the lodge, and for giving me a little time to try to come up with a way to keep it. Not everyone would be so understanding, and I appreciate it, more than you know."

THE SMALL LOT at the edge of the park had filled with cars by nine forty-five the next morning. Malcolm pulled his truck around to the street side and expertly parallel parked between an orange pickup pocked with rust holes and a Cadillac Escalade still sporting dealer's plates. Amanda climbed out of the jump seat in the back of the cab and walked around to the edge of the park. Easily a dozen adults and several children and teenagers already milled around the new playground area. "Wow."

"I know." Nathan came to stand next to her. "When something needs to be done, the people of Swan Falls really come through."

"That they do," Malcolm agreed as he opened the topper on the back of the truck. "Nathan, give me a hand here with the tools?"

Nathan turned to help, and Paisley slipped her hand into Amanda's. "That's a lot of people," she whispered.

"Yeah, but they're nice people," Amanda whispered back, "here to build a playground for kids like you. Come on, let's help Nathan and Malcolm carry the tools." Loaded down with shovels, rakes, and wrenches, the four of them crossed the park toward the crowd.

Vince waved and came to meet them. "Good, you're here. We're ready to get started, but first Mayor Johanson wants to say a 'few words.'" This pronouncement was accompanied by a good-natured eye roll. "He's running for reelection this fall," Vince added in a quieter voice.

The mayor introduced Nathan, Amanda, and Paisley and then thanked the Swan family for the equipment and all the volunteers for being there. While he spoke, Amanda scanned the crowd. Bethany from the ice cream store was there, with two teenage boys beside her. Two elementary-aged kids fidgeted next to a woman carrying a tote bag, probably their grandmother. A couple of the men she'd seen at the post office stood with their heads together near the open tailgate of a pickup, pointing at a diagram. The mayor seemed to realize he was losing the crowd. "So, without further ado, let's build this playground."

After a few seconds of polite applause, Vince stepped forward, bringing with him a man holding a stack of hard hats. "I'd like to introduce Bruce Taylor, a structural engineer from Anchorage. He'll be overseeing everything, making sure it's all installed properly to keep us and our kids safe. Everyone in the construction area will need to wear a hard hat. We'll need three teams, one to install the central climbing tower and attachments, plus two smaller teams for the playhouse and the spring animal." He walked through the crowd with a smile and a word for everyone as he assigned them to their tasks.

Amanda found herself on the playhouse team along with a woman about her mother's age. Before she could introduce herself, the older woman with two kids approached. "Good to see you, Mary," she said before turning to smile at Paisley and Amanda. "I'm Janice Cooper, and these are my grandkids, Max and Lyla."

"Hi. I'm Amanda, and this is my daughter, Paisley."

"Hi. Paisley, the kids were wondering if you'd like to go feed the ducks with them."

Paisley looked up at Amanda. "Can I, Mommy?"

"Sure. Just stay where you can see me, but don't get close to the construction, okay?"

"Okay." Paisley moved toward the other kids.

"Here's the duck food." Janice handed over the shopping bag to the boy who looked to be a year or two older than his sister and Paisley. "You can pass it out to all the kids."

The three kids immediately took off for the pond. As they left, Amanda could hear the girl telling Paisley, "It's corn and vegetables. Never feed ducks bread. It's bad for them. Vegetables and seeds are much healthier." Paisley seemed to be hanging on to every word.

"Lyla is a bit of a science nerd," Janice told Amanda. "She's nine. Max is twelve. I told him if he'd keep an eye on the younger kids while we work, we could go to Raven's Nest Pizza for dinner. They're both excited about the new playground."

"I'm excited, too," the other woman told them.

"It's just like Eleanor to arrange for something like this. I'm Mary Youngblood, by the way," she said while offering her hand to Amanda.

Amanda shook her hand. "Nice to meet you, Mary. Oh, Youngblood. You must be the artist whose pictures are in the museum."

"Yes." The woman smiled. "You've already seen the museum?"

"The mayor let us in the day before yesterday. I love your paintings."

"Thank you. We're planning to keep the museum open all day during the Feather Festival. If either of you are interested in taking a shift, I have a sign-up sheet in the car."

"Sure. I could do that." Janice agreed, and Mary went to fetch it.

"Mary's a big promoter of the museum," Janice commented. "Eleanor was, too. Vince said she had donated her Deanna Somers sculpture to the museum if it's ever recovered."

"Such a shame the sculpture was stolen," Mary said, handing a clipboard and pen to Janice. "Deanna Somers went on to make quite a name for herself. Having a piece like that could put our little museum on the map."

Once Janice finished, Amanda signed her name in a time slot for early afternoon on a Friday. She was tempted to tell the ladies about the ransom letter they'd discovered, but figured there was no reason to get their hopes up.

"Will Emily be back in time for Feather Festival?" Mary asked Janice.

Janice shook her head. "No, she has to miss it this year. She's bummed." To Amanda, Janice added, "Emily is my daughter-in-law, Lyla and Max's mom. She's an engineer on the North Slope, working two weeks on and two weeks off. I take care of the kids while she's working."

Before Amanda could comment, Vince came over, dragging a cart holding two large boxes. "Team Playhouse. You're over there." He pointed to a spot where Bruce was standing about twenty feet from where Nathan was helping the largest group unpack and sort the parts of the main climbing tower. He dragged the cart toward Bruce, and the three women followed.

"Hello, ladies. These are the anchors for the playhouse already installed." Bruce pointed to some pipes embedded in concrete sticking up from the ground. "Basic tools are in this bucket, and the assembly directions are in the box. Are you comfortable with tools?"

"I've done my share of furniture assembly," Amanda assured him.

Janice looked amused. "I think we're good."

"All right, then. I'll leave you to it. Call if you need a hand."

"We will." Mary smiled sweetly. As soon as he'd moved on to the third group, she muttered,

"I was building cabins while he was still playing with alphabet blocks."

"He couldn't know that," Janice pointed out as she produced a well-worn and fully stocked tool belt from her tote. She strapped it around her waist and took out a razor knife. "Let's open the boxes and see what we have here."

Amanda found herself acting as assistant to the two women as they made short work of bolting the floor of the miniature house to the anchors and then assembling the white walls and bright red roof. The house stood about five feet high at the ridgeline and was just big enough for three or four small children. Blue trim outlined the arched doorway, which they decided to orient toward the rest of the playground. The small window on the back faced the duck pond. Openings on each side held built-in toys small children could manipulate. The left side was filled with columns of spinning blocks with letters and numbers embossed on the sides. Horizontal dowels filled the opening on the right, with ten large beads on each row that children could move back and forth. Preschoolers were going to love this.

Amanda frequently looked up to check on Paisley, but the kids were doing fine. They'd moved from the duck pond to the open grassy area between the new playground and the cabin museum and joined several other kids in a game of tag. Paisley's cheeks were flushed, and she giggled as she dodged away from the girl chasing her. She needed more of this. Paisley was such a quiet, self-contained child, it was easy to forget she was a child, not a little adult. She needed playmates who would encourage her to run and laugh and make new friends.

When Amanda turned back, Mary was walking around the new playhouse, nodding to herself. "If it's all right with you," she told Amanda, "I have some ideas to customize the playhouse."

"What did you have in mind?" Amanda asked.

"I'll show you." Mary went to her car and returned with a caddy filled with paints and brushes. She removed a folder and handed it to Amanda.

Amanda opened it to find a sketch of the playhouse, with a colorful border of flowers painted around the bottom edges. "This is gorgeous. It's like an enchanted cottage."

"Love it." Janice was looking over her shoulder. "A Mary Youngblood original right in our own playground."

Mary smiled. "Vince sent me a picture of the playhouse in advance. He didn't say anything, but I suspect he was hoping I would see those plain white walls and feel compelled to do something about them. And, of course, his diabolical plan worked perfectly."

"How long for the paint to dry?" Janice asked.

"I'll be using acrylics, so only an hour to touch. In about a week, I'll come back and give it a clear coat, just to make sure it lasts. I'll probably need to touch it up every year or so, but I'm willing to do that."

"Then let's get started," Janice said. "How can we help?"

But Mary shooed them away, saying she could concentrate better by herself. Bruce checked the bolts holding the central tower, slide, stairs, and climbing bars in place. Amanda and Janice stood to one side, waiting for him to finish so that he could assign them to other duties, but before he was done, Peggy drove up in the Swan Lodge van, double-parking in the lot near them.

"Let's go help Peggy unload," Janice suggested.

Peggy had the rear doors of the van open to reveal stacks of folding tables and chairs. "Let's set up under those trees." Peggy pointed. Like magic, two teenage boys showed up and hoisted one of the tables, carried it to the spot, and set it up. Amanda and Janice followed with chairs. In a matter of minutes, they had the van unloaded and Peggy was spreading tablecloths over the tables and clamping them at the corners. Then came the food—platters of sandwiches and wraps, bowls of salads, a lavish charcuterie board, pickles, chips, bowls of fruit, cookies and brownies—enough to cover one entire table. Janice brought a stack of plates and set it at the end of the table, and Peggy set baskets of silverware and napkins on the other end. Pitchers of water and plastic cups went on each dining table.

At Peggy's signal, Vince put two fingers in his mouth and whistled, bringing conversation and work to a halt. "It looks like Peggy has provided us a feast. Nice work this morning, everyone. Let's take a lunch break, and we'll start up again in forty-five minutes."

"I'll get the kids," Janice told Amanda, and so Amanda walked over to the playhouse, where Mary continued to paint, leaning in close to add some tiny detail to the wall.

"Aren't you coming to lunch?" she asked the artist, as she took in the amazing scene on the sidewall. Mary had painted the wall to look like logs, with tall stalks of fireweed and Jacob's ladder growing against them. Daisies, lupines, and sweet-faced yellow-and-purple pansies edged the border. Somehow, despite being painted on a flat wall, it gave the illusion of a bed at least three feet deep. "This is gorgeous!"

"Thanks. I'll finish this side while the lunch crowd dies down. Let the kids eat first. They'll be hungry after all that play." Mary stepped back and surveyed what she'd just painted.

Amanda moved to stand beside Mary and gasped at the image before her. There, among some reeds, were two swans. One stood protectively, neck extended in a graceful arc. The other sat, her bill tucking a stray stick into the edge of a nest. "Oh, wow!"

"In memory of Eleanor and Harry," Mary explained as she added a tiny highlight in the standing swan's eye.

"It's perfect," Amanda told her. "It reminds me of the Swan Lodge logo, only instead of a stylized design, these swans look like they could step out of the painting any second."

"I designed that logo." Mary added some shading to the swan's breast. "That was way back, only a few years after they'd started the lodge. A gallery offered to do a show of my art, but I needed money for framing. Eleanor and Harry suddenly decided the clip-art logo they'd been using was all wrong, that they needed a custom design, and that I was the only one who could do it for them. That wasn't the first or the last time they were there for me when I needed them."

"Well, it's a lovely logo, and this painting is absolutely gorgeous. Eleanor would be thrilled."

"Mommy!" Paisley came running over. "Lyla's grandma says it's time for lunch. Can we eat now? Oh, wow. Swans. They're soooo pretty, just like the ones at the marsh." She turned back to Amanda and took her hand. "Can I sit by Lyla at the table? She's my new best friend."

"Sure." Amanda threw Mary an apologetic smile and allowed Paisley to tug her toward the buffet table, where her friends were already filling plates. Paisley glanced at Lyla's plate, which contained a turkey wrap, a fruit kabob, and a cookie, and chose the same foods for herself. Amanda took two mini bagels with smoked salmon spread, some bean salad, and a few strawberries. Peggy was a magician. That was Amanda's only explanation as to how she had managed to put together such a spread in one morning.

Amanda followed Paisley and her friend to a table where Janice and Lyla were already sitting with some of the other workers, including Nathan. The girls chose chairs beside each other at the end of the table, leaving the one next to Nathan free for Amanda. As soon as she sat down, Nathan leaned closer and asked, "How did it go for you this morning?"

"Very well," Amanda told him. "The playhouse is even cuter than it looked in the catalog, and Mary Youngblood is making it into something really special. How about your crew?"

"Now that we've got the central tower in place, it shouldn't take long to add the climbing net and swings. Vince says the truck is bringing the rubber mulch at two, which should take about an hour to spread with all of us helping. Then we'll be done."

Sitting across the table from Nathan, a man who looked to be in his late twenties took a bite of one of the bagels and groaned in appreciation. "Peggy's salmon dip is the best. What would I have to do to get her recipe, do you think?"

Nathan held up his hands. "You'll have to ask her. I don't get between Peggy and her recipes."

"Wise man. I'm Mike Donovan, by the way. I run Raven's Nest Pizza. I was wondering what the plans are for the lodge. Will it be opening back up this summer at all?"

Nathan exchanged a quick glance with Amanda before answering. "Things are still kind of up in the air. Right now, we're in the middle of painting and repairs."

"But you are going to keep the lodge?" Mike pressed, and Amanda realized a substantial portion of his business probably came from guests from the lodge.

"That hasn't been decided yet," Nathan reiterated. "Sorry."

"Understood. Just, you know, I'm putting in an order today and wondered if I should order extra pepperoni. But with the Feather Festival coming up, we'll get a lot of traffic anyway. You know, if you were to open up just for the festival, you could probably fill the rooms."

"We'll keep that in mind," Nathan said.

Amanda changed the subject. "How long have you been in Swan Falls? When I last visited eight years ago, I don't remember seeing a pizzeria."

"No, we opened three years ago. Things were

slow at first, but we're starting to build enough of a reputation that people will come from Wasilla."

"I can see why. We picked up a pepperoni pizza from your place the other day and it was wonderful."

"Try the Swan Falls Special sometime," Janice suggested. "But be warned, once you taste it, you'll be back. Max can't get enough. I swear if I didn't slow him down, he'd eat a whole one by himself."

They continued to chat, while the children whispered and giggled. Amanda noticed Max going back for seconds. She couldn't imagine he would be hungry for pizza after this lunch, but then he was twelve and probably about to start a growth spurt. They had almost finished eating when Paisley asked, "Mommy, can Lyla come over and play at the lodge tomorrow? I want to show her the beavers and the reading tent."

Two sets of pleading eyes looked up at her. Amanda glanced at Janice, who gave a slight nod, before telling Paisley, "Sure."

"Can I, Grandma?" Lyla asked.

"I don't see why not," Janice said. "You have a dentist appointment in Wasilla in the morning, but I could take you to the lodge right after lunch, if that works."

"Works for me," Amanda told her.

The two girls beamed, and Paisley gave a happy sigh. "I love Swan Falls."

CHAPTER FOURTEEN

THE NEXT DAY, Nathan and Amanda worked together to get the hallways painted, with a break to accompany Paisley and Lyla to the beaver pond. Nathan smiled at the look of pride on Paisley's face when she showed Lyla the beavers, as though she was sharing something truly special. The two girls chattered away the whole time, as if they had known one another for years, not just a day. When they got back to the lodge, Peggy invited the girls into the kitchen, while Nathan and Amanda tackled the final hallway.

"How's that list coming along?" Amanda asked as she brushed paint into the narrow space between the door molding and the corner. She had already painted around all the doorframes and baseboards, and Nathan had followed up with the easy job of rolling the paint onto the walls in between. Now he just needed to do the ceiling.

"Once we're finished here, the lodge is done, and we can shift focus to the cabins." He loaded his roller, lifted it overhead, and painted the first swipe a little too enthusiastically, splattering paint onto his hair and face.

Amanda laughed and handed him a wet cloth. "Getting a little carried away?"

"Apparently." Nathan tried to take the paint off his face. "Did I get it?"

"Here." Amanda took the cloth. Nathan held still while she gently wiped along his cheek, her lovely denim-blue eyes focused on his face. A few locks of hair had escaped her ponytail and fell in fiery waves onto her forehead. If he leaned forward, just a little bit, he would be within kissing distance.

As though she'd read his thoughts, she stepped back. "There. You'll need to wash your hair later, though."

Nathan nodded and looked around. "Did I get any on the wood trim?"

"Just this one spot," she said, wiping a splatter from a nearby doorframe. "Better wipe up that splatter on the drop cloth too, so you don't get paint on your shoes."

Nathan bent to do the cleanup. After a moment, Amanda asked, "How do you feel about Mike's suggestion of opening up just for the Feather Festival next week?"

"I've been thinking about that," Nathan admitted. In fact, he'd had a tough time getting to sleep the night before, turning it over in his mind. He'd decided not to bring it up, not wanting Amanda to feel like he was pushing, but now that she'd mentioned it, "It would be an opportunity to bring in a little extra cash."

"Is it too late to pull everything together, though?"

"We could do it if we put our minds to it. Right now, the online reservation system doesn't say we're shut down, it just shows no available rooms for any dates. We don't have the staff to service the entire lodge, but if Ava Burke is willing to take on some extra hours, and we're willing to do some of the housekeeping ourselves, we could accept reservations for one wing as kind of a trial run."

"What about food? Would we still include breakfast? Would that be too much for Peggy to handle alone?"

"We'd have to talk with Peggy, but judging by the smorgasbord she put out yesterday, I don't think it would be much of a stretch for her, especially if I'm willing to work as dishwasher, which I am."

"It would be an opportunity for you to try things out," Amanda suggested. "To see if the reality of running a lodge matches your fantasy."

"Yeah, although after all those years of staying here, I feel like I have a pretty good grasp of what's involved. It is a lot of work, but it's also a lot of fun."

"What if nobody comes?" Amanda asked.

Nathan shrugged. "Then we're no worse off

than if we didn't open the rooms. I say let's try it, assuming Peggy, Malcolm, and Ava are on board."

"I'm in," Amanda told him. "After dinner, let's sit down and make a plan."

Paisley came galloping around the corner, calling, "Mommy? Nathan?" Lyla was right behind her.

"Down here," Amanda called. "Don't touch the walls. The paint is still wet. Did you help Peggy in the kitchen?"

"We made you a surprise," Paisley said.

"What is it?" Nathan asked.

Lyla grinned and hopped with excitement. "Come to the kitchen and see."

"Okay." Amanda put her brush into a plastic bag, while Nathan set his roller aside. They followed the girls back to the kitchen.

"Ta-da." Lyla gestured to the table, where a plate was piled high with marshmallow treats.

"Ooh, I haven't had one of these in ages," Amanda told the girls. "Let me pour us some milk to go with them. Nathan, Peggy, you want milk?"

"Sure. Thanks," Nathan replied.

"I've got coffee," Peggy said, pouring herself a cup.

When Amanda went to get glasses, she picked up a book from the countertop. "Is this yours?" she asked Peggy.

"Yes, it's for our book club. It takes place in England during World War II. Really good."

"I agree. I love the heroine." Before Amanda could say more, the kitchen door swung open.

"Knock, knock," Janice called as she peered in. "I'm back for Lyla."

"Can we stay just a little longer?" Lyla begged. "We made marshmallow treats, and we were just about to eat them."

Janice checked her watch. "Just for a little while. I have to pick up your brother from soccer practice in thirty minutes." She noticed the book in Amanda's hand. "Have you read it?"

Amanda nodded. "About a year ago. Loved it."

"Great! You should come with Peggy to our book club," Janice said, accepting a cup of coffee from Peggy. "It's at my house tonight."

Lyla jumped up from her chair. "Can Paisley come, too? We'll stay in my room and be real quiet, I promise."

"Fine with me," Janice said, "if it's okay with Paisley's mom."

"I, uh, was planning to help Nathan with something—" Amanda looked toward him.

But Nathan realized this would be an excellent opportunity to advance Peggy's plan of getting Amanda involved with the people of Swan Falls. "You should go to the book club. Have some fun. I can handle that other thing."

"Come with me tonight," Peggy urged. "You already know Janice, Helen, and Bethany. It'll be fun."

"Can we, Mommy?" Paisley wheedled.

Amanda glanced down at the book in her hand and then at all the people at the table. "Okay. We'll come. Thanks."

RAINDROPS DOTTED THE windshield as Peggy pulled up in front of a sprawling cedar-sided house, next to several other cars. Ignoring the rain, Lyla jumped up from the porch steps and ran to them, squealing. Paisley squealed, too, and dashed to meet her friend. They hugged as though they'd been separated for years, rather than a couple of hours.

"We've got mac and cheese, and corn dogs, and baby carrots and dip, and Grandma says we can watch a movie in the den instead of staying in my room." Lyla's voice sounded as though someone had sped up a recording. "Let's go!"

"Bye, Mommy and Peggy." Paisley turned and the two girls ran inside the house.

Peggy laughed as she handed Amanda a tray of crackers and salmon dip to carry in. "Oh, the enthusiasm of the young." But as soon as she and Amanda walked in the door, everyone called a greeting every bit as warm if not quite as frenetic. Dining chairs had been set between upholstered chairs and couches in the living room. Through an archway, Amanda could see a dining table loaded with food. Janice took the salmon dip from Amanda and carried it to the table.

Peggy introduced Amanda around. "You know

Bethany and Janice, and Helen from the bookstore will be coming. This is Amy, whose family runs the diner, and Melissa, who owns the bed-and-breakfast on East Main."

Both women greeted her, with Melissa following up to say, "So you're the new owner of Swan Lodge."

"Well, half owner," Amanda said. "I was shocked when I found out."

"You didn't know Eleanor was leaving you the lodge?" Amy asked. "Wow. That's life-changing."

"You could say that."

"What can I get you to drink, Amanda?" Janice interrupted to ask, and the other two women went to find chairs. "We have white wine, sparkling cider, and sodas."

"A glass of wine sounds nice, thanks." Peggy had moved on to talk with Bethany, and so wineglass in hand, Amanda looked around for a chair. Melissa encouraged her to take the empty one next to hers. Amanda sat down. "Yours is the yellow house with all the beautiful hanging baskets on the porch?" she asked Melissa.

"That's right. Every year I try out a new combination. This year it's purple lobelia, chartreuse creeping Jenny, and white daisies."

"So pretty. I'll have to take a closer look. Have you been busy this summer?" Amanda asked. At least here was one business that had probably benefited from the lodge's temporary closure.

"We're busy every summer," Melissa told her. "After I inherited the house, I was toying with the idea of starting a B&B, but I wasn't sure it would make money. But then Eleanor told me she'd decided to stop renting out the cabins at the lodge and urged me to take the overflow. The first couple of years, it was really her referrals that kept me full, until we could find our own clientele."

"Will it hurt your business if the cabins reopen?" Amanda asked, concerned.

"I don't think so, really. The Swan's Nest B&B has developed a reputation as a getaway for couples or women's gatherings. The cabins cater more to families with children. Different niches."

The front door opened, and two more women came in, Helen and a younger woman with short dark hair who Amanda hadn't seen before. Janice got them drinks and then introduced the woman. "Kailee, this is Amanda, one of the new owners of Swan Lodge. Kailee manages Wildwood Wonders, the art co-op."

"Oh, I have money for you, then." Kailee plopped into the chair on the other side of Amanda.

"You do?"

"Don't get too excited," Kailee said, laughing. "It's just a hundred bucks or so. Eleanor licensed the Swan Lodge logo to me, and I sell souvenir T-shirts, hats, sweatshirts, that sort of thing, and the lodge gets a cut of each sale. I told Eleanor she ought to run a gift shop in the lodge, but she said it was too much work, but if I wanted to do it, go ahead. So I did."

It sounded like Eleanor had done more to encourage local business than Amanda ever realized. "That's great. I'll have to stop by and see your store."

"Super. I can give you the money then. We've got some really wonderful things in right now. The local artists bring their best stuff in just before the Feather Festival. Today we got some amazing beaded earrings."

"Did you get in any more of those thyme-and-citrus-scented beeswax candles?" Melissa asked Kailee.

"We did. Want me to set some aside for you?"

"Please. Six should do. I'll be in tomorrow."

"Will do. I'll just send myself a note." Kailee pulled out her phone, but before she could type in anything, it chimed. Almost simultaneously, phones all around the room began alerting or buzzing, all except Amanda's. "Uh-oh," Kailee said as she read the text. "Are you all seeing this?" Gasps and groans from around the room were her answer.

"What?" Helen said. "I left my phone in my car."

"It's from the mayor," Janice announced. "Apparently there was a leak in the roof of the barn where they keep the swan float, and nobody noticed until today."

"Oh, no," Peggy said. "After that extra-heavy snow load this winter, they should have known to check."

"Well, they didn't. He says the trailer bed is fine, but all the papier-mâché is mush and the bench is damaged."

"What are we going to do?" Melissa asked as she dug her phone from her bag. "The Feather Festival King and Queen always ride on that float. It's tradition."

"He's looking for volunteers to completely rebuild it before the parade."

"I'm in," Kailee announced as she typed a reply. "I have a shift at the store tomorrow afternoon, but I'll put in some time in the morning."

"Same here," Bethany said, typing.

Helen leaned toward Bethany. "Tell him I'll come if I can get someone to cover the store."

"I'm not much of an artist," Amanda said, "but—"

"It's all hands on deck at this point," Janice told her. "I'm bringing the kids to help tomorrow morning."

"In that case, Paisley and I will come, too," Amanda said.

"I'll tell the mayor and give him your cell number, so you'll get the group texts about when and where." Janice sent the text and waited until everyone had settled a bit before tapping the side of a glass with a spoon. "Well, we can't do anything more about the float until tomorrow, so let's move on to our book club meeting. Welcome to our newest member, Amanda Flores. We're glad you're here." There was a smattering of applause.

"Thank you. I appreciate the invitation, and I loved the book. I look forward to discussing it with you." Now was not the time to explain that she and Paisley would be going home right after the Feather Festival, and quite possibly never coming to Swan Falls again. A depressing thought, but she kept the smile on her face.

Janice smiled back at her before lifting a wine bottle and one of sparkling cider. "Now, does anyone need a refill before we get started?"

AFTER HEARING ABOUT the float emergency from Peggy and Amanda when they got home from the book club, the entire contingent from Swan Lodge had decided to volunteer. The next morning, Nathan drove the Swan Lodge van a couple of miles east of town to a farmhouse with a large metal barn behind it. Cars and trucks were already parked all along the driveway. Nathan pulled into a spot near the main road. "Looks like this is as close as we're going to get."

"The walk won't hurt us," Yolanda said as they all climbed out of the van. Malcolm reached into the back for a toolbox, and they all made their way down the driveway to the barn, where the doors stood wide open. The sound of hammering echoed off the walls.

"Paisley!" Lyla called. "Over here." Lyla, her brother, and Janice were sitting at a folding table holding scissors with piles of what looked like white paper in front of them. Paisley ran over to join them. Peggy and Yolanda followed.

In the center of the barn, someone was scrubbing the decking of a flatbed trailer. Another group was doing something with a power saw and lumber. A pickup truck backed up to the doors and a woman with short dark hair climbed out and opened the tailgate. "Amanda, hi," she called. "Can you guys give me a hand with this chicken wire?"

Nathan went with Amanda to help her unload several rolls of wire and carry them to one side of the barn. Once they'd finished, Amanda said, "Kailee, this is Nathan Swan. Kailee runs the art co-op in town and makes the souvenirs with the Swan Lodge logo I told you about."

"I'm glad to meet you, Nathan," Kailee answered. "I knew Amanda was coming, so I brought that check for you. Just a sec." She took an envelope from the passenger seat and passed it to Nathan, who was nearer. "I hope we can continue this arrangement. Swan Lodge shirts are one of our biggest sellers."

Nathan looked toward Amanda, who nodded. "We're good with that, at least for now."

"For now?" Kailee pressed.

"If someone else buys the lodge, they may have other ideas," Nathan explained.

Kailee frowned. "I didn't realize you were putting the place up for sale. People were saying— well, obviously they were wrong."

"Nothing has been decided yet," Amanda hurried to say. "Nathan and I are exploring our options."

"I see," Kailee said, although her puzzled expression belied her words. "Well, anyway, we have a float to build, and somehow I got put in charge." Kailee shut the tailgate. "I'll park and be right back to get everyone organized."

While they were waiting, Amanda said softly, "Thanks for not throwing me under the bus about selling the lodge."

Nathan shrugged. "What you said is true. We are exploring our options. I haven't heard anything from the bank yet, but no news is good news, right?" He doubted that was true, but it sounded positive. "Maybe I will be able to buy you out and we can both get what we want."

"I hope so." Amanda sighed. "I didn't realize just how intertwined the lodge and the town are. Our being closed for a month has been hard on the local businesses. I gather they're hoping to make up some of that during the Feather Festival. I felt bad dragging all of you here to work on this float when we have so much to do at the lodge, but it seems like we owe it to the town to help make the festival a success."

"I agree one hundred percent," Nathan replied. The lodge and the town were intertwined—one couldn't succeed without the other. Besides, Peggy's plan to get Amanda involved with the townspeople seemed to be working. That didn't resolve her dilemma over greenhouses, but maybe they could come to some agreement.

Kailee returned, carrying an armful of pool noodles and a bucket of tools. "Okay, everybody, gather up," she called. While the volunteers assembled, she dumped her load and went to stand beside a large paper pad set on an easel. She opened the cover, to reveal a sketch of a giant swan float. "We can't replicate the old papier-mâché float we had before, because we don't have enough time to let it dry and paint it," she explained. "So we're going with the classic chicken-wire-and-tissue float design, but we've decided to reuse plastic grocery bags instead of tissue, one because they would just go into the landfill otherwise, and two in case it rains during the parade. Always a danger, right?"

Nathan laughed along with the rest of the crowd, because he couldn't remember a Feather Festival where it didn't rain at least once.

"So basically, we're building a swan boat on a trailer. The carpenters—" Kailee pointed toward the group that had been sawing and hammering earlier "—are building a support frame to go along the sides and back of the float, which we'll cover with chicken wire to create the body and wings. We'll make the swan's neck and head from pool noodles wrapped in chicken wire. We can reuse the bench in the middle where the king and queen sit, but it needs to be sanded and repainted. Bethany, your group is handling that, right?"

"We're on it." Bethany nodded at Malcolm, Helen, and a man Nathan didn't know. They separated from the crowd and went over to a high-backed bench in the corner.

"Janice, Peggy, and their crew—" Kailee smiled at the kids "—can work on cutting the bags into squares. Meanwhile, I need someone to staple chicken wire all around the perimeter of the trailer and attach fringe to the bottom. Nathan and Amanda, can you handle that?"

"Sure," Nathan agreed, glad she hadn't put him in charge of anything artistic. Everyone went to work. Once he and Amanda finished attaching the wire skirt and fringe, Kailee brought over a stencil and paint, which they used to mark letters spelling out "Swan Falls" on both sides of the skirt. Then Nathan helped a group lift the heavy wooden frame they'd created onto the trailer and bolt it in place.

While Kailee supervised the group on how to mold the swan's body from wire, Nathan, Amanda, Janice, Yolanda, and the kids all went to work stuffing squares of paper into the holes of the chicken wire on the skirt, creating a ruffled white texture that really did look a lot like feathers. At Kailee's direction, they used dark blue squares to fill in the letters. It was tedious work, but with so many hands it went fast, and by noon the skirt was three-fourths of the way covered, and one wing of the swan was complete.

"I'm calling lunch," Kailee announced. "I have to lock up before I go to work, but Lars will be here at one to open up for the next shift. Great job, everybody. Thanks!"

As they all collected their gear and filed out of the barn, Helen asked Paisley, "How did you like the ending of *Treasure Island*?"

Paisley lowered her chin. "I haven't finished it yet," she admitted. "I've been reading the two books we got at your store instead. But I'm going to finish."

"It's harder to read old books like that, isn't it?" Yolanda responded with sympathy. "Did you ever figure out what the map was about?"

"What map?" Nathan asked.

"There's a hand-drawn map in the back of Paisley's copy of *Treasure Island*," Yolanda explained.

"Someone probably drew a map of the island based on the description to keep it all straight," Helen speculated. "Paperback or hardback?"

"Hardback," Amanda confirmed.

Helen gave a rueful smile. "I hope it wasn't a

collector's edition. Was it your own book or from the Swan Lodge library?"

"From the library," Paisley said. "But the map was already there. I know not to draw in library books."

"I never doubted you," Helen assured her. "I could tell from our first meeting that you're someone who takes care of books. Happy reading." She gave a little wave and turned toward her car.

But Nathan wasn't ready to let go of the topic. He touched Amanda's shoulder and motioned for her to drop back with him while the others went on ahead to the van. "Helen mentioned some of her more valuable books disappearing from her store the same summer as the sculpture was stolen," he murmured.

"Uh-huh."

"And there's a map in the back of Paisley's book, which happens to be a nice hardback copy. And Derrick, our top suspect, spent a lot of time in Helen's store."

Amanda stopped. "Do you think there's a connection between the map in Paisley's book and the ransom letter?"

It sounded farfetched when she said it aloud. "Probably not."

"But it could be," Amanda said thoughtfully. "Let's get back to the lodge and take a look at that map."

CHAPTER FIFTEEN

ONCE THEY RETURNED to the lodge, they all gathered in the kitchen. Amanda sent Paisley up after the book while Nathan mentioned their idea to Peggy, Yolanda, and Malcolm.

"Wouldn't it be wild if the key to this whole debacle was there in the library all these years?" Peggy mused as she filled bowls with chicken soup she'd left simmering in a slow cooker that morning.

Nathan got up to help her serve. "It's a long shot," he warned, as he carried two bowls to the table and set them in front of Yolanda and Malcolm. "The ransom letter implied that they would send directions once they got the ransom."

"But the directions could have been to look in the book." Amanda passed the breadbasket to Yolanda.

Nathan thought back. "You know, Helen said Derrick liked to discuss classic literature, and I remember him teasing Krista about reading romance novels. I could picture him hiding the clue in a classic book as sort of a joke, because he figured nobody else would be 'cultured' enough to read it."

"That does sound like him," Yolanda agreed.

Paisley came rushing into the kitchen, carrying the book. "I've got it." She climbed into a chair on her knees and set it on the table, back cover open. "See?"

Nathan and Peggy brought the other bowls of soup to the table and sat down to inspect the book. The drawing seemed to be of several rectangles, a curved sweep with a shaded area, and a few other markings.

"Nothing is labeled on this map," Peggy complained.

"The X is where the treasure was in the story," Paisley said, pointing to the mark about halfway between two of the rectangles. A line with three dots arranged in a triangle at the end formed an arrow that pointed directly at the X.

"This could be the lake." Amanda pointed toward the shaded area. "And this wavy line looks like a river. The rectangles could be the cabins. But our creek doesn't flow between two cabins like this. We pass the last cabin before we follow the creek to the beaver dam."

"Hmm. Maybe this map is of some other lake around here. There are a couple of ponds and lakes between here and Swan Falls," Nathan said. "After lunch, I'll pull up satellite views on the computer and see if we can find a match."

They all stared at the map while they ate a few spoonfuls of soup. Malcolm suddenly set down his spoon. "Was that beaver dam there twenty years ago?"

Nathan exchanged glances with Peggy. "Not that I know of," he said.

"Beavers can completely change the path of a river," Malcolm pointed out.

Nathan blinked. "You're right! There's a spot in the road to the last cabin that goes over a drainage culvert. I'll bet that's where the creek fed into the lake before the beavers dammed it up and sent it off to the northeast instead."

"Which would put the X about halfway between cabins five and six," Amanda said.

Paisley jumped up. "Let's go look!"

"Eat your lunch first," Amanda told her. "If the sculpture has been there twenty-two years, it can wait another ten minutes, and we'll need our energy to find it."

Nathan was on Paisley's side on this one, but he managed to finish his soup and even helped Peggy clear the dishes before announcing, "Okay. Let's grab some tools and go treasure hunting!"

Twenty minutes later, after a stop by Malcolm's toolshed, they were standing on the road connecting the cabins, eyeing the area between cabins five and six, where a thick stand of old birches grew. There had been a brief shower that morning, leaving the ground damp, but now patches of blue sky appeared between the clouds.

"Let's make a line and start walking as straight ahead as possible, to make sure we cover all the ground," Nathan said. "Maybe there's some sort of marker or something we can spot. But be careful. Wet leaves are slippery." Amanda reached for his hand and squeezed it. He squeezed back. They might be close!

Together, they all stepped forward off the road, but almost immediately they had to drop hands and separate to detour around rocks, trees, and bushes. Ferns and clusters of bunchberries grew over parts of the forest floor, with a thick layer of composted leaves blanketing the space in between. They made several passes covering the area between the two cabins, but if there was a marker indicating where to dig, it had long since disappeared. Dozens of rocks, ranging in size from ping-pong balls up to yoga balls were scattered through the woods. Could one of them mark the spot to dig? None seemed to have been stacked into cairns, and if any had been marked with paint, the mark had weathered away. It was frustrating to think they might be within feet of their goal and not even know it.

"Maybe we should just eye it and start digging," Nathan said. "On the map, it looks like it's right in the middle between the cabins."

"Let's find the center," Malcolm suggested.

They threaded measuring tapes through the branches of several small trees and bushes to discover that exactly seventeen and a half feet from each cabin, there was a relatively clear spot below a tree with a double trunk. Amanda grabbed a rake and pulled back the forest duff to expose the soil, and Nathan started digging. Malcolm joined him, and even Paisley grabbed a trowel and tried to dig. Unfortunately, they mostly hit tree roots, but when they did, they just moved to the side and kept digging. Soon they had a dozen or so holes each a foot or so deep, but they hadn't come across anything more interesting than buried rocks.

"How deep would it be buried?" Amanda asked.

"Knowing Derrick, no deeper than it needed to be," was Peggy's answer. She was looking at the map. "I think we're giving him too much credit, assuming this map is to scale. Just because it shows to be in the middle, doesn't mean it's exactly here. What we need is a metal detector."

"Great idea," Nathan said. "I don't suppose you know anyone in Swan Lake who has one?"

"I could make some calls," Peggy offered.

"Or I could run into Wasilla and buy one," Yolanda suggested.

"Hello," came a voice from overhead.

All eyes looked up. "Hi, Maggie," Paisley called. "Do you know where the treasure is?"

"Say please," was Maggie's answer.

Amanda laughed. "Please." She took a step toward the tree where Maggie perched, but because she was looking up, she tripped and only stayed upright when Nathan grabbed her arm. Their eyes met, and there was a long beat before Amanda gave an awkward laugh. "Thanks. Guess I'd better look where I'm going." She let go of his hand and kicked some of the decaying leaves out of the way. "Oh, no wonder. I stepped on the rotten log buried here and it gave way under my foot." She dusted leaves off her jeans and pushed away some of the debris that had settled over to expose more of the log. Suddenly, she bent down and cleared away the leaves at the end of the log, revealing three rocks, each about the size of a loaf of bread. "Nathan, look!"

It took him a few seconds to realize the rocks were in the form of a triangle at the end of the log. "It forms an arrow," he whispered.

Paisley squealed. "It must be pointing to the treasure."

They all gathered in the area there. Malcolm grabbed a rake to clear the fallen leaves from the soil, but the tines of the leaf rake caught on something. "Hold on," Amanda said, kneeling on the forest floor. "There's something square poking out here." She brushed away the dirt to expose a rounded corner. "It's plastic. Could it be what we're looking for?"

"Let's find out." Nathan dropped to his knees and began scraping away dirt with a trowel. Paisley quickly joined him. Before long, they'd uncovered a rectangle of pitted plastic about two feet across and four feet long. "It looks like a big ice chest."

"Harry used to have one like that," Peggy said. "He never used it because it was too big and heavy to carry once it was loaded. He liked to use two smaller chests instead."

It didn't take much longer to dig down far enough that they were able to lift the plastic ice chest from its hole in the earth. It was pitted and stained but had held up surprisingly well considering how long it must have been buried there. A padlock held the hasp closed.

"I'll go get a hacksaw to cut the lock," Malcolm offered, but Nathan shook his head. "No, look, the plastic hinges have cracked. We can open it from the back."

"Open it already!" Peggy demanded.

Slowly, Nathan pulled the lid open, and there, lying at the bottom of the ice chest, was the sculpture that had gone missing so many years before, looking no worse for having been hiding underground for two decades.

"We did it!" Paisley cried. "We followed the map and found the treasure. Can I take it out?"

"I'll help you lift it," Nathan told her. Together they took the sculpture from the chest and set it on a nearby boulder with a flat surface. Overhead, a cloud drifted away, and a shaft of sunlight pierced the leafy canopy to spotlight the swans rising gracefully from the reeds.

"I never thought I'd see it again," Peggy admitted.

"Sure is a pretty thing," Malcolm said, almost reverently. "Eleanor told me all about it, but the picture in my mind was never as grand as this. Eleanor would be tickled pink."

Peggy grinned. "You know who else is going to be tickled pink? The mayor, once he finds out he's got a fancy new tourist draw for the museum."

"No use carrying that heavy thing all the way back to the lodge," Malcolm said. "I'll go get my truck."

"I'll come with you," Peggy said, "and grab a quilt to wrap it in. We don't want to take any chances of putting a dent in it after all this."

Yolanda accompanied them back to the lodge, leaving Nathan with Amanda and Paisley. Paisley ran her fingers over the bronze feathers of a swan's wing. Amanda slid an arm around Nathan's waist. "You did it," she said softly. "You brought the swan sculpture back to where it belongs."

"We did it." He put an arm around her shoulders and squeezed. "It never would have happened without you and Paisley."

She smiled. "We do make a pretty good team."

"I couldn't agree more."

THE NEXT MORNING, Peggy begged off float building, saying she needed to prepare a dozen pie shells for the pie auction during the Feather Festival. Yolanda decided to stay and help, and Malcolm had already gone to assist the mayor with some emergency project, according to Peggy. Amanda suspected these last-minute emergencies might be the rule rather than the exception at Feather Festival time. That left Amanda, Nathan, and Paisley to help Kailee with the float.

When they arrived, Kailee was unlocking the door, but she turned when she saw them. "There are the heroes of the day."

"Why heroes?" Nathan asked.

"You recovered the swan sculpture and now you're donating it to the town. I heard all about it from Lars. That's so exciting."

"Eleanor is the one who donated it," Amanda insisted. "It was in her will that if it was ever recovered, it should go to the museum."

"Well, in that case," said Kailee as she slid the door open, "you're even more heroic because you worked so hard to solve a mystery that didn't even benefit you."

But it did benefit them, Amanda realized. No matter how much anyone tried to reassure him, Nathan had been carrying the guilt of losing the sculpture all these years. The joy and relief on his face when he'd opened that old ice chest and found the sculpture inside—Amanda would never forget it. "We're thrilled," she told Kailee.

"I can only imagine. Where is the sculpture now?"

"I dropped it off at the mayor's house yesterday," Nathan told her. "He said he'd take care of it until they could get a case for it at the museum."

"I hope they can find a good way to display it before the Feather Festival. Between the Deanna Somers sculpture, and Mary Youngblood's paintings, we're starting to get a respectable collection of art in the museum. I told Lars we need to start treating it like a real museum with set hours, at least in the summer. It could draw a steady stream of visitors." She grinned. "And hopefully, looking at all that lovely art in the museum will put them in the mood to buy something from Wildwood Wonders."

Amanda laughed. "Always on the job."

Kailee flipped a switch to light up the interior of the barn. Amanda was surprised to find how much progress the afternoon shift had made. The freshly painted bench had been moved into place in the middle of the swan's body, and a gracefully curving neck and head had been fashioned out of wood, pool noodles, and chicken wire. Shiny black eyes covered with satin were already attached to the head. Yesterday's team had even made a start on stuffing, with the bill already covered in orange, and white covering the head and the upper half of the neck.

A minivan drove up and Janice and her two

grandkids spilled out. Paisley ran over to meet them and was soon answering all their questions about treasure hunting.

"If you guys want to start stuffing the front of the swan," Kailee told them, "I think we can finish this by noon."

They went to work, although Paisley's efforts were hampered by having to use her hands to act out digging up the ice chest and opening the lid. They had almost finished covering the swan when the mayor came striding into the barn. "This looks great. Thanks for all your efforts."

"Glad we could help," Nathan told him.

"I'm sorry to take half of your crew," Lars said to Kailee. "But I need these three—" he pointed to Nathan, Amanda, and Paisley "—at the museum."

Why? Amanda's stomach tightened, like it might have if she'd suddenly been called to the principal's office when she was a student. Was there a problem? She tried to guess from Lars's expression, but his face was neutral. Was there something wrong with the sculpture? Maybe it wasn't genuine?

Kailee didn't seem to sense anything wrong. "All right," she told Lars. "But if we don't get finished, you'll have to make it up this afternoon."

The mayor gave her a thumbs-up. "Deal."

"Can I stay with Lyla while you go?" Paisley asked Amanda. "I've already seen the museum."

Before Amanda could answer, Lars shook his head. "I need the whole family."

"Lyla will give you a call later," Janice told Kailee. "And we'll make a plan for you two to get together again."

That seemed to placate Paisley, but she dragged her feet as they walked out of the barn.

"Can you follow me over?" Lars asked Nathan.

"Sure." Nathan placed a hand on Amanda's back to guide her toward the car. It was just a casual gesture, but somehow it felt like more, as if it somehow bound them together.

Once they'd closed the car doors, Amanda asked, "What do you think this is about?"

"My guess," Nathan said, "is that he needs us to sign something to officially transfer ownership to the museum."

"Then why not just bring the papers to us to sign? And why would he need Paisley?"

"Maybe they have to be notarized or something. But as for why he needs Paisley..." Nathan shrugged. "That is a good question."

"I wish I didn't have to come," Paisley grumbled. "Me and Lyla only have a few days before I have to go back to Albuquerque. Lyla says their whole school goes on a hike to Swan Falls every year. I wish my school did that."

"We could plan a hike to the falls this week, before all the tourists show up for the Feather Festival," Nathan suggested.

Amanda shot him a grateful smile. "Good idea. And maybe Lyla and Max would like to come along."

Paisley was instantly intrigued. "Can we do it tomorrow?"

"Tomorrow might work," Amanda told her. "Then we'd have Friday clear to get ready for the guests. But it depends on weather and your friends' plans."

Nathan followed the mayor's SUV into the parking lot near the playground. "Let's go find out what's so important. Maybe we can get it done quickly and get back in time to help finish up the float."

Children were enjoying the playground. A preschooler peeked out the window of the playhouse, calling excitedly to his mother, while older kids climbed on the net and slid down the slide. Paisley looked longingly toward them. "Can I go play on the swings?"

"Not right now," Amanda told her. When they reached the museum, Lars held open the door. Nathan touched Amanda's back, indicating that she should go first. She stepped through the doorway to find a well-dressed woman with chin-length brown hair waiting and a man fiddling with a movie camera on a tripod in the corner. In the middle of the room, Malcolm polished the glass of an octagonal case that topped a new wooden pedestal. As Nathan and Paisley stepped into the room behind Amanda, Malcolm moved to the left to reveal the swan sculpture in its new home. A spotlight in the lid of the case highlighted all the delicate details of the swans.

"So this was Malcolm's mystery project," Nathan murmured. Amanda glanced back to see him staring at the sculpture in awe. "It looks great, doesn't it?"

The woman stepped forward. "I'm Leslie Gorshek from Channel 5 news. Call me Leslie. Mayor Johanson has told us the history of this sculpture, but our viewers would love to hear the details of how you were able to recover it after all these years. Are you willing to give us an interview?"

Amanda glanced down at the sneakers, jeans, and faded UNM Lobos sweatshirt she'd worn to work on the float. Thankfully, she'd put on a little makeup that morning, but had she known she might be on television, she would have spent more than the thirty seconds it took to tie her hair into a ponytail. She cast a rueful look at Lars, but he was beaming proudly. At least Paisley looked adorable with her dark curls and purple top, and Nathan was more handsome in a ratty old T-shirt than most men would have been wearing a tux.

She eased back a step. "Nathan is the one you want. He knows the whole story from the very beginning, and—"

But Lars cut her off. "They want the whole Swan family for the interview, to make it a fea-

ture on the news. Getting out the word that people can see the famous sculpture here during the
Feather Festival would be great for the town." He
didn't add, "to help make up for the lost business when the lodge closed," but Amanda heard
it, nonetheless.

"Okay," she told the reporter, "if you'll give me
a minute to comb my hair."

"Of course." The woman gave an understanding
smile. "The closest bathroom I found was in the
post office. We'll just get set up while we wait."

Fortunately, the mirror in the post office bathroom revealed that Amanda's appearance was less
dire than she'd feared. When she took the elastic
from her hair, it settled into soft waves around her
face, and a coat of the cherry lip balm she carried in her small cross-body bag added a touch of
color. When she returned to the museum, Nathan
and Paisley were standing to one side, talking with
Lesley, while the camera operator arranged four
folding stools in an arc in front of the sculpture
with his camera on a tripod pointing at it.

Leslie directed Amanda to sit on the leftmost
stool, and she took the one on the right, so that
Nathan was to her immediate right and Paisley
between Amanda and Nathan. The cameraman
adjusted a couple of supplemental lights, checked
the view through his camera, and gave Leslie a
go sign.

The reporter projected a professional smile toward the camera. "We're here with Nathan Swan and Amanda Flores, the owners of Swan Lodge at Swan Falls, Alaska, and with Amanda's daughter, Paisley, who I understand played a key role in recovering a Deanna Somers sculpture called *Swan Trio* that went missing more than twenty years ago." She winked at Paisley before turning to Nathan. "But we'll get to that in a minute. First of all, Nathan, I understand you have a long history with Swan Lodge."

"Yes, I do." Nathan's voice was a little stiff, but then he cleared his throat and grinned. "I was probably the luckiest kid in Phoenix, because every summer, I got to spend a month at Swan Lodge with my great-uncle Harry and his wife, Eleanor."

"What a treat. So do you know the story of how the sculpture came to Swan Lodge in the first place?"

"Yes, in fact, I was there when the package arrived. The summer before, Deanna Somers had been commissioned to create a swan-themed fountain for a hotel in Las Vegas, but she was having trouble finding inspiration. So she came to stay at Swan Lodge for a few weeks and spent her days at the marsh, watching the swans and talking with Eleanor, who was a total bird enthusiast. She left with all kinds of ideas and made several smaller sculptures in preparation for designing the huge one that's currently in the lobby of the Swanson

Regal Hotel. She sent one of those sculptures to Eleanor and Harry as a thank-you for helping her find her inspiration."

"What a special gift." Leslie was a skillful interviewer, and soon Nathan relaxed as he told her all about the theft of the sculpture. He didn't belabor the point, but it was clear that he blamed himself. "Now, how long ago was this theft?" she asked.

"Twenty-two years ago. I had just graduated from high school," Nathan replied.

"And that was the last anyone knew until recently, when you and Amanda inherited Swan Lodge, correct?"

"Yes. Everyone assumed the sculpture had been sold on the black market, until Amanda found a ransom letter."

"How did you find it?" Leslie asked Amanda.

"Just luck. We moved the reception desk away from the wall to paint, and found an unopened letter that had apparently fallen into the crack twenty-two years ago. It said if Harry and Eleanor would pay a ransom, they would receive directions on how to find the sculpture, which made us think it might be hidden somewhere nearby."

"So you went looking for it?"

"We did some random searching," Amanda answered, "but we didn't find anything."

"Until it turned out your daughter had the key, is that right?"

"Yes." Amanda smiled at Paisley, who wriggled in her chair.

"Can you tell us about that, Paisley?" Leslie asked.

Paisley nodded eagerly. "There's a big library at Swan Lodge and it has all these books, and you can read whatever you want, and there's a reading tent, and it's really cool. Anyway, I found this real old book called *Treasure Island*, and the people talk funny, so it took a long time to read it, but at the back of the book somebody drew a map."

"A treasure map?" Leslie prodded.

"Yeah. At first, we thought it was a map of the treasure in the book, but then Mommy said it might be a map of Swan Lodge, and it was. We went to the place on the map, and found an arrow made from a log and rocks hidden under all the old leaves in the forest, and it pointed right to the place where the sculpture was buried."

"And nobody had come across that place for the past twenty-two years, so if you hadn't decided to read that book, *Swan Trio* might never had been found. You're a hero!"

"Well." Paisley gave a little shrug. "Mommy and Nathan figured out what the map went to. I just found it."

"Still, they never would have figured it out without you." Leslie looked directly at the camera. "So, kids, one more reason to read. You never know what treasures you might find in a book."

"And cut," the cameraman said. "Good job. I want to get some more close-up footage of the sculpture. Can we take it out of the case?"

"Of course." Lars, who had been standing next to Malcolm behind the cameraman, rushed forward, pulling a ring of keys from his pocket as he came. "Oh, and Nathan, there's something you'll want to see."

"What's that?" Nathan asked as they stood and moved the stools out of the way.

"Just a sec. I'll show you." Lars pushed a key into a concealed lock under the rim of the pedestal top and turned it. Then he pushed on one of the panels on the side of the pedestal and it swung open. Inside there seemed to be some sort of mechanical device. "Now, how does this work again?" he asked Malcolm.

"It's just a jack." Malcolm reached inside for a handle, which he fitted into a slot in the mechanism, and began cranking. Slowly, the platform at the top of the pedestal lowered, and the sculpture sank from view in the glass case until it came to rest on the floor of the base.

Malcolm removed the handle and Lars reached inside to lift the sculpture out and set it on the floor. "Oof, that's heavy."

"Where do you want it?" Nathan asked, reaching for the base.

"Over by this wall would be good," the cameraman directed. "We can get natural light from the window, and I'll set up supplemental light on the other side."

"Before you move it," Lars said, "take a close look on the inside wing of each of the swans."

Amanda and Paisley crowded in, but Amanda couldn't see what he meant until the cameraman switched on a light and pointed it toward the spot. "There's an E worked into the pattern on the wing of the standing swan," she pointed out. "Oh, and an H on the one with its wings spread. Harry and Eleanor! That's so sweet."

"Now look at the top swan," Lars directed.

The cameraman switched his spotlight to the trailing foot of the swan that was lifting off from the surface. "It's an N," Paisley shouted.

"An N, for Nathan. On the younger swan who is taking flight, while the swans that taught him how to fly look on." Amanda grabbed his hand and squeezed it.

"Wow. I never knew." Nathan blinked, and his eyes grew shiny.

"No wonder Eleanor was so keen to recover the sculpture." Amanda smiled at him, although her eyes misted as well. "So special."

CHAPTER SIXTEEN

SUNNY SKIES GREETED them the next morning, perfect weather for a hike. Max had declined the invitation due to soccer practice, but Lyla was thrilled to come along. Which is how Amanda found herself at the trailhead to Swan Falls, applying mosquito repellent to herself, Nathan, and the two girls. They each had a small backpack holding the lunches Amanda had prepared and their water bottles.

With a sudden cacophony, Nathan pulled a tangle of large jingle bells from his pack. "Turn around, Paisley, and let me attach some of these to you."

"What are they?" Paisley asked as she turned.

"Bear bells."

"So the bears will know we're here and stay away," Lyla explained, as she turned to get a set of bells for her pack.

"Grizzly bears?" Amanda asked, thinking of the enormous bear they'd seen at the airport with claws the size of a steak knife blade. She did not want to meet one of those face-to-face.

"Not likely," Nathan reassured her as he added her bells. "The grizzlies are only around here during the salmon run in late June, then they move on to other creeks with later runs. But there are a few black bears in the area, so it's better if we don't surprise them. I've also got bear spray." He patted the spray can in a low mesh pocket on the side of his backpack. Hanging below was an aluminum pot that Peggy had thrust into his hands just before they left the lodge that morning.

"I heard the blueberries are ripening early this year along the power line trail," she'd told them. "If you can fill this up, I can make two wild blueberry pies for the auction."

Nathan zipped his pack and announced, "Let's head out."

Amanda let the two girls follow Nathan before falling in behind them. Each step created a merry jingle, although in Nathan's case, it was more of a clank as the bells banged against Peggy's pot.

Amanda felt a little guilty about leaving Peggy alone to bake all the pies, but Peggy had laughed and shooed them out the door. "I've been doing this for thirty years. You go have fun. If you can get me those fresh blueberries, that's the best help you could give me."

The trail to the falls wasn't steep but it was a steady uphill. At about the halfway mark, they reached a Y in the trail. "That's the power line trail," Nathan pointed out, "where the blueberries grow. Should we pick now, or do it on the way back from the falls?"

"Let's do it on the way back," Amanda answered. "That way the berries will be their absolute freshest for Peggy's pies."

They continued on, the trail rising and falling, but the trend was clearly uphill. As they climbed, the girls talked less, leaving only the jingle of bells to blend with the birdsong of the forest. The forest smells of foliage and damp earth surrounded them. Between the tree roots and rocks, they had to keep their eyes on the trail rather than their surroundings, so it was a surprise when Nathan suddenly stopped, and they got their first glimpse of Swan Falls.

They were all breathing hard by that time, but the view was more than worth the climb. Water cascaded over the edge of a bluff above them, onto a ledge about halfway down, and then again into a pool below them. Ferns and bunchberries covered the forest floor on the shady side nearest them, while a border of hot pink fireweed bloomed on the far side of the pool, the image reflecting into the water in a moving mosaic of bright color. A series of flat boulders beckoned them to come and sit in the sun beside the water. So many of the sights of Alaska seemed bigger than life, but Swan Falls was intimate, just the right size for a small group to enjoy together.

Lyla and Paisley stepped out onto the rocks.

"We should have brought our swimsuits," Paisley said, but Nathan laughed.

"Put your hand in the water."

Paisley did and drew back with a gasp. "It's so cold!"

"That's because it comes from a glacier. Do you know what a glacier is?"

Paisley nodded. "We studied it in school. It's a river made of ice, and it moves real slow."

"Glaciers are so heavy that the ice inside gets squeezed and squeezed until it's blue," Lyla added. "My class took a field trip to the Matanuska Glacier last year."

"Still want to go swimming?" Amanda asked Paisley.

"No." Paisley pretended to shiver. "But can we have our picnic here?"

"Sure." Amanda had kept it simple. After checking for tastes and allergies, she'd made peanut butter and jelly sandwiches, plus carrot sticks, apples, and oatmeal cookies Peggy had stashed in the freezer from the batch she and Paisley had made together. Paisley and Lyla sat cross-legged on one of the biggest rocks, facing each other. Lyla spread out her napkin between them, and they carefully arranged the food they took from their packs, almost like a tea party.

"Let's sit over here," Nathan suggested to Amanda, pointing at some rocks that were closer to chair height. Nathan unpacked his food and bit into his sandwich. "This is good. Raspberry jam?"

"Yes. Peggy said she gets it at Wildwood Wonders, where Kailee works. I've been meaning to check it out." She should pick some up next week to take home as a gift for Harley. She'd been so wrapped up in everything going on in Swan Falls the past few days, she hadn't even taken the time to call and check on the nursery. Not that she was worried—she trusted Harley's judgment completely—but Zia Gardens was her responsibility.

"Look over there." Nathan stood and pointed toward a steep slope coming down off the mountain behind the falls. "Can you see them?"

Amanda got to her feet and squinted toward the rocky slope. "I see some white shapes. What are they, rocks?"

"Dall sheep." Nathan stepped behind her to rummage in his pack and pulled out a pair of binoculars. He removed the lens covers and handed them to Amanda. "Take a look."

Amanda lifted the binoculars to her eyes, but the scene was a blur. "How do I focus?"

"Here." He put one hand on her shoulder to steady her and reached around her with the other to cover her hand with his and show her how to adjust the focus wheel. She caught his woodsy scent, felt his warmth on her back, his breath against her neck. If she leaned back, just a little, she could rest against that solid chest. "Can you see them now?" Nathan asked, apparently unaware of the effect his closeness was having on her.

Amanda refocused her attention as well as the binoculars, and suddenly the blurs on the hillside coalesced into sharp-pointed rocks and scraps of vegetation. She raised the binoculars slightly, and spotted a half-dozen animals grazing or milling around on the steep rocky slope. Each of them had a heavy set of horns curving back from their faces. She focused on the biggest one in the middle, bulky and muscular, whose horns swept out from his head to curl so that the points at the ends faced forward. Wide-set eyes and alert ears gave him a look of noble intelligence. "They're beautiful!"

She returned the binoculars to Nathan. "Take a look."

He peered through the lenses. "Wow, did you see the big guy with a full curl?"

"Handsome fellow," Amanda commented, enjoying the excitement on Nathan's face.

"He sure is." Nathan didn't seem to notice she'd been looking at him and not the sheep. "Hey, girls. Want to see some Dall sheep?"

"I do!" Paisley got up and scrambled over the rocks to him. "Where?"

"There they are." Lyla pointed toward the hillside. "Can I use the binoculars, please?"

Nathan handed them to her, and she focused

like a pro. "Six rams," she announced. She handed the binoculars to Paisley. "Rams are boy sheep."

"I knew that," Paisley said as she raised the binoculars to her eyes. "And girl sheep are ewes. Baby sheep are lambs." She moved her head around. "I can't find them."

Nathan guided the binoculars so that they were pointed in the right direction. "How about now?"

"No, I—oh, there they are. They don't look like the sheep I saw at the fair. They have really big horns! Are they bighorn sheep?"

"No, but they're close relatives," Nathan explained. "Bighorn sheep are brown, and they live in the Rockies. I think there are some in New Mexico, where you live. Dall sheep live here in Alaska and the Yukon. Bighorns have even thicker horns than Dall sheep."

"They're so pretty." Paisley gave the binoculars back to Lyla, who passed them to Amanda.

As Amanda focused the binoculars for one last look, the sure-footed animals scrambled around the hill out of sight. She returned the binoculars to Nathan. "Thank you. That was amazing."

He replaced the lens caps and tucked the binoculars in his backpack. "Are we ready to find some blueberries?"

"Yes!" the girls called.

"But first, I want a picture," Amanda told them. "You three stand here." She snapped a picture with her phone and the girls started to move away, but Nathan stopped them.

"Wait." Nathan crossed to a boulder and set up a pair of flat rocks in an L shape. "Put your phone here on a timer, so you can be in the picture, too."

The support he'd rigged worked surprisingly well, and Amanda got a great shot of everyone, with Swan Falls in the background. Nathan looked over her shoulder. "Great pic. Can you send it to me?"

"Sure. Oh, I just realized I don't have your cell number." He gave it to her, and Amanda texted him the photo. Once the girls had gathered the remains of their lunches and put on their backpacks, they started down the trail. It was easier going downhill, and they got to the intersection to the powerline trail much quicker than Amanda would have expected.

The trail took them through the woods for the first bit, but soon opened onto a swath cleared through the forest about thirty feet wide. Low foliage covered the ground, and almost immediately, Lyla called, "Here's some blueberries," and bent to pick them.

"Here's more," Paisley replied, squatting among another patch a few feet away. "Can we eat them?"

"Of course," Nathan replied, before Amanda could mention washing them first. "That's part of the process."

The girls popped a couple in their mouths and

looked so happy, Amanda didn't have the heart to stop them. She supposed eating a little dirt wasn't going to kill anyone, and it wasn't as though she hadn't eaten a few cherries directly from the tree that grew next to their farmhouse when she was a girl. She chewed a couple of berries, and when the sweet juice touched her tongue, her taste buds danced. No wonder Peggy wanted wild blueberries for her pie.

Nathan shed his backpack and untied the pot from it. "Peggy says we're supposed to fill this. Think we can do it?"

"Sure!" Paisley dropped in a small handful of berries. "There's millions of blueberries here!"

Maybe not millions, but there were certainly dozens of patches scattered across the area, Amanda noted. Still, they were smaller than domestic blueberries and only a few grew on each plant. She had a feeling the girls would lose interest long before the pail was full. However, it turned out that there was something quite satisfying about finding a new patch, picking the ripe berries there, and dropping them into the pot that held the girls' attention as well as hers. The sun was warm on their backs as they drifted along the pipeline clearing, and the girls' faces and hands became streaked with purple juice while the pot slowly filled.

As they wandered higher on the hillside, the trees thinned, and the berry plants became more prolific. Amanda found a particularly lush patch just past the tree line and stopped for a few minutes to gather all the berries. When she looked up, Nathan and the girls had moved on past her into the alpine meadow. A snow-capped mountain pierced the blue sky behind them. Everything was picture-perfect.

She started toward Nathan, but a sudden movement in her peripheral vision made her turn. A furry shape emerged from behind a boulder not far from the girls. For a moment, Amanda thought it was a big dog, but then she recognized the shape. A bear!

She froze, staring at the huge animal with a deceptively benign expression that seemed to be sniffing the air. Nathan had his back to the bear, but Amanda's sudden stillness must have alerted him because he turned. Unlike Amanda, he immediately jumped into action, rushing forward to put himself between the girls and the threat. "Bear!" he shouted.

Paisley and Lyla jumped up. Nathan reached toward his hip and came up empty. "Shoot. I left the bear spray in my pack." He grabbed a stone from the ground and beat it against the side of the pot he was holding. "Hey, bear!" he yelled. "Move along now!" In a gentler voice, he called, "Amanda, take the girls and get them down the hill. Don't run. Just walk away."

Something about his calm instructions released

Amanda's frozen muscles, and she made her way to Paisley and Lyla as quickly as she could without running. "Come on, girls. You heard Nathan. We need to go." She dropped the berries she'd been holding and grasped the girls' hands, guiding them across the meadow. All the while, she never took her eyes off the bear.

"Sorry we interrupted your lunch," Nathan was saying to the bear as Amanda and the girls reached the tree line. "I understand you need to build up a nice layer of fat before you hibernate this winter. We'll just leave you to it." He slowly began backing down the hill.

The bear, black with a brownish muzzle, continued to sniff the air and moved a couple of steps closer to Nathan. Nathan tripped, stumbling a short distance before righting himself, which must have startled the bear. It raised onto its back legs. The girls gasped, and an icy bolt of fear shot down Amanda's spine. She looked around and spotted Nathan's pack on a flat rock not too far away. She slowly made it to the pack and pulled out the can. "I've got the bear spray."

"Stay there," Nathan called. He held the pot high over his head and beat on it with the rock, making a tremendous racket. The bear tilted its head in confusion. "That's right, bear," he said between clanks. "Nothing but noise and chaos here. You should move along, now, and come back for more berries after we're gone."

For what seemed like hours but was probably less than a minute, the bear and Nathan stared at one another. Finally, the bear dropped to all fours and loped off in the opposite direction. Amanda let out the breath she'd been holding and went running toward Nathan. "Are you okay?" she called.

"Fine," he told her, but she didn't stop until she'd wrapped her arms around him in a fierce hug. Laughing, he held the pot away from his body. "Careful, you're going to make me spill all these blueberries we worked so hard for." But his other hand ran up and down her back, soothing her.

"You were so brave," she whispered. "I really thought that bear was going to attack you."

"He was probably more interested in what other berries he could find, fortunately," Nathan told her. "Are the girls all right?"

"We're okay," Paisley told him, as she and Lyla came running up.

"Do you still have the blueberries?" Lyla asked.

"I do." Nathan showed her the almost full pot. "And I think that should be enough for Peggy's pies, so let's head down the hill before that bear changes his mind." He accepted the bear spray from Amanda. "And the lesson here is bear spray doesn't do any good unless it's within reach." He shuddered, probably thinking about how the situation could have ended badly.

Amanda squeezed his arm. "I'm impressed. You managed to dissuade the bear without anyone getting hurt or sprayed. You should be a professional diplomat."

He smiled. "Sure. I can just see the business card. 'Bear negotiation specialist.'"

Amanda turned to reassure the girls, but neither of them seemed particularly traumatized by the events. They fell in line behind Nathan. "That was so cool," Paisley told her friend. "I can't believe I saw a real, live bear. I still haven't seen a moose, though."

"There were two in the park in town yesterday, a mama and a baby," Lyla said, "but they're gone now. I'll bet you'll see one soon."

Paisley and Lyla continued to chat casually as they followed the trail, secure in their faith that Nathan could protect them from any and all danger. Amanda knew better, of course. If that bear hadn't backed down, Nathan would have come out much the worse for wear. Still, the way Nathan unhesitatingly stepped between the girls and the bear was awe-inspiring. He truly was a hero.

CHAPTER SEVENTEEN

SATURDAY MORNING, Amanda helped Peggy provide breakfast for the seventeen people who had checked into the lodge the evening before. Three more rooms were booked for check-in this afternoon. Yolanda held court at the largest table in the dining room, advising first-timers about what to do and see at the Feather Festival and comparing experiences with returning guests. Peggy had outdone herself with her caramel French toast casserole, three kinds of quiche, an elaborate fruit platter, and savory reindeer sausage. This was in addition to a bar with coffee, tea, and cocoa, cereal, milk, yogurt, and three kinds of bread for toast. Somehow, Peggy made the cooking look almost effortless, probably because she'd done the prep for the casserole and quiches while the rest of them had been picking berries and dealing with bears.

It was a lot of effort, but Amanda enjoyed it. She worked hard at the nursery, too, but somehow it always felt like it was David's business, and she was just helping out. Even after he died, before she'd hired Harley as manager, she'd used David's calendar as a guide as to when to plant, repot, and prune. Here, she understood the guests' needs instinctively and how to provide for them.

Paisley contributed, too, filling pitchers with orange juice, bussing tables, and answering questions. She enjoyed her role as insider, telling the families with children about the joys of the beaver pond and marsh, and of course, the library. Amanda's usually self-contained daughter had somehow morphed into a social creature. Nathan, meanwhile, was off helping one of the guests get their Wi-Fi working, but he'd promised to return shortly to wash dishes.

Amanda checked her watch. Still plenty of time before they all needed to head out for town for the Feather Festival parade. Ava Burke, the housekeeper, would be coming in an hour to clean the occupied rooms and cover the front desk while they were gone. She'd claimed she never watched the parade anyway—too crowded. The old lodge was once again coming to life, sheltering people from as close as Anchorage and as far away as Romania in warmth and comfort. Just like Eleanor and Harry had envisioned when they built the place.

After checking the buffet table, Amanda went to the kitchen to replenish the sausage tray and take out another broccoli cheddar quiche if Peggy had one. The phone hanging on the wall rang. Peggy had her hands full pulling another casserole pan from the oven, so Amanda picked up. "Swan Lodge. How can I help you?"

"Amanda, this is Lars Johanson."

"Hello, Mayor Johanson."

"Lars," he insisted. "Say, is Nathan around?"

"Just a minute and I'll see if I can find him," she answered, but the swinging door opened, and Nathan stepped into the kitchen. "Oh, here he is. I'll get him for you."

"Actually, I need to talk with both of you. It's about the parade today."

"Okay, just a sec." She covered the receiver with her hand. "Nathan, the mayor is on the phone. He says he needs to talk to both of us. Something about the parade."

"Okay." Nathan came to the phone and pressed the speaker button. "Hi, it's Nathan and I'm here with Amanda on speaker. Is there a problem with the float?"

"No, no problem," Lars answered. "But we'll need you to come a little early because the two of you have been voted Feather Festival King and Queen. Congratulations. Oh, and Paisley is more than welcome to ride with you, of course."

"What?" Amanda looked at Nathan, who seemed just as mystified as she was. "But we weren't in the running. I saw the nominees on the poster at the mercantile."

"Yes, but after you put in the new playground at the park, somebody started a write-in campaign for you."

Nathan immediately corrected him. "Eleanor was the one who provided the playground equipment, not us."

"Nevertheless, you pitched in to get it installed, and you've been pitching in ever since. Plus your recovery of *Swan Trio* got a lot of coverage. The way the poll is set up, it allows people to change their votes up until midnight last night, and you got the most votes." He chuckled. "And no need to ask for a recount. You won by a landslide. Now, can you be at the school parking lot by nine thirty?"

Nathan shrugged. "We should be able to manage that."

"Excellent. See you then."

Nathan hung up the phone and turned to Amanda. "Wow."

"I know. I can't believe it. Why would the people here choose us, especially me? They know you—you used to come here as a boy. But I just came for Eleanor's memorial service."

"And yet you've helped build a playground, rescued a parade float, picked berries for the pie auction, and gotten to know a lot of the people here. They like you, and apparently, they want you in the parade."

Peggy came bustling in the swinging door, with

Yolanda and Paisley right behind her. "I just heard! Congratulations!"

"What? How—" Nathan shook his head. "Never mind. I forget how fast news travels around here."

Paisley was practically vibrating with excitement. "Peggy says we get to ride on the swan float in the parade. That's awesome!"

Amanda squeezed her daughter's shoulders. "I thought you'd like that."

Yolanda hurried over and gave Nathan, and then Amanda, hugs. "It's so exciting to have Swan Falls royalty here. What are you going to wear?"

"Oh." Amanda stopped in her tracks, mentally going through her suitcase. "I have no idea."

"Well, keep in mind that we don't wear a lot of fancy clothes here. Jeans or work pants are the usual attire for the parade," Peggy advised. "And you might want to take a rain jacket. Rain's supposed to hold off until late this afternoon, but you never know. Take a look in Eleanor's closet if you need to."

"What about those fancy rubber boots of Eleanor's?" Yolanda asked Peggy.

"Yes, those would be perfect," Peggy agreed. "And I'll bet you could find a Swan Lodge shirt in her closet, too. Good advertising."

"Let's take a look." Yolanda practically dragged Amanda from the kitchen, stopping only to get the key from Nathan.

Paisley tagged along. Once they were inside

Harry and Eleanor's private suite, Paisley paused to look around the room, her head jerking back and forth like a curious bird's. "I've never been in here before." She stepped closer to the eclectic collection on the shelves. "It's neat."

"It's cozy, isn't it?" Yolanda called from the bedroom where she was already opening the closet doors. "I've shared many a pot of tea with Eleanor and Harry here. Harry was a big fan of afternoon tea and cookies, you know."

"I remember that from when I was a kid," Amanda said as she joined Yolanda in front of the closet. "But I thought he was just indulging me with a tea party."

"Oh, no. He and Eleanor always had afternoon tea, but it was a privilege to be invited. Obviously, you were special." Yolanda pulled a royal blue top from the closet. "Here we go." She passed the hanger to Amanda.

Amanda held it in front of her and checked the mirror over the dresser. The top, a long-sleeved T-shirt with the Swan Lodge logo on the front, looked to be the right size. She rubbed the soft fabric between her fingers. "It's nice."

"Yes, Kailee does good work. The first year she began making shirts with this logo, Eleanor bought one for herself and all the staff. She liked to do that, you know, help out creative people just getting started. That's how she came to have these boots, too." Yolanda reached up to take a pair of heavy rubber boots from the upper shelf. "When she heard about the women starting a business adding fancy liners to these fisherman's boots, she ordered some right away. And now they're selling them in all the outdoor stores." Yolanda folded down the cuff of the boot to reveal an exquisite print of coral-pink sea stars floating in stylized waves in shades of blues and purples. "What size shoe do you wear?"

"Seven."

"These are seven and a half. I'll bet they'll work fine with socks. What do you think?"

Paisley had joined them in the bedroom. "Those are so cool!"

"They really are." While Amanda tried on the top, Yolanda unearthed some thick socks. The black rubber boots pulled easily over her slim-leg jeans, with the cuff turned down over her calf to display the colorful lining. When she looked in the mirror, a genuine Alaska woman looked back. "These are great."

"Eleanor would get a big kick out of you wearing them for the parade," Yolanda told her.

Nathan appeared at the open doorway. "We'd better head out. Hey, look at you. Great boots. And I love the shirt."

"Thanks," Amanda said, as they followed him out and he locked the door behind them. "Let me just run up and grab our rain jackets, and we'll be ready to go."

"I'll get them!" Paisley took the key card Amanda handed her and scurried off up the stairs.

"She's excited," Amanda commented.

Nathan chuckled. "I can tell. Just wait until she finds out about the candy we get to throw from the float."

"Tell her I'm particularly fond of Tootsie Rolls." Yolanda winked and walked back toward the dining room.

Paisley returned with the jackets, and they got into Nathan's car to head to town. "I wish I had a Swan Lodge shirt like yours," Paisley said.

Amanda had a thought. "Let me call Kailee. I know Wildwood Wonders carries them. If they're open early, maybe we can swing by and grab you one before we meet at the school."

As it turned out, the shop didn't open until ten, but after Amanda explained the situation, Kailee offered to meet them at the school with a Swan Lodge hoodie for Paisley. "What's your favorite color, Paisley?" she asked over the speakerphone. "I think I have blue, purple, red, and yellow."

"Purple," Paisley called.

"Will do."

"Thanks. See you soon." Amanda hung up the phone. "Talk about excellent service."

"Small towns do have their advantages." Nathan drove slowly past the cars and floats already lined up on the edge of the street and found an empty spot in the school parking lot. A tile mosaic on the side of the building featured a view of Swan Falls, with a wedge of white birds, presumably swans, in the blue sky overhead.

"Nice," Amanda commented as they got out of the car. "Is this the elementary school?"

"Kindergarten through eighth grade. The kids go to Chugiak High School after that."

Amanda spotted Kailee from across the parking lot and waved. Kailee waved back and came running over. "Hi, guys. Paisley, I've got you covered." She reached into a shopping bag and pulled out a hoodie in a soft purple color with the logo in white on the front. "Voila. Hope it fits."

"I like it!" Paisley immediately pulled it on over her head and then struck a model pose. "Yes?"

"Perfect fit," Amanda said.

"Awesome. You, too, Amanda. Love, love, love the boots. Now, Nathan," she said, shaking her head as she looked at his flannel shirt over a basic white T-shirt. "We can do better." She pulled out a forest green long-sleeved polo with the Swan Lodge logo embroidered on the chest.

"Nice." Nathan replaced the flannel with the new polo. Amanda would have sworn he couldn't get any more handsome, but the color brought out the reddish tones in his hair and made those brown eyes seem even warmer.

When he smiled at her, Amanda found it hard to look away. "You look great," she told him.

"Thanks." A beat later, as if he'd just remembered they weren't alone, he added, "And thank you, Kailee."

"Yes, it was so nice of you to bring these to us." Amanda reached into her pocket for her wallet. "What do I owe you?"

Kailee jumped back. "It's on the house. Good advertising for Wildwood Wonders."

"No, I know things have been harder for the businesses this summer with the lodge closed for so long. You need to make your profits," Amanda insisted, and thrust some bills into Kailee's hand. Nathan took out his wallet, too, but Amanda waved it away. "I've got it covered."

"Thank you," Kailee and Nathan said simultaneously, and laughed.

"One more thing." Kailee reached into the bag again. "Lars will have your crowns—"

Amanda blinked. "Crowns?"

"Yes, crowns. You are the Feather Festival King and Queen, and that involves the proper headgear. But anyway, this is our first year to have a Feather Princess." She smiled at Paisley. "So I thought you might like to borrow this for the day." She pulled out a sparkling tiara.

"Wow!" Paisley gasped.

Amanda chuckled. Paisley had never been a big fan of frills and lace, but she had a thing for tiaras. The box of old Halloween costumes in the top of Paisley's closet in their apartment held several.

The mayor came striding over. "Good, you're

here. These are your crowns, and the candy for you to throw from the float, which will be the grand finale. It's back there." He pointed. "My wife is waiting to get you settled."

They moved past a float made by the Swan Lake Tourism Association, with a fake grass surface and a miniature of a waterfall in the front. A man sat on a stool in front of a folding easel, which held a half-completed painting of the falls. A teenage boy wearing waders and holding a fly rod was helping a middle-aged woman with a floppy hat and binoculars hanging from her neck climb aboard. Next in line were two reindeer. A woman held the ropes attached to their halters while a man was arranging blue banners with gold fringe over their backs. A white vintage convertible with a sign identifying the Swan Lake City Council stood empty. A marching band in costume milled around behind them, still in the stages of unpacking their instruments and finding their places. Following that was another vintage car, or rather a pickup truck, with the mayor's sign on the side, followed by a bunch of young gymnasts practicing their cartwheels, and a baton twirler warming up.

Paisley stared as they walked past. While this certainly wasn't her first parade, it was her first time seeing the controlled chaos involved in preparing for one, especially a small-town parade like this one. One of the gymnasts waved at her. She waved back. As they reached the swan float, which was hooked up behind a white SUV at the back of the parade, a woman with fading reddish hair and smile lines around her eyes came hurrying up.

"You're Nathan, Amanda, and Paisley, right? From Swan Lodge? How are you this morning? I'm Delia Johanson, Lars's wife. We need you right over here, on the swan float." Without pausing for answers to any of her questions, she turned and walked briskly toward the float, leaving them to follow.

"I'll be driving the truck that pulls your float. Don't worry, I pull our travel trailer all the time, so I know how. Besides, we only go about three miles per hour. Do you have your crowns?" Delia asked, finally pausing.

"I think so." Nathan opened the bag Lars had given him and removed two boxes, handing the one marked "Queen" to Amanda. She opened it to find a crown made from thin sheet metal, but instead of zigzag points, each of the uprights was embossed in the shape of a short feather. It had been painted gold, and then glazed to make it look antique, and to bring out the detail of the feathers. Cute.

Delia pointed to the padded purple velvet strip that lined the bottom of the crown. "I added this a few years ago after I spent the parade trying to keep the crown from slipping down over my ears. It makes it more comfortable, too. Go ahead. Try it on."

Amanda set the crown in place. Delia nodded her satisfaction. "Good. You, too, Nathan." She watched until Nathan had set a similar crown on his head. "Looks like it fits. And Paisley, I see you've decided to join in on the wearing of the crowns."

Paisley touched her tiara. "Ms. Kailee gave it to me."

"Oh, it must be one of her beauty crowns. I hear she won a few pageants down in the lower forty-eight before she moved up here."

Amanda was surprised to hear Kailee was a former beauty queen. Sure, she was gorgeous, but her style of minimal makeup, short hair, and casual clothing was about as far from pageant ready as Amanda could imagine.

"Now, let's get you on this float," Delia said. "There's a step stool in the back of the truck."

"We're good," Nathan told her, cupping his hands to give Paisley a boost onto the trailer. Amanda followed, and then Nathan vaulted up from ground level.

"All right, then. Once we're ready to start, you just sit there on the bench and wave. Oh, and throw candy to the kids along the parade route. Be sure and throw it far away from the float—we don't want any little ones running out into the street and getting hurt. I'm just going to go get the band lined up, and I'll be back." She scurried off.

Amanda watched her go. "Energetic lady, Delia. I wonder if she ran Lars's campaign for mayor."

Nathan chuckled. "I suspect she runs a lot of things in Swan Falls. Let's get settled."

Paisley led the way around the swan's wing and to the bench seat. Nathan put his hand on Amanda's back to signal her to go next. Warmth seemed to spread from his hand all through her body. She looked back at him and smiled. "A month ago, if anyone had told me I'd be in a parade in Alaska—"

"I know. And yet, here we are." He circled the hand on her back in a small caress.

"Yes." Their eyes met and held for a long beat, before Amanda repeated, "Here we are."

CHAPTER EIGHTEEN

THAT EVENING, Nathan, Amanda, and Paisley were still on the go in downtown Swan Falls. Responding to an urgent text from Peggy, Nathan went to the parking lot two blocks from the park to meet Malcolm and a van-full of excited guests. As they exited the van, Malcolm handed them cards with his cell phone number to coordinate their rides home, and Nathan pointed out the way to the park, where the street dance was due to start shortly. Once the guests were on their way, Malcolm opened the back of the van and lifted out a cooler. "Peggy says she forgot to bring ice for the drinks earlier. Can you take this to the park?"

"No problem," Nathan told him. "Thanks for driving the van. I don't see a single parking space open."

"My pleasure," Malcolm replied. "I'll go pick up the next group. If you need anything else from the lodge, give me a call and I'll throw it in."

"Will do." Nathan hefted the heavy cooler to his shoulder and carried it up the block and across the street to the park, where tables had been arranged under a tent near the new playground.

Amanda was there, setting up a row of urns for drinks. "Yay, ice. Thanks for bringing that over." She scooped cubes from the cooler into the urns before filling them from the jugs of strawberry lemonade, iced tea, and fruit punch he and Amanda had assembled that afternoon, using Eleanor's handwritten notes, while Peggy boxed up all the pies she'd made for the auction.

Nathan paused to watch Amanda in action. Other than their time on the float, she'd hardly had a chance to sit down all day. After the parade, they were informed that one of the duties of Feather Festival royalty was to serve lunch at the big hot dog cookout in the park, which actually turned out to be a lot of fun, but it did take time. Then they'd hurried back to the lodge, washed all the breakfast dishes, cleaned three rooms that Ava hadn't had a chance to get to yet, checked in six more guests, taken some of the guests on a guided tour of Swan's Marsh, fulfilled Eleanor's traditional role of preparing beverages for tonight's street dance, and made it back to town in time to stand in the rain and cut a ribbon that officially dedicated the playground to Swan Falls.

Since kids had been using the playground for almost a week, a ribbon-cutting ceremony seemed superfluous to Nathan, until Lars had unveiled a plaque on one of the uprights honoring Harry and

Eleanor. Amanda had burst into happy tears, and he might have shed one or two himself.

Fortunately, the rain stopped before the pie auction, where Peggy's wild blueberry pie set a new record when a man from Anchorage and another from Paris drove the bidding up to $160 before the local man conceded. Nathan managed to snag one of Peggy's strawberry-rhubarb pies for a slightly more reasonable fifty bucks. Since the proceeds went to fund PTO projects for the school, everyone benefited.

Afterward, they'd grabbed dinner from one of the food trucks gathered in the lot at the edge of the park, before throwing themselves into preparations for the street dance, which was due to begin any minute. One would think, after all that, Amanda would be exhausted, but if she was, it didn't show. Her cheeks were pink, her smile bright, and her amazing coppery hair twisted and twirled in a cloud around her face. To Nathan's relief, they'd been allowed to ditch the crowns after the parade, but Nathan had to admit that it had looked right at home on Amanda's perfect head. She was a queen, not in a haughty way, but in the sense that she felt a genuine affection for the people of Swan Falls. Whether it was riding on a float or shoveling mulch onto a playground, she'd been ready and willing to do whatever needed to be done.

She smiled at him. "Ready for the big dance?"

"I'm not much of a dancer," he admitted.

"Me, neither, but I don't think it matters. From what people tell me, it's just all good fun."

Nathan looked around. "Where's Paisley?"

Amanda gestured toward the playground. "She's with Lyla and a whole group of kids. Between that and riding on the float, I'm not sure she's ever had such a great day. I'm so glad I decided to stay for the festival."

It was a gentle reminder that Amanda and Paisley were due to fly out on Monday, but Nathan didn't want to think about that right now. He was having too much fun. Even with all the work involved, he was loving Swan Falls, loving having guests at the lodge once again, and loving having Amanda and Paisley there to share it with him.

The band began tuning up, and the hum of conversations rose a notch. People began drifting from all around the park toward the entry where some familiar faces were collecting a small admission fee and providing people with bracelets so that they could go back and forth between the dance and the park. Despite clouds and occasional showers throughout the day, people from all over had turned out for the Feather Festival. Nathan hadn't had a chance to get to the outdoor market in the meadow at the edge of town, but he was hearing reports from the vendors that this was their best year ever for sales of baked goods and craft items.

Paisley came running up, her face pink from exertion and her smile almost ear to ear. She still wore the tiara Kailee had given her, but it was listing to one side. "Hi, Nathan. Mom, can I have money for the dance? Everybody's going. Lyla's waiting for me." She gestured toward the gate, where Janice was waiting in line with her two grandchildren. She waved, and Amanda waved back.

"Sure." Amanda dug a ten from her wallet, but before handing it over, she straightened the tiara. "Be careful with this. You'll need to return it to Kailee tomorrow."

"I know." Paisley took the money and galloped off to join her friend. "Thanks," she added, over her shoulder.

"Have fun," Amanda called after her. "I'll be along soon."

Most of the people had moved to join the line for the street dance, leaving Amanda and Nathan alone at the beverage tables. The sun dropped below the level of the clouds in the west, sending a flood of golden light streaming across the park. Drops of water that still clung to some of the leaves glistened, and the warm copper highlights in Amanda's hair gleamed like a new penny. Her skin seemed to glow in the warm light, or maybe just from the smile of contentment on her face as she watched her daughter run joyfully across the park.

Without thinking, Nathan stroked Amanda's

silky-smooth cheek. She turned to him, and their eyes locked. Somewhere far, far away the band played their first song, an old Western waltz. Children squealed, conversation buzzed, dogs barked, but nothing seemed to matter except for the energy humming between the two of them. Slowly, slowly, he leaned closer until their lips met. She pressed her hands against his chest and then slid them up to encircle his neck. He wrapped his arms around her waist, and when he broke the kiss, he pulled her close and they swayed to the music.

She rested her cheek against his shoulder and closed her eyes. "This is nice," she murmured.

"Very nice." He stroked his hand up and down her back and inhaled her fresh scent of lavender and orange.

"I wish—" She paused.

"What?" he whispered.

"Never mind." Her lips brushed against his ear. "For tonight, I have everything I need."

ONCE AGAIN THE next morning, Nathan, Amanda, Peggy, and Paisley rushed around serving breakfast, but since they didn't have a midmorning parade to attend, the guests seemed more inclined to linger over an extra cup of coffee. Everyone seemed to be enjoying themselves, and Nathan counted their first weekend open a success so far.

Paisley was exchanging an empty milk pitcher for a full one when she overheard a family mention they planned to hike to Swan Falls that day. She immediately chimed in, telling them all about their encounter with the bear in the blueberry patch. Nathan wasn't sure bear stories were great for business, but he supposed it was better that people understood the risks of hiking in wild country. The family, a mom, a dad, and two young teenagers, seemed more entertained than alarmed by the story. But then, Nathan recalled they had driven up from Valdez, and living on the coast next to a fish hatchery, they probably saw more bears in a week than he was likely to run into around Swan Falls in a year.

"Did you say there are blueberries to pick?" a woman sitting with a man at the next table asked. A small terrier who had been snoozing at her feet lifted its head.

Nathan nodded. "Along the powerline trail that branches off from the Swan Falls trail. But do be aware of wildlife and don't let Milo there wander off by himself. Just a second and I'll get you a trail map." He jogged across the lobby to the registration desk and returned to hand out maps, hiking bells, and bear spray that came with a belt holster, so his guests wouldn't be inclined to set it down somewhere like he had.

Amanda worked nearby, her spirits seemingly bright given her wide smile and bobbing head. After clearing an empty table, she filled a carafe with coffee and started around the room, offering refills. She paused at the table with the couple and the dog and pointed at the map. "The Feather Festival market is here, next to the road to the trailhead, in case you want to stop in either coming or going. Paisley and I are planning to visit it this afternoon."

The woman looked up at her. "Do they sell shirts like the one you had on yesterday?"

"I'm not sure," Amanda told her, "but I do know they sell them at Wildwood Wonders, along with all kinds of local arts and crafts. It's on Main, a block east of the mercantile. There's a great bookstore across the street from the mercantile, too, if you're into reading."

"I'll definitely check it out," the woman said, accepting a refill.

Before too long, the guests had all cleared out and Nathan and Amanda moved to the kitchen. Peggy was on one side of the huge room, wiping down her cooking area, so Nathan and Amanda tackled the dishes. "I see you're taking your role as Feather Festival Queen seriously." Nathan lifted a rack of hot dishes from the washer and set them on the counter.

"How so?" Amanda asked as she finished loading the next rack.

"The way you were promoting local businesses out there."

"Oh, that." She laughed. "It's just that I realized recently that our being closed for a month was hard on them, and I know they're counting on the Feather Festival to make up for some of the lost sales. Besides, our guests will love them."

"Our guests." He smiled at her. "I like that."

"Well, they are our guests, technically. I guess they'll be your guests if you get that loan. Any word on that?"

"Not yet. I'd like to believe no news is good news, but—" He shrugged. He'd been trying not to worry about the delay, but it hadn't been easy.

"Maybe we can find another way. I was thinking—" But before Amanda could finish her sentence, Paisley burst through the swinging door. "Mommy, that lady with the dog wants to talk to you."

"Okay. I'll be right back," she told Nathan before following Paisley to the dining room.

Peggy crossed the kitchen toward him, a sly smile on her face. "You and Amanda seem to be getting along nicely."

"She's easy to get along with." Nathan set the next rack in the washer.

"Uh-huh. I heard a rumor that there was some kissing going on at the park last evening," Peggy continued.

"That wouldn't surprise me," Nathan replied, his lips twitching as he tried not to chuckle. "People were having a good time at the dance."

"Are you saying you have no personal knowledge?" Peggy cocked her head. "Because a reliable source told me something different."

"I'm saying I don't kiss and tell." Nathan collected a stack of clean plates and stored them in the cabinet.

Peggy grinned. "Well, regardless, Amanda has certainly thrown herself into the community here at Swan Falls. I think she was really touched that the people voted her Feather Festival Queen. It shows her how much the Swan family means to the people here. I'd say Operation Amanda is a rousing success."

The sound of the door swinging shut made them both look up. Amanda stood, just inside the doorway, a puzzled expression on her face. How much had she heard? Nathan quickly asked, "Did you get Mrs. Knowles taken care of?"

"Yes. She just wanted the name of the bookstore." Her eyes went from Nathan to Peggy and back again. "Would anyone care to tell me what Operation Amanda is all about?"

"Oh, dear. This is my fault. We were just—" Peggy started to say, but Nathan laid a hand on her arm and shook his head.

"Peggy, could Amanda and I have a few minutes alone, please?"

She opened her mouth as though to argue and then thought better of it. "Of course. I'll just be…" Peggy started for the door, but before she left, she added, "Don't blame Nathan. It was all my idea." The door swung closed behind her.

Amanda turned to Nathan, her eyes pinning him. "You were saying?"

He huffed out a breath. "Operation Amanda goes back to when we first realized you wanted to sell the lodge and I wanted to keep it. Peggy suggested that if you were to become more involved in Swan Falls and got to know the people here and how much the lodge means to this town, you wouldn't want to sell."

"You and Peggy were manipulating me?"

"No!" Nathan said, but then backtracked, "That is, not exactly. I mean, at first—"

But Amanda wasn't listening. "Who else was in on it? Was this whole Feather Festival Royalty thing part of the plan, too?"

"No," Nathan declared, but after thinking about it, he added, "At least, I don't think so." Were the people of Swan Falls in cahoots with Peggy to change Amanda's mind? It didn't seem likely, and yet...

"It doesn't really matter. What I really need to know..." Amanda licked her lip in a nervous gesture. "What about you and me? Were those kisses we shared just a part of Operation Amanda, too?"

Nathan jerked his head backward. "Absolutely not." Knowing the way Priscilla had used him for her own financial gain, how could Amanda believe he would do something like that? But his outrage quickly died when he considered it from her point of view. Seeing the evidence, how could she come to any other conclusion? "Amanda, no. I would never do anything to hurt you. Just the opposite." He took a step closer, but Amanda held up a hand.

"I thought you understood." She gazed at him, her expression now grim. "It's not that I *want* to sell Swan Lodge. I've always loved it here, and now that I've spent time getting to know the people of Swan Falls, I do understand that there's a lot at stake." She drew in a breath. "But I'm a mother first, and I have to do what's best for Paisley. There's no one to look after her interests except for me, and Zia Gardens is her legacy. I have to keep it up and running until she's old enough to take over. And if selling my portion of Swan Lodge is the only way to make that happen, then that's what I have to do. Even if it means that other people get hurt."

"I do understand. But let me be clear—I care about you. Those kisses were never, ever about trying to change your mind. You're special to me, and so is your daughter, and I only want the best for you." He straightened his shoulders. "So if selling the lodge is what you need to do, and I can't get the loan to buy you out, then I won't fight you. We'll put it up for sale."

Amanda met his eyes. "You mean that?"

"I do. I'll call tomorrow and find out the status

of that loan application. And if they say no, we'll find a real estate agent to list the lodge."

"Paisley and I fly out tomorrow afternoon," she reminded him.

"I know." As if he'd been thinking of anything else all day except for how much he would miss them. Desperately trying to figure out how to keep them here. But he had to face the truth, that he and Amanda were never meant to be. "Despite all evidence to the contrary, you can trust me to handle everything here. I won't cheat you."

"I know you won't. I trust you." Amanda blinked, her eyes suspiciously shiny. "I'm sorry it has to be this way."

CHAPTER NINETEEN

IN A CORNER of the basement, Amanda had unearthed a floral brocade rolling suitcase of Eleanor's as a replacement for her own ruined suitcase. While she packed their belongings, Nathan took Paisley for one last visit to say goodbye to the beavers.

Now Amanda rolled the suitcase out of the elevator on the ground floor and looked up at the freshly painted walls and soaring wood ceiling above her. The guests had checked out, leaving the lodge quiet once again. She would miss this place. Chances were, she would never be back, never again visit the people she'd come to care for here. It felt like losing Eleanor all over again.

And Nathan. How was she going to say goodbye to Nathan? His experience with his former fiancée could have turned him into a skeptic, and yet his innate kindness kept bubbling to the surface. Just look at how he had offered to give her the last rental car at the airport, even before he'd known who she was. How he'd gone out of his way to show Paisley the beavers and show her the wonders of Alaska, even to the point of shielding her from a bear. How he'd jumped right into helping with the float for the Feather Festival parade. He'd come away with some scars, but underneath, he was still that boy with the warm brown eyes who had helped her find her way home when she was lost. She'd never forgotten that boy, and she would never forget the man.

Her time here in Alaska, working and playing side by side with Nathan, had been more fulfilling than she could have imagined. But it was time to get back to her real life. David had worked so hard to build Zia Gardens, and it was her responsibility to keep it going. And, thanks to Eleanor's generosity, the new greenhouses she needed to make it happen were within reach. But it meant leaving all this behind. At least, she had some good news. After Vince had answered a legal question for her over the phone this morning, she had a plan.

The back door opened, and Paisley rushed in, followed by Nathan. "Mommy, the littlest beaver swam right up to me and looked at me. He's not scared anymore. He knows me!"

"That's amazing!" Amanda answered, looking over Paisley's shoulder to share a smile with Nathan.

"Yeah." Paisley dragged the toe of her sneaker across the floor. "I wish we didn't have to go."

"I know, but I have to get back to work, and you'll be starting school soon."

"But I didn't even see a moose. Everybody said I'd see a moose in Alaska, but I never did."

"I'm sorry," Amanda told her. "But you got to see swans, and beavers, and a talking magpie. And even a bear. That's pretty impressive, don't you think?"

Paisley shrugged.

"We're all packed. Nathan and Helen both said you can keep *Treasure Island*, so I put it in your backpack. Let's go say goodbye to Peggy, Malcolm, and Yolanda."

"Wait. I think I left my other book in the library. And I have to say goodbye to Shadow."

"Okay," Amanda told her, "but don't take too long. We have a plane to catch. I'll meet you in the kitchen in a few minutes."

Nathan stepped closer and together they watched Paisley trudge up the stairs. Once she was out of earshot, Nathan turned to her, his face serious. "Can we talk?"

"Of course. I have something to tell you, too, but go ahead. What did you need to talk about?"

"First of all, I heard from the bank a few minutes ago. It's a no. They tried to soften it, saying I could reapply in four years when my bankruptcy goes off my record, but—" He shrugged. "We knew it was a long shot."

"I'm sorry," she told him, but she wasn't surprised, given what he'd said about his finances. "But it's okay. I've been talking to Vince, and we've come up with a plan. It doesn't have to be me who's your partner. Vince says I can sell my share of the lodge to someone else who is willing to partner with you. He says it might take a little longer than an outright sale, but there should be investors out there who are willing to be a silent partner. Ideally, they would share in the profits, but you could run the place however you wanted."

She waited, expecting him to latch onto the idea, but his response was half-hearted. "Yeah. That could work."

"I thought you'd be more excited. This would solve both of our problems. I can get the money to pay for the greenhouses, and you can keep the lodge. It's a win-win."

"No, I am. I deeply appreciate what you're trying to do." He rubbed the back of his neck. "It's just—"

"Just what?"

"Okay, I'm just going to throw it out there." He reached for her hand. "Amanda, I don't want another partner. I want you."

She studied his face, trying to get a read on him. "What are you saying?"

"I'm saying I love you, Amanda Flores. I love you, and I love your daughter. I want us to be together. Why can't you both stay here, with me? I know you love it here, in Swan Falls, and so does

Paisley." He grinned. "You fit in so well, Eleanor would say it's your natural habitat."

"Oh, Nathan." She reached up to touch his face and sighed. Everything in her heart longed to tell him that she loved him, too, and that they could live happily ever after. But she couldn't simply follow her heart. She had responsibilities. "I wish we could. But you don't understa—" she started to say, but he shook his head.

"I think I do understand. I know it's important to you to keep Zia Gardens up and running so that someday Paisley can take it over. Go ahead and sell your share of Swan Lodge to buy those greenhouses you need, but that doesn't mean you have to go. From what you've told me you have an excellent manager who can run the business for you. Don't go back to Albuquerque. Stay here, with me."

She gazed into those warm brown eyes, reading the sincerity there, and hating herself for the heartbreak she was about to inflict. She loved him—but he could never know. It would only make things harder. "Nathan, as wonderful as that sounds, I can't." How could she make him see? "Paisley needs to be around the business, to learn it from the inside out, the way I learned about farming following my dad around when I was a child. Zia Gardens is her heritage, and I can't take her away from that. It would be so easy to stay, to let myself fall in love with you, but I have to do what's best for my child."

"Even if it's not what's best for you?" he pressed.

"What's best for me," she insisted, "is to put my daughter first."

He held her gaze for a long moment before he nodded and dropped her hand. "I do understand. I'm sorry if I made things awkward—"

"Never awkward." She pulled him into a hug. "You are the kindest, most wonderful man I know," she whispered. "If it was just me, I'd be all over that offer. But I have to do what's right for Paisley."

He closed his eyes and gave a deep sigh. "I respect that." He gave her one last embrace, and then let her go, just as Paisley came down the stairs, her steps dragging. "Did you find Shadow?" he asked as she reached the lobby.

Paisley nodded. "She's sad I'm going away."

"We all are," he said, laying a hand on Paisley's shoulder, but his eyes met Amanda's for one more brief moment. "Swan Lodge won't be the same without you."

CHAPTER TWENTY

NATHAN SAT ON the leather club chair in Vince's home office, trying to make sense of the listing contract in his hands, but the words kept swimming around. Since Amanda left a week ago, he couldn't seem to focus on anything. Vince busied himself at the credenza in the corner, pouring coffee. "Cream or sugar?" he asked.

"What?" Nathan looked up. "Oh, no thanks. Black is fine."

Vince nodded and set two cups on a tray. "The broker says he has a couple of prospective buyers in mind. Amanda has already signed electronically, so he just needs your signature to get started." Vince set the tray on the tile-top table between them and settled into the chair next to Nathan. "Any questions I can answer for you? It's a fairly standard listing agreement that sets the asking price and the commission the broker will receive when he finds a buyer for Amanda's share of Swan Lodge. The commission comes out of Amanda's sale price, so it doesn't affect you at all."

"Uh-huh." Nathan turned to the next page and took a sip of coffee.

"The only reason you need to sign at all is because Amanda has given you the power to accept or reject the sale." Vince pointed to a paragraph typed in at the end of the page. "She didn't have to do that. Legally, she can sell her share to whomever she likes, but she made it clear to me that she wants you to have a partner you can work with, preferably a silent partner."

"A silent partner," Nathan repeated. That's what he'd wanted, wasn't it? He'd even said as much to Amanda once, that she could be a silent partner and leave the management of the lodge to him. So really, it shouldn't matter whether the silent partner was Amanda or some stranger.

It shouldn't, but it did.

He didn't want a silent partner; he wanted her. Here, in Swan Falls. Insisting on sage green paint instead of sticking to the safe cream color he'd chosen. Doggedly continuing the search for the swan sculpture, even when it looked like they'd reached a dead end. Encouraging her daughter to expand her horizons while appreciating and supporting her strengths. Playing badminton with little skill, but endless enthusiasm. And laughing, always laughing, with that joyful chortle that never failed to make him smile.

He loved her. Shouldn't that count for something? He really and truly loved her and Paisley, and with a feeling stronger than anything he'd ever experienced. He'd tried to make her understand, but Amanda had rejected him. To be fair, she'd been straight with him from the very beginning. Her first priority was Paisley, just as it should be. And she sincerely believed that Zia Gardens, Paisley's legacy from her father, was more important than her own inheritance from Eleanor. More important than any attraction he and Amanda might have for each other. More important than love.

Maybe she was right. Maybe love shouldn't dictate decisions. Falling for the wrong person had derailed his life once before. Maybe it was better if he stuck to his original plan to stay far, far away from romance. He could certainly live a fulfilling life following Harry and Eleanor's example of warm hospitality here in Swan Falls, sharing this special piece of Alaska with outsiders and locals alike. He should concentrate on that.

He turned to the last page, scrawled his signature on the line, and handed the contract to Vince. "Here you go. Anything else?"

"Nope, that does it. Now we just sit back and wait to see what offers come in."

"Right." Nathan set his almost full cup on the tray and stood. "In that case, I'll be heading out."

"Stay and finish your coffee," Vince suggested. "And you can tell me about your plans for the lodge."

A week ago, Nathan would have been eager to

share, but he just couldn't seem to find the enthusiasm he'd felt before, when he and Amanda were painting and fixing up the place together. But the work still needed to be done, whether he was in the mood or not. "Another time," he told Vince. "I have stuff to do."

"Okay, but don't be a stranger. If you need someone to talk to, about the lodge—" Vince paused and caught his eye "—or anything else, I'm always here."

"I appreciate that," Nathan told him, but the last thing he wanted right then was to share his feelings. "See you 'round, Vince."

AFTER DROPPING PAISLEY off at soccer practice, Amanda returned to Zia Gardens, but instead of going right in, she paused to really look at the place. Out front, in the xeriscape garden of drought-tolerant plants, Texas sage and brown-eyed Susans bloomed brightly among gray-leafed shrubs and succulents. As she passed under the archway at the entrance to the garden, she brushed against the rosemary bush, releasing a burst of fresh, almost piney scent. David had planted it there for just that reason. Last year, Harley added lambs' ears along the edge of the path for children to touch. Neither of those things would have occurred to Amanda. She'd grown up on a farm, but farming and gardening were not quite the same.

She walked to the front door, where Harley had

set up a display featuring all sorts of ornamental sunflowers, from shaggy dwarf doubles to tall stalks with flowers in jeweled shades of mahogany, orange, and yellow—the perfect accent for a Labor Day barbecue. The bright blooms drew attention away from the patched cracks in the greenhouse walls.

Her phone rang—her sister. After catching her mother up a couple of days before, Amanda had been expecting this call. "Hi, Jess."

"Hi. So, from what I hear from Mom, all those old movies were right—it does pay to butter up rich old relatives, so they'll put you in the will."

Amanda shook her head. "I did not—"

"Kidding." Jess laughed. "I know you loved Aunt Eleanor, and you even like that monstrosity of a hotel she ran. Seriously, I'm happy for you. Even though Mom says you're going to blow all the money on frivolities like new greenhouses and Paisley's college education." She clicked her tongue. "So shortsighted."

"Oh, yeah? What would you spend it on?"

"Easy. An around-the-world cruise."

Amanda scoffed. "A cruise?"

"For sure. I believe it would be highly educational for my niece and her mother to travel the world. And if they wanted someone along to share the experience…"

"Yeah, no. I think I'll stick to the original plan."

"Oh, well, it was worth a try. Was the place still

the same—all rustic wood and antlers, with that creepy swamp next door?"

"Swan Lodge is lovely, and it neighbors a marsh, not a swamp."

"To-may-to, to-mah-to. It's a wet place crawling with mosquitoes and quite possibly alligators or other creepy crawlers."

"Too cold for alligators, or reptiles of any sort, actually. But it does have birds, including trumpeter swans."

"Oh, I'd forgotten about the swans. They were pretty. They're still there?"

"Probably not the same swans, but yes, there was a whole swan family living there. They're gorgeous." Amanda sighed.

After a short pause, Jess said, "You hate it, don't you? The idea of selling that place."

Amanda blinked. "How did you—never mind. Yeah, I wish I didn't have to sell. After all, it's been in the family for years and years. But we need those greenhouses."

"Hmm. Is the family connection the only reason you don't want to sell?"

"What other reason would there be?" Amanda asked.

"I don't know. Just wondering why you're not more excited." In the background, someone called Jess's name, probably because her Frappuccino was ready. "Listen, I have to go. But for real, congratulations, Amanda. You deserve this. Talk to you later. Bye."

"Bye, Jess," Amanda said, but the call ended before she could finish her sentence. That went better than expected. Maybe she underestimated her sister. She slipped the phone into her pocket and stepped inside the greenhouse.

In the back, Logan, a college student working for the summer, watered the potted roses and shrubs. Harley would need to find a replacement for him soon, but Amanda was sure he was on top of that. She drew in a breath of warm, moist greenhouse air, but it only served to remind her of the crisp, clean air of the Alaska outdoors. She shook her head to clear the memories. She'd been home for more than a week now, plenty of time to get into her normal rhythms. There was no use looking back, wondering what might have been. She'd made her decision. Her focus needed to be on Zia Gardens, and on Paisley.

Three or four people browsed among the plants, which wasn't bad for a weekday afternoon. Harley was at the front register, checking out a customer with a wagonload of five-gallon pots holding sage, yarrow, and junipers. He finished the transaction and followed the woman outside to help her load the pots into her car. When he returned, he came to find Amanda, who had been straightening up a table of bedding plants. "Did you find the field okay?"

"Yes, thanks to you." She'd signed Paisley up for an autumn soccer league, hoping her daughter would find some new friends on the team. The first practice had started today, and despite having lived in Albuquerque for most of her life, Amanda had never heard of the practice field and couldn't find it with her phone's navigation. Fortunately, Harley, who had grandkids in soccer, knew that the field had recently undergone a name change, which hadn't been noted in the team handout. Once again, his knowledge had saved her. "I'll need to pick her up in an hour."

Harley nodded. "Hope she has fun. She's seemed a little…subdued since you got back from Alaska. Maybe she was just tired from traveling."

Amanda would have liked to believe that was all it was, but she knew the truth. "She misses Alaska. She made some good friends in the short time we were there, and it was hard on her to leave them." She blew out a breath. "But hopefully, there will be some nice kids on her team."

"What about you?" Harley asked.

"What about me?"

"Was it hard for you to leave Alaska and the people there?"

"I—I mean, sure it was. I've always been fond of Aunt Eleanor, and it was hard to say goodbye to her and to the people at the lodge. Peggy, the cook, has been there for so many years she's prac-

HER ALASKAN SUMMER

tically grown roots. I have some great memories at Swan Lodge."

"What about Nathan?"

She glanced up, sharply. "How do you know about Nathan?"

"You mentioned him, remember? When we talked on the phone." Harley's expression was suspiciously innocent. "And Paisley was telling me all about him this morning. How he chased a bear out of a berry patch."

"Yeah, he did do that." Amanda remembered how he'd stepped right between Paisley and the bear, risking his own life to make sure her daughter was safe.

"Sounds like a courageous man." Harley nodded approvingly. "Paisley also mentioned that once, she saw the two of you kissing."

"Did she?" When did that happen? She and Nathan had always been careful about public displays of affection. Except, now that she thought of it, that night in the park, during the Feather Festival street dance when the feeling grew so strong they hadn't cared who noticed.

Harley's eyes crinkled up at the corners. "She seemed pleased with the notion of you and this Nathan person together."

Amanda shrugged, trying to appear casual. "Well, she'll just have to let go of that idea." Just like Amanda herself was going to have to let go. Her head kept telling her she was doing the right thing, but her heart—at some point, she'd given her heart to Nathan. She wasn't sure exactly when she'd fallen in love with him. Maybe it was when he'd stood up to the bear. Or maybe when they kissed in the park. Or maybe the feelings had started that very first day, when he'd offered to give them the last rental car even before he knew who they were.

She hadn't gotten a good night's sleep since she'd left Alaska. Instead she lay awake, tossing and turning, remembering the heartbreak in his brown eyes when she'd refused to stay. All day long, she would pretend to be cheerful, pretend she was glad to be home, when all she really wanted to do was to watch sad movies and eat anise-flavored *biscochitos* until she burst. Scratch that. What she really wanted was to get herself and Paisley on the next plane to Alaska, and hold Nathan in her arms once again, but that couldn't happen. She had responsibilities, and they were here.

"Why?" Harley asked. "What happened?"

"Nothing happened," Amanda assured him. "It was never going to happen. He belongs in Alaska, and Paisley and I belong here."

"Hmm." Harley reached over to snap off a few faded petunia blooms from one of the hanging baskets. "You know, I never knew your husband, but from what I've gathered from you and from some of your longtime customers, David was a good man."

"Yes, he was."

"Then I can't imagine he would have wanted you to be alone for the rest of your life out of some misguided sense of loyalty."

She looked at Harley. "Is that what you think is going on?"

He turned his hands palms up. "You tell me. There must be some reason why you're avoiding relationships."

"I have a daughter to raise and a business to run. I don't have time for dating. Besides, I'm nearly forty. From what I've heard, finding a decent guy at that age is like winning the lottery."

Harley snorted. "You're thirty-seven, practically still a pup. And what about this Nathan fellow you were kissing? Did he turn out not to be a decent guy?"

"That's not what I meant. Nathan is a great guy, but we're in different places. Literally."

"I see." Harley moved to the next row of baskets. "You got another offer from that real estate developer, by the way, ten percent higher than the one he made last week. He really wants this property."

"I'm not selling." Amanda realized she sounded harsh, so she softened it with a smile. "Besides, if I sold, you'd be out of a job."

"Yeah, I know, but my wife will have her twenty-five years of working for the city as of January, and she's making noises about moving away from Albuquerque, fixing up that cabin on Abiquiu Lake we bought back in '08, during the crash."

"You're leaving me?" Tears welled up in the back of her eyes. Harley was the one who had pulled this place together and got it back on the road to profitability. How could she run it without him?

"Not yet," he told her in a soothing voice. "But I'm getting on up there. One day soon, if you're going to keep going, we'll have to find someone to take my place."

Amanda shook her head and hugged him. "Nobody could ever replace you."

"That's sweet of you to say," he told her as he patted her gently on the back, "but things change, and we have to adapt. That's just life."

Amanda's cell phone rang, again. She glanced at the screen. "Sorry, I have to take this. It's the estate lawyer from Alaska."

Harley nodded toward the front desk. "Looks like I have another customer anyway." He walked toward the register and Amanda answered the phone.

"Hi, Vince." She glanced over at Harley, who was laughing with the customer as he answered her questions about the two rosebushes she carried. The man had certainly earned his retirement, but how could this place function without him?

"Good afternoon, Amanda." Vince sounded cheerful. "I have news. The broker has found a buyer willing to pay you the full asking price."

"Oh." She hadn't expected it to happen so quickly. "What does Nathan think of the buyer?"

"Nathan showed him around the property, and he tells me he thinks it's someone he could learn to work with."

Learn to work with? "That doesn't sound like a ringing endorsement," Amanda commented.

"Well, as I'm sure you realize, Nathan doesn't trust easily. But he knows you're eager to sell and he doesn't want to hold you up unnecessarily. I just spoke with the broker, and he said if you want to talk to the buyer before you make the decision, he's available to take your call right now."

Amanda checked the time. "I have thirty minutes before I need to leave to pick up Paisley from soccer practice. I'll give him a call." After getting the number from Vince and thanking him, she ended that call and dialed the new number. "Hello, Mr. Garrets? This is Amanda Flores. I understand you'd like to buy my share of Swan Lodge." Wow, it sounded so final when she said that.

"Amanda, so nice of you to call. Please, call me Tristan." His was a salesman's voice, smooth, almost slick. "Yes, after seeing the property, I think it has a lot of potential, and, of course, having a Swan descendant running Swan Lodge is a great hook. I think, with time and effort, Nathan and I could develop it into a jewel of a property."

It was already a jewel, in Amanda's opinion, but maybe she couldn't be objective. "What changes did you have in mind?" she asked, keeping her voice neutral.

"It's already a lovely little rustic lodge in an awesome setting, so I'd go with small changes at first. Basics, like televisions in all the rooms and a coffee bar with an espresso machine and baked goods for sale. The very minimum people expect when they travel. But the guest rooms are large enough that, over time, we can upgrade the furnishings, and make them into mini suites. Tear down those old cabins—which I gather haven't been used in several years anyway—and eventually add a spa on-site."

"A spa?" Amanda tried, and failed, to imagine Eleanor indulging in facials or seaweed wraps.

"Spas have a very nice profit margin, and an on-site spa with windows looking out on that serene lake could draw an upscale crowd to Swan Lodge. Especially once we use that undeveloped acreage, to put in a nine-hole golf course."

"You mean the forest between the lodge and the marsh?" The woods, with all the hiking trails, filled with birds and wildlife?

"Yes, right there. It would be a beautiful setting. I'd use a professional course designer, of course, but I envision it with groves of trees and some of the tee boxes overlooking vistas of the marsh."

"But Swan's Marsh is a bird sanctuary. Don't golf courses require all kinds of fertilizer and chemicals that might run off into the water?"

"No, no, not at all," he rushed to answer. "Sure, permitting is a concern, but we can work through that. There are ways to mitigate any problems and facilitate approval. It will be fine." He was a master of the reassuring tone.

Amanda was not reassured. "What did Nathan think of these ideas?" she asked. Nathan had told her he wanted to continue Harry and Eleanor's brand of rustic hospitality. She couldn't imagine he would be inclined to jettison all the guests who had returned to the serenity of Swan Lodge again and again in favor of high-maintenance upscale clients. And he certainly wouldn't be on board with possible contamination of Swan's Marsh.

"We didn't really get that far," Tristan admitted. "At the time I was with Nathan, I was just touring the property. It wasn't until after I'd studied the plat map that I was able to envision the feasibility of a golf course."

"I see." Amanda didn't need to hear any more. "Well, Tristan, this has been most informative, but I have to go pick up my daughter from practice, so I'll need to go now. Thank you for your time."

"Of course. I'll look forward to hearing from your broker. Goodbye, Amanda."

"Goodbye." Amanda ended the call and immediately texted Vince not to sell to this man under any circumstances. Maybe she couldn't be Nathan's partner, but she wasn't going to saddle him with someone who wanted to tear out the natural beauty surrounding Swan Lodge and turn it into a manicured imitation of nature. There was nothing wrong with golf courses or spas, but they didn't belong at Swan Lodge.

She wasn't in so much of a hurry that she couldn't wait a little longer to see if a better partner came along, one who could understand what Swan Lodge meant to the community and to the guests who returned again and again. But could anyone who hadn't stayed at Swan Lodge, who hadn't known Eleanor and Harry and felt the particular magic of the place, truly understand? She would love to be that partner, to work side by side with Nathan, but her duty was here, and so the least she could do was find someone who respected Nathan's vision for Swan Lodge. And if finding the right partner for Nathan meant she had to take a lesser offer, it didn't really matter, as long as she made enough to pay for the two greenhouses.

She owed Nathan that much.

CHAPTER TWENTY-ONE

Two days later, Amanda and Paisley climbed the stairs to their second-floor apartment. Paisley carried the take-out pizza they'd picked up on the way home, while Amanda lugged the bags of school clothes and supplies they'd spent all afternoon shopping for. Usually, back-to-school shopping was something they both enjoyed, but today, Amanda could tell Paisley's heart hadn't been in it. She was probably tired from the soccer practices, plus the stress of meeting new people could be exhausting for an introvert like Paisley.

In the meantime, Amanda figured they could both use a little treat—thus the pizza. They reached their door, unlocked it, and went inside. Amanda set the bags on the sofa. "I like the backpack you chose," she told Paisley, pulling the lavender pack from the biggest bag. "Especially the furry little balls on the zipper pull."

"Me, too." Paisley set the pizza on the kitchen counter and came to stroke the fur. "Lyla has one just like it, except hers is blue."

"Really? How do you know that?"

"I remember from when we went hiking. We could be twins—" her smile faded "—if we were in the same school, that is."

"Well, it's a really nice backpack. Let's eat that pizza before it gets cold. Pour us some milk, please, while I make the salad." Since it was a bagged salad, Amanda just had to dump some in a bowl, add a few cherry tomatoes, and toss it with bottled dressing. By the time Paisley had the milk poured, they were ready to sit down at the kitchen bar for dinner.

Paisley reached into the box for the first piece of pizza. "Too bad Nathan's not here. He likes pepperoni. Remember when we all got pizza from Raven's Nest in Swan Falls?"

"That was good pizza," Amanda admitted, "but so is this." She took a big bite to demonstrate, but honestly, it wasn't nearly as good as Raven's Nest pizza. They ate in silence for a few minutes.

"Don't forget your salad." Amanda pointed to the untouched pile of greens on Paisley's plate.

"I wish—" Paisley sighed. "Never mind."

"What do you wish?" Amanda asked. If Paisley didn't want salad, she could give her carrot sticks instead.

"I wish we were still in Alaska, and I could go to school with Lyla, and live at the lodge with Nathan and Peggy and Malcolm," Paisley blurted out.

"Oh." Where did that come from? "Did Nathan talk to you about staying?"

"No. Why?" Paisley brightened. "Does Nathan want us to live there?"

Amanda avoided the question. How did she handle this? She knew Paisley missed the lodge and all the people she'd gotten close to in Alaska, but she thought her daughter had understood going in it was all temporary. But saying that wouldn't help. Instead, she rubbed her hand over Paisley's shoulder. "I understand how you feel. We had a really fun time in Alaska, didn't we? And Lyla was a good friend to you."

"I never did get to see a moose," Paisley complained. "Everyone said I would, but I never did."

"I'm sorry. But we can't control things like that."

"Will we go back?"

"I don't know," Amanda answered honestly. "It's a long way to fly to Alaska, and expensive. Right now we need to focus on our life here in Albuquerque."

"Why?" Paisley asked. "Why do we have to live here? Nathan lived in Arizona, but he's moving to Alaska. Why can't we?"

"Because Zia Gardens is here, the business your daddy started, and that will be yours someday. That's important. That's why I'm selling my share of Swan Lodge, to pay for new greenhouses so Zia Gardens can continue."

When Paisley looked skeptical, Amanda added,

"You remember how I told you I grew up on a farm that had been in my family for generations?" Paisley nodded.

"Well, when my daddy died, my mother sold the farm, and that meant I could never be a chili farmer like my dad, and his parents, and our family before that. It made me sad that I never had that chance. I don't want that for you. I want you to be able to continue the business your daddy started someday."

Paisley wrinkled her nose. "I don't like being at Zia Gardens that much. I like talking to Harley, but hanging around plants is boring."

"You think so?" Sure, Paisley had never seemed terribly excited about spending time at the garden center, but she'd never complained. Usually she escaped to the office to read or hung out with Harley, unless Amanda or Harley specifically assigned her a task. "Well, maybe you'll change your mind about that when you're older." David had loved everything about the business: planting, pruning, advising customers on the best plants for their situation. Surely Paisley's green thumb would kick in at some point. Wouldn't it?

"I want to be a librarian when I grow up," Paisley declared. "Do they have a library in Swan Falls? I could work there. Or I could work for Helen, in her bookstore. Or maybe I could have a bookstore of my own. And it could have a reading tent, like the one at Swan Lodge."

"Hmm, well, you've got a lot of years before you need to make that decision," Amanda told her. "Now, eat your salad."

Paisley took a bite of salad, but after a moment she asked, "Aunt Eleanor was your family, right?"

"Yes, she was my great-aunt. Your great-great-aunt."

"Then if it's important to keep a family business, why are you selling it?"

"Because—" Amanda struggled to find the words to explain. Why was she selling it?

Maybe Paisley was right. Maybe the lodge she'd inherited from her family was every bit as important as David's business. Maybe she needed to find a way to keep both. Or maybe—maybe in her determination to keep Zia Gardens, she was projecting her own feelings about losing the farm onto Paisley.

Amanda had always loved the farm, loved riding with her dad in the pickup truck to check out the fields. Sometimes he'd even let her sit in his lap and steer the tractor. But Paisley had never shown any real interest in Zia Gardens. What if pushing Paisley toward a business she had no real interest in was more of a curse than a blessing?

It wasn't as though David had ever expressed a desire that his daughter would follow in his footsteps. No, this decision was all on Amanda. She'd thought she was putting Paisley and her future first, but what if she was wrong? Had she made the biggest mistake of her life?

"Mommy?" Paisley tilted her head and studied her. "Are you okay?"

"Sure. I just—" But before Amanda could come up with an excuse, someone knocked on the door. Probably Mrs. Garcia from down the hall. A widow who had raised four kids, Mrs. Garcia often defaulted to making *pozole* or enchiladas in the same quantities she used to make for her family, which she would then distribute to her neighbors up and down the hall.

But when Amanda looked through the peephole, it wasn't Mrs. Garcia's face she saw. Instead Nathan stood in the hallway, nervously running a hand over his hair. She opened the door. "Nathan!"

"Nathan's here?" Paisley jumped down from her seat, galloped to the door, and threw her arms around his waist. "Nathan!"

"Hi, Paisley." He hugged her with one arm, his other one occupied by a cellophane-wrapped bouquet of flowers in his hand and a satchel hanging over his shoulder. He looked up and those wonderful brown eyes met hers. "Hello, Amanda."

Amanda just stared for a long beat. Had her imagination conjured him up somehow? But no, he was really here. She stepped back out of the way. "Hi. Come in."

"Thanks." He dislodged Paisley long enough to

step inside the door so that Amanda could shut it. He handed the bouquet to Paisley. "These are for you and your mom."

"Flowers! Wow, Mom, he brought us flowers."

"I see that. They're beautiful." And they were, a colorful bouquet of white-and-yellow daisies, purple asters, roses, carnations, and baby's breath tied with a deep red ribbon. "Thank you. Paisley, why don't you fill that vase on the bookcase with water and put the flowers in that?"

While Paisley was busy, she asked in a quiet voice, "Nathan, what are you doing here? Not that I'm not glad to see you, but..." She let her voice trail off.

"I'm here because I missed you," he said. He glanced toward Paisley, who was running water. "Both of you."

"We missed you, too." He had no idea how much. "Here, sit down." Amanda gestured toward the couch. He sat in the corner, and she settled in the chair beside it and leaned forward toward him. "Did you just fly in today? Where's your luggage?"

"I dropped it at a hotel before I came." He fixed his gaze to her face. "Amanda, I need to talk with you."

"And I need to talk with you," she said softly. "But not in front of Paisley."

"Right," he replied, as Paisley finished stuffing the bouquet, plastic and all, into the vase and carried it toward them.

"Paisley, I have one more thing for you." Nathan reached into his satchel and pulled out a small book. "It's a collection of mini mysteries, all about Alaska. It gives you a story and then gives you a chance to solve the mystery before you turn the page for the solution."

"Wow. Thank you!" Paisley set the flowers on the coffee table and took the book. She immediately opened it and started to sit on the couch next to Nathan.

"Why don't you take it to your room?" Amanda told her. "Nathan and I need to talk about something."

Paisley hesitated as though she planned to protest, but apparently the lure of a new book was enough to gain her compliance. "Okay. But Nathan can't leave without saying goodbye to me."

Nathan placed his hand over his heart. "I promise."

Paisley nodded and drifted off to her room, her nose already in the book. Amanda got up and followed behind her to shut the door before returning to the living room. She paused at the corner of the couch, hardly able to believe he was really there. "Nathan," she whispered.

"Amanda." He stood and, in a flash, they were in each other's arms.

Amanda closed her eyes, breathing in his familiar woodsy scent and relishing the warmth of his embrace. Despite the hot weather of late August in New Mexico, she felt like she hadn't been truly warm since leaving Nathan in Alaska. After a long moment, she looked up at him and his lips brushed hers, light as a feather, before capturing her mouth under his, the kiss gentle and yet somehow fierce.

"Oh, Nathan," she whispered when they broke the kiss. This was where she needed to be, close enough to feel his heart beating. Did the fact that he was here mean it wasn't too late?

"Nathan, I—"

"Wait." He held up a hand. "I've been practicing what I was going to say in my head all day, so let me go first. Okay?"

She smiled. "Okay. But I have to sit down."

"Good idea." This time they both sat on the couch. He took her hands in his and looked into her eyes. "Let's start with the basics. Amanda, I love you. I know I sort of sprang that on you at the last minute when you were leaving, but it's true. I love you, and I love Paisley. Do you think—"

Amanda squeezed his hands. "I love you, too. I've missed you, so much." She leaned forward and they shared a small kiss.

Nathan let out a nervous chuckle. "That's reassuring, because if you didn't the rest of what I have to say wouldn't make much sense. Amanda, Swan Lodge was a wonderful surprise, but the real gift Eleanor gave me was to bring you and Paisley into my life." His eyes grew solemn. "You and Paisley are my first priority. Not Alaska. Not Swan Lodge. It took a lot of stewing, but it finally hit me—I can stay in Alaska and maybe eventually I'll be sort of okay, or I can be with you and know for sure that I'd be happy."

Amanda tilted her head, not sure she understood. "What are you saying?"

"I'm saying I'm moving here. I have a real estate agent's agreement with me for you to sign so that we can put the lodge up for sale, and I have a couple of job interviews scheduled here in Albuquerque for tomorrow. I finally understand. It's people, not places, that matter."

Hot tears gathered in her eyes. "You would do that for us? Sacrifice your dream of running Swan Lodge?"

"It's not a sacrifice if it means being able to be with you." He released her hands and reached into his satchel to pull out a stack of papers, but she took them from him and tossed them on the coffee table.

"No. We're not selling Swan Lodge." She took his hands once again. "I had a little talk with Paisley earlier, or more accurately, she had a little talk with me. She made me understand that my determination to hold on to Zia Gardens was really about me having to move away from the farm I loved when I was a child, not about what was best for her. She has no particular bond with Zia Gardens, and she doesn't need the business to remind her of her father. But she does feel a bond with Swan Lodge. And so do I. You're right, people matter more than places, but sometimes people and places are perfect complements to one another. Swan Lodge is that place for you, and it can be that place for Paisley and me, too."

"But—"

"Cancel those interviews tomorrow. You already have a job. And so do I." She grinned. "We've got a lodge to run. Together."

The joy reflected in those warm brown eyes validated her decision. This was right, for all of them. She slid her arms around his neck, and he wrapped his around her, pulling her into a long and satisfying kiss. Finally, he pulled back just far enough to smile at her. "There's just one more thing I need to ask you."

"What's that?" she asked.

He reached into the open satchel and pulled out a small box. In the same motion, he dropped off the couch to rest on one knee and opened the box to reveal a gorgeous diamond ring. "Amanda Flores, will you marry me?"

A sudden squeal erupted from the hallway. "Mommy, say yes!"

Amanda erupted in laughter. "How long have you been standing there?"

"Just a little while. Long enough to hear you say we're going back to Alaska." Paisley hurried over to them, quivering with excitement. "Say yes, Mommy. Say you'll marry Nathan."

"Yes," she said and enveloped the two most important people in the world in a group hug. "Yes, let's get married."

CHAPTER TWENTY-TWO

NATHAN AND AMANDA waited in the pickup line outside of Swan Falls Elementary and Middle School in Nathan's new vehicle, a three-year-old SUV much more suitable to life in Alaska than the sports car rental. He'd purchased it sight unseen, based on a recommendation from Mayor Lars. Lars had even arranged, somehow, to have it waiting in the parking garage of the Anchorage airport when they'd arrived back on Saturday.

They'd had a hectic couple of weeks in Albuquerque, but once Amanda had made up her mind that she was leaving, it all fell into place. Nathan had been extremely impressed with her manager, Harley, even more so when Harley had seemingly pulled a developer eager to purchase Amanda's property from his hip pocket. Harley had negotiated an arrangement whereby the sale could go through right away, but Amanda could continue to lease the place until the end of the year, which would give Harley time to sell off their current inventory and rehome the plants in the demonstration garden before he retired.

Amanda seemed a little sad when Harley mentioned ordering a "Going Out of Business" banner, but at least she didn't have to say a permanent goodbye, since Harley and his wife were already booked for two weeks at Swan Lodge next summer. Nathan suspected they would be frequent visitors.

Amanda's all-wheel-drive minivan was in transit from Albuquerque, as were her furniture and household goods. In the meantime, he had no problem driving her and Paisley wherever they needed to go. The school doors opened, and students poured out. After a moment, Nathan spotted Paisley, accompanied by Lyla and several other girls, all talking excitedly and waving their hands around.

A teacher corralled the girls over to the pickup line. Paisley spared a moment to see that his SUV was four cars back before she resumed chatting with her friends. When it was their turn at the front of the line, Paisley climbed into the back seat. "Hi."

"Hello," Amanda answered as Nathan pulled forward to allow the next car to advance.

"How was your first day of school in Swan Falls?" he asked Paisley.

"Awesome," she answered immediately. "Ms. Englund is really nice, and she let me sit at the desk right across the row from Lyla. At recess we all played kickball, and every day after lunch, Ms. Englund reads to us, and she has a whole bunch of books we can read if we finish our work early. Next week, we're going on a field trip to a museum in Anchorage. Mommy, you need to sign my permission slip. It's in my backpack. And they need parents to go, too. Lunch was chicken nuggets with sweet potato tots, and I got chocolate milk. We had a spelling test and Ms. Englund said I didn't have to take it if I didn't want to because it was my first day, but I did and I only missed two words."

"That does sound awesome," Amanda replied. "And I don't see any reason I couldn't be a chaperone on the field trip. Are you hungry? Nathan and I thought to celebrate your first day, we might stop by for ice cream."

"Ice cream! Yes!"

Nathan pulled into the parking lot, and they walked over to Glacier Scoops. Bethany greeted them from behind the counter. "Nice to see you back in Swan Falls. How long will you be staying?"

"We're here for forever," Paisley told her. "I started school here today."

Bethany looked delighted. "First day of school in Swan Falls? That definitely calls for a celebration cone on the house. What flavor for the first scoop?"

"One scoop is enough," Amanda said, laughing.

"Don't forget, we told Peggy we'd make spaghetti for dinner to give her a night off."

"Spaghetti is my favorite," Paisley explained to Bethany. "I'd like a scoop of Mud Flats on a pointy cone, please."

"Coming right up." Bethany made it one scoop, but it was a very generous scoop.

Once they all had their cones, they crossed the street and strolled along the path in the park, peeking into the windows of the museum to see the swan sculpture in the center of the room. It warmed his heart to think that, working together, they'd been able to recover the sculpture and fulfill Eleanor's wish to display it here. After they finished their cones, Paisley noticed some kids she'd met at school on the playground and ran over to join them, leaving Amanda and Nathan to walk on alone.

They reached the tree where the drinks table had been set up for the street dance. Where they'd shared not their first kiss, but the kiss that made Nathan realize they were connecting on a deep level. Judging by the blush rising on Amanda's cheeks, she was remembering the same thing.

"What do you think?" Nathan whispered. "Should we try to repeat history?"

Amanda pretended to be shocked. "In broad daylight? What will the good citizens of Swan Falls think?"

"Probably that I'm in love with my fiancée.

Besides," Nathan said with a grin as he looked around, "the kids are busy playing, and nobody is paying any attention to us."

"You've convinced me." Amanda slipped her arms around his neck.

He took her in his arms and pulled her closer, taking a moment to admire the curve of her lips, the fiery strands in her hair, the humor and affection in her eyes. But it wasn't long before she pulled his head down and kissed him, a soul-baring kiss that he experienced all the way to his toes. No one had ever kissed him like that before Amanda, and he knew with certainty he wanted to spend the rest of his days sharing kisses with her.

Amanda pulled back just far enough to make a quick check on Paisley, and then kissed him again. This time the kiss was shorter, but full of promise.

"Welcome back to Swan Falls." The mayor's booming voice made them both jump. How had he managed to sneak up on them like that? Lars laughed and reached for Amanda's left hand, nodding approvingly at the ring there. "I see the rumors are true. Congratulations to both of you."

"Thank you." Amanda smiled at him as she reached for Nathan's hand. "We're very happy."

"By the way, you know Ted, the postmaster? He mentioned this morning that this will be his last hitch on town council, and so there will be a seat coming open. Since you two are officially citizens of Swan Falls now, you'll be eligible to run after three months of residence. It would be an honor to have another Swan on the council." Before either of them could answer, the mayor raised his hand. "Just food for thought. The election isn't for another six months, so you have plenty of time to consider. In the meantime, we're glad you're here." And with that, he was heading off toward the post office.

Amanda laughed. "He doesn't let any grass grow under his feet, does he?"

"Nope. That's probably why he keeps getting elected mayor. From some of the stories Eleanor told me, this is his MO. Plant the seed of an idea, then pop back in to water it a few times, and before you know it, you're volunteering and thinking it was your own idea. That's how Eleanor came to be in charge of the community Thanksgiving dinner a few years back, as well as the head of the Christmas decorating committee." Nathan squeezed her hand. "Don't worry. You don't have to run for council unless you want to."

"Oh, I know. Besides, I'm pretty sure he was talking to you. I'm not a Swan."

"But you will be, sooner than later if I have anything to say about it."

"Sooner sounds good." She kissed him once more and then looked toward the playground, where the three kids that had been playing with Paisley were loading into a car. "Let's collect Paisley and go home. *Home.* Isn't that a lovely word?"

She gave a delighted laugh. "You know, the first day I ever came to Swan Lodge, I got lost and you showed me the way home. And now you've done it again."

He grinned. "Glad to be of service."

Paisley came running, and they returned to the car. Back at the lodge, Nathan let Amanda and Paisley out in front before parking in the big garage in the back. As he headed toward the lodge, something on the lake drew his attention. He hurried to the back door. "Paisley, Amanda, come quick."

"What is it?" Amanda asked as they stepped outside.

"Look." He pointed toward the lake.

"A moose!" Paisley squealed and ran to the edge of the patio overlooking the water. The trees cast long shadows from their side of the lake, but the low sun sparkled over the ripples and dips and lit up a point of land where a bull moose was drinking. After a moment, he raised his head, his spectacular antlers silhouetted against the water.

Amanda and Nathan went to stand behind Paisley. Nathan set a hand on Paisley's shoulder, and slipped his other arm around Amanda's waist, drawing his family together. The moose held his pose for several long minutes and then, with a shake of the head, moved forward, into the lake, and began swimming across, cutting through the water with his powerful legs while keeping his head and those enormous antlers clear. They watched in awed silence until he had disappeared from view behind some trees on the other side.

The spell was broken when above their heads, a raucous voice said, "Go on. Shoo."

"We love you, too, Maggie," Nathan called to the bird, who squawked and flew away.

"I finally got to see a moose," Paisley announced happily. "We're real Alaskans now."

"That's us." Amanda laughed and pulled Paisley and Nathan into a group hug. "The real Alaskans of Swan Lodge."

* * * * *

*For more great romances from author
Beth Carpenter and Harlequin Heartwarming,
visit www.Harlequin.com today!*